SEVEN SECOND DELAY

TOM EASTON

Holiday House / New York

For Ella

Library of Congress Cataloging-in-Publication Data
Easton, Tom (Children's fiction writer)
Seven second delay / by Tom Easton. —First American edition.
pages cm
"First Published in the United Kingdom in 2014 by Andersen Press, London."
Summary: In a future where few places are still habitable and people share their entire lives
on the Web, Mila illegally enters the Isles, is captured and has a telephone implanted in
her brain, and escapes but government agents are after her and her greatest asset is a seven
second delay from the time she acts until they receive the signal.
ISBN 978-0-8234-3209-7 (hardcover)
[1. Science fiction. 2. Technology—Fiction.
3. Fugitives from justice—Fiction.
4. Adventure and adventurers—Fiction.
5. Environmental degradation—Fiction.] I. Title.
PZ7.E13159Sev 2015
[Fic]—dc23
2014007804

Prologue

Julian tumbles. Slowly, it seems. Twisting down, down through the thin, gray air. Mila clings tightly to the safety wire and watches him get smaller. His body turns lazily, and as it faces upward she glimpses the pale face, the dark O of his mouth as he screams. Then he turns again, hiding his face from her. He is tiny now, shrinking, shrinking. All she can make out is the dark blue of the Agency uniform she stole for him in Sangatte.

He hits the main span of the bridge and ricochets off, spinning furiously. He must be dead, she thinks. That must have killed him. Please let it have killed him. But it is another few seconds before his body hits the water and she can be sure. He has fallen a quarter of a kilometer into the freezing waters of the English Channel.

At the speed he is traveling, water is like concrete. This she knows. It is one of the many things she has learned in her short life. Her stomach, already cramped with fear, knots and gnarls as she tries to comprehend what has just happened. She has lost him. Simultaneously, another part of her mind, uncomfortably lacking in compassion, is asking a plaintive question. What now, Mila? What are you going to do now that Julian is dead?

How will you survive?

1

A clock ticked slowly, legato seconds checked off one by one.

The woman. Attractive, older, blonde. In her mid-thirties, Mila guessed. She'd learned to adjust her estimates in the brief time she'd been on the Isles. Everyone here looked younger than they were. Or maybe everyone back home looked older. The mean had shifted.

The woman sighed. She hadn't given her name. Mila would have remembered, like she remembered everything. She waited for the woman to follow the sigh with a question, but it was the dark-haired man who spoke, wrong-footing her.

"Let's try again," he said calmly, a fake smile forced into his voice, slightly out of sync with the equally fake smile plastered across his face. It was a good face, Mila thought. Handsome. He was properly young, mid-twenties probably. He was the good cop, which was a role that seemed to suit him. Mila was skilled at reading people, though the occasional misjudgement had taught her not to trust herself entirely.

"What's your name?" The good cop looked at her earnestly, a little sideways grin appearing. *Come on*, his expression said. *Why fight this?* "What harm could it do to tell us your name?"

Because giving you my name gives you a measure of power

over me, Mila wanted to say. If I give you what you want, you'll use it against me. Otherwise why would you ask?

So she said nothing and kept her head down, staring at a spot at the center of the plastic table, her chosen focus point. It was the only thing she controlled, that square inch of off-white thermo-plastic; the only thing she owned in the world, and they couldn't take it away from her.

She knew enough about the Agency to know that you couldn't improve your position by cooperating. You couldn't negotiate. If they wanted something from you, they'd let you know about it. Julian had taught her that; it was just one of the million things she'd learned from him. Thinking about him brought pain, and she shut the memory down before it could take hold.

"We're not evil, you know," Good Cop said. "You think we are, but we're not. It's common for foreigners to believe the worst about us. We've heard all the stories before."

Mila had heard the stories too. About the Centers, the Hulks, the rough justice. She was curious to see for herself just what was fact and what was hysterical fiction. It couldn't be as bad as what she'd gone through in the U, could it?

"You have food and clothes, don't you?" he asked. "And a bed. The Center is warm and safe, is it not?"

What he said was true. Mila had been held in a dozen camps, or prisons, or "Centers" over the last three years. Some were better than others. Some had nearly killed her. The Center she was in now was by far the most comfortable. So why was she so full of dread here? she wondered. Was it because Julian was gone? Or was there more to it? There was something about these people that scared her. They were different.

"We've given you books to read," he went on. "You have a screen to watch the Channels."

Mila looked back at her spot. She blinked. Sluggish seconds ticked by on the clock.

Then a *crack!* as the woman slammed her palm down on the table, directly over Mila's focus point, as though Mila's gaze had burned a spot there, revealing its location. Mila flinched, her heart pounding.

"What's your goddamn NAME?" the woman yelled.

And a sudden torrent of fury loosened Mila's tongue.

"What's YOURS?" she roared back.

The man and woman sat back as one, smiling. They'd made progress.

"So at least we know you speak English," the man said, pausing for a moment, probably making an internal note on his device. Neither of the Agents carried anything for the purpose. No one did in this country. They kept it all inside.

"It's important to know names, isn't it?" the good cop said, with another smile from his smile bank. A warm, conciliatory one this time. "My name's Adam, I . . ." He stopped, looking alarmed. Mila caught a brief roll of the eyes from the older woman. She guessed that the man hadn't intended to reveal his real name.

Adam went on. "This is . . ." He hesitated again.

"Eve?" Mila asked, unable to resist.

The older woman's eyes flicked heavenward in annoyance at her colleague. He was clearly junior, inexperienced. He should have had a false name already prepared for himself and his colleague. Now Mila had been granted a small victory.

"Rebecca," he said, resignedly, and Mila thought she saw a slight flush of his cheeks. He looked down at the table, perhaps seeking his own spot.

"Where were you born?" he asked, quietly.

Mila laughed, a sharp bark which said quite clearly that this was a question she would never answer.

He waited a moment, then tried a different tack.

"Okay, then tell me this," he said. "How did you get onto the Isles?"

Mila stared at her spot and tried to zone out. He spoke like no one else she'd ever met. Perfect English, of course, but more than that. His voice had a confidence, a strength that she'd not come across before in her travels. He didn't borrow language, to use it apologetically. He owned it, and handed it over like a gift, wrapped in intent.

"Did you come over the bridge?"

The bridge. The word was enough to send her tumbling back in time to the day she'd lost Julian. A word, a scent. Even a simple gesture. It didn't take much for her to be back on the weathered island of memory.

She stands, half crouching, on the wire-strand cable. It is thick enough to walk on, perhaps a meter in diameter. Nonetheless, she is unable to stand fully, half rigid with fear. The span of the bridge, the section carrying the cars and the trains, is one hundred meters below her, and the freezing gray water of the Channel is 150 meters below that.

"Come on," he says. He is a few steps ahead of her, standing sideways, holding out a hand. His scarred, creased face is smiling encouragement. His curly black hair, shot through with salty white streaks, ruffles in the stiff breeze. They'd waited nine days for a time when the wind wasn't too strong.

He smiles and steps toward her, and then suddenly there is a wind. A gust. An eddy. And he sways slightly. His left foot lands too far to the side, where the surface begins to slope. Then he is down, quickly. Too quickly. He clutches at a thin electrical wire running along the walkway. This holds him for a moment. But Mila can see it is already stretching. It is not designed to hold the weight of a man, even a gaunt, malnourished man. Cleats pop and the cable begins to pull away from the span.

"Get a phone," Julian says firmly, as though prepared for this moment. "Once you have a phone, call Beverley Minster. But only if you're in real trouble."

"Julian, I . . ." she says, inching toward him. She is too far away.

"There's something in . . ." he begins, but with a sickening jolt the cable comes fully away and for a tiny instant their eyes meet, his filled with nothing but sorrow, as he disappears over the side, silently.

6

"It was the bridge, wasn't it?" Adam repeated. "I can see by the way you reacted."

Mila shook her head. "No, not the bridge," she said.

"Then how?"

Mila leaned forward and fixed him with a conspiratorial look. "Okay, I'll tell you," she said.

Adam leaned forward too, unable to help himself.

"Giant swans," Mila whispered. "I was carried by giant purple swans."

Adam pulled a wry smile from the smile bank. "That's funny," he said. "You have a sense of humor."

Mila sat back and arranged her features into what she hoped was a look of utter blankness.

"Adam, let's step outside for a moment," Rebecca said. "Please excuse us," she said, coldly. "My colleague and I would like a private chat."

"If you want to chat privately," Mila replied quietly, "you could just talk to each other using those machines in your heads." She looked up at the woman, trying to pierce her with her gaze. "You're just leaving to let me stew for a while. I'm familiar with the process."

She knew she was talking too much. She'd broken her resolve to say nothing. She was bored, which was part of their tactic. They'd been doing this for hours, days in fact, asking a few questions before leaving the room. Leaving her alone to listen to the incessant ticking of that damn clock, driving little nails of wasted time into her skull.

"We'll be back in a few minutes," Adam said. "Then we'll have some more questions for you."

"Missing you already."

The heavy door slammed shut, rattling the walls with its solidity, and Mila was left alone with her spot on the table. And the clock, of course.

"Everything's recorded," Julian tells her, one cold night, as they huddle over a fire in a paint tin in an abandoned farmhouse somewhere in the country that used to be known as Germany. He is eating the leg of a lamb they stole and killed. Messily, cruelly. The meat is half burnt, half raw and tangy with the taste of the paint chemicals. Nonetheless it is a feast; it's all they've eaten this week apart from a few tins of beans and some tart cooking apples, six weeks from ripening.

Julian wipes his mouth, which is smeared with fat, shiny in the firelight. He looks, for a moment, like a caveman ten thousand years ago. "Everything," he repeats.

"There are cameras?" she asks. "Like in Prague?"

Julian shakes his head, shuddering at the memory. "No, they record everything in their heads. They have phones in their heads."

She looks at him skeptically.

It sometimes seems that Julian knows everything, can do anything. He is much older than her. He knows the U well, has spent time on the Isles themselves. He has also traveled the other way, through China and into the gleaming technocracies of the East Coast. He doesn't like to talk about China. On his torso he has a map of China in scars. His left eye was thumbed out by a guard in a prison cell there.

Julian knows things, but sometimes Mila gets the impression he is exaggerating a little to impress her. The stories he tells about the First World can't possibly all be true. He wants her to like him, to admire him, to stay with him for his wisdom and skills. She wonders if he wants her in that way. But he's always kept his distance and protected her. Guardedly, she trusts him. He is a good man.

And she has heard rumors of these phones in their heads before.

The next day, they leave the farmhouse and Julian begins talking again, picking up from where he left off the night before. Mila smiles. They've been traveling together for months, nearly a year in fact, and she is used to his oddities.

"The weakness they have," he tells her, "is that they have no crime. They have no poverty, they have no . . . you know, political problems."

They are walking along a country lane. A rusted tangle of

twisted metal and cabling fills the field to their right. An old pylon, brought down during one of the countless wars. Something squeaks in the wind as it swings back and forth. Mila wrinkles her nose at a sudden vile stench, brought their way by the breeze.

"Why is that a weakness?" she asks, squinting up at the blood-red sun, hanging low and bloated over the horizon. It seems to shimmy a little as it sinks, like a fat lady lowering herself onto a stool. Mila is aware that the sun hasn't always looked that color. It is the emissions that make it look this way. It used to be bright yellow, her teacher told her, in a pale blue sky, and Julian claims it looks like that on the Isles. Mila can't imagine it. To her, the sun is dark orange, or red, in a purple sky.

"It's a weakness," Julian tells her, "because once you're in, you're in. Nobody suspects you; everything's free. You can live where you want, eat what you want. Get drunk, chase the ladies." He laughs, a little self-consciously.

"They threw you out twice," she points out. He is easy to tease, thick-skinned and good-natured.

"Yes, this is true," Julian says. "I may have got a bit carried away. Let myself down."

"They have libraries there, don't they?" Mila asks after a while. She's heard all about them so many times, she can picture them in her head. Big red buildings filled with books. Unlimited access to everywhere on the Web, all the information in the world. The thought makes her dizzy sometimes.

"Yes. And you know what they don't have?" Julian says. "CCTV. No monitoring, nothing."

"Why not?" Mila asks. The rank smell is getting worse. She breathes shallowly, not wanting to take in more of the foul air than necessary.

"They have two political parties," Julian goes on. If he's noticed the smell he is ignoring it. "One of the parties calls for more privacy, the other calls for less. That's the only thing they argue about."

He stops, holding out an arm to let Mila know she should follow suit. Following his gaze she sees a tumbled pile of military-green metal lying in the field. It is half crushed by the fallen pylon. It takes her a moment to make sense of the shape but then she recognizes it as a Waldo. An armored, walking monster operated from within by a man. The smell is worse now and Mila guesses the source of the smell is the corpse of the luckless soldier within the mechanical beast.

Julian is cautious. "Sometimes they have automated weapon systems," he explains. "They keep firing even when the operator is dead."

He moves slowly, watching for movement from the machine, but there is nothing. He beckons Mila and they continue, grateful to escape the stench of death. It has been like this ever since they left Köls. Twisted, burned-out war machines. Collapsed houses and destroyed churches. Ordinary people struggling to survive. Starving refugees wandering aimlessly, ending up in camps or worse. Mila and Julian have had to escape from such places more than once.

"A few years ago," says Julian, continuing his potted history of the Isles, "the Privacy Party got in and took away all the cameras. They said everyone's recording everything on their phones anyway, so why bother. So once we're in, no one's going to be able to follow us. I'm not going to get caught this time."

"But won't we need phones?" Mila asks. One of her soles is flapping a little, and makes a rhythmic beat as she walks. Step, swish-step, step, swish-step. "You told me everyone has a phone. And without one you can't live there."

Julian nods. "Yes," he says. "That's true. But you can get phones illegally, of course."

"From where? From a camp?" She glances over at him and he shakes his head. His face is filthy. They stink. She can smell him; she can smell herself. How can they get onto the Isles like this?

"Not from a camp on this side," he says. "It needs to be a phone from the Isles. That's how they know if you're a Citizen or not. It's not easy. They're all coded. You see, when someone is born, they create a phone specifically for that person. When the child is, I don't know, six or so, it gets implanted. The tech will get upgraded, replaced many times, but the code, the phone number—that stays the same always."

"So they know how many people there are, and how many numbers there are?"

"Yes. Getting the phone is not so hard. But if you don't have a registered number, then it doesn't work. You can't get food or shelter. The Agency comes to find you and they send you back. Or somewhere else."

"So how do you get them? Phone numbers?"

Julian doesn't answer for a while. They keep walking. Step, swish-step.

Unable to wait for a response, Mila prompts him. "Do you steal them? From factories? Or off the Web?"

Julian seems to be thinking. He says nothing. Mila sniffs. "If you don't know . . ."

He stops suddenly and stands in the middle of the road. She stops too, a few paces on and turns to look at him, standing in his rags on the cracked, pitted tarmac. A mess of a man, but her only hope.

"They get them from babies," Julian says. "Babies who die."

Mila purses her lips and shuts her eyes, closing herself off from the distasteful thought.

"If the baby dies then they don't give the number to someone else," he says. Mila wishes he would stop. "The baby is buried with it. You can hack into the list of the numbers and assign it to new, illegal hardware."

"You steal the identity of a dead child?" Mila asks, arms folded, angry at him for even knowing about such a thing.

Julian nods.

"Why not an adult? Adults die too."

"Because the phone number is associated with a Citizen. If you use the number of someone else, even if they're dead, all their old records come up, all their old pictures, videos, conversations. I told you, Mila, they record everything; they show their whole lives to each other on the Web."

Mila thinks about this. She can't imagine why anyone would want other people to watch everything they did. But she could imagine maybe wanting to watch others.

"So if you take on the phone number of an adult," she says slowly, "you take on their whole life, all their history, all their baggage."

"Yes," Julian says. "That's why you need a baby's number. Unfortunately, not so many babies die on the Isles."

Mila winces. "I didn't mean it like that," Julian says, embarrassed. "I don't want babies to die. Just . . . I'm just saying."

Mila nods. She understands. One of the things she's learned during this never-ending journey is that you just have to take the opportunities life presents. If the rules are set against you, then you have to cheat a little, just to even things up. There is no room for sentimentality in a dying world.

They carry on walking.

"But don't they check?" Mila asks. "Don't they realize that the phone number you're using belongs to a baby that died?"

"I told you," Julian replies. "They're weak. Not many police and hardly any cameras. At least, not security cameras. They spend their whole time watching each other, sharing everything they do. The last thing they suspect is a secret. As long as there aren't a bunch of old pictures of you looking like someone else on your phone memory, they don't go digging."

He stops as a bird takes flight from within a dark stand of trees to their left. Birds aren't common, and Mila has noticed Julian seems fascinated by them. The bird, a large black specimen, flaps off toward the mid-morning sun and Julian turns his attention back to the conversation.

"Of course, if you screw up—you know, kill someone or something else dumb—then they'll start to probe and they'll catch you. But they have these Privacy Laws." He sniffs.

"You say that as if it's a bad thing," Mila says, wondering what it might be like to have a little privacy once in a while.

"No," Julian replies. "Not for us, anyway."

The kitchen down the hall was a stark contrast to the interview room. Fat leather sofas, mood lighting, walls decorated with huge black-and-white images which changed when you weren't looking.

"Remind me, is this your first day on the job?" Rebecca asked as Adam ordered coffees. A semi-intelligent, or SEMINT, barista whirred into life, pulling levers, pressing buttons, flipping cups gently onto saucers.

"No," Adam replied, sighing inwardly.

"She's running rings around you."

"She doesn't want to talk," Adam shrugged.

"You fancy her, don't you? You like those Slavic girls? Sharp cheekbones."

"Jesus, leave me alone. Who cares, anyway?" he said, turning to her. "She's going to get sent off somewhere on a Hulk. We'll never see her again."

"She may have something," Rebecca said. "She's got an air about her. . . ."

"Do you fancy her?" Adam asked.

Rebecca sucked in air sharply.

"We've been asked to pay special attention to this girl," she said. "Considering where she was found, and who they found nearby."

"Who's asked us?" Adam asked. "The Minister?"

Rebecca said nothing.

"My god, it is the Minister," he said. "No wonder you're being so intense."

"Look, Adam," she hissed. "I know you've had some . . . tough times lately, but all we're asking for is a little professionalism, okay? You have a job to do. Everyone has to make a Contribution. This is yours; do it properly or you'll get a flag."

Adam passed a latte to Rebecca and lifted his own to his nose, closing his eyes at the scent, relishing the bitter-sweet memories it produced. For an instant, he was at home in London and Clara was with him, laughing, bright with happiness.

He opened his eyes to find Rebecca studying him doubtfully.

"Can you handle this?" she asked. "Or should I get someone else?"

"I'll be fine. . . . I am fine," he said quickly. He sipped his coffee. "I'll get something useful, I promise."

"Just find out how she got in, okay?" Rebecca said. "I'd do it myself, but now I'm established as the bad cop. . . ."

He nodded. "I know."

"Come on," she said, more gently this time. "Let's have another crack before lunch."

They set down their cups and a robot arm whipped them off the table.

If it were up to me, I'd just let them stay, Adam thought as they returned to the interview room. Maybe not all of them. Not the violent ones, or the ones who won't wash. But I'd let this one stay. He was careful to check his settings were on "hide." These were not the sort of thoughts an Agent of the Security Ministry should be having, much less Showing.

Rebecca was waiting for him at the door. With a nod she indicated he should go first.

Adam applied a new smile before turning the handle and opening the door.

Mila reckoned she had around four and a half minutes after Adam and Rebecca left the room.

There were two reasons they might leave a room mid-interview. The most likely was that they wanted to chat about tactics, in which case they tended to grab a coffee while they did so. She knew this by the smell of their breath and the mocha moustache Adam sported when they returned. If so, she had just under five minutes.

The other possibility was that they were leaving her to stew, in hopes that boredom would loosen her tongue. Sometimes these stewing periods lasted an hour, which would be plenty of time to get up to no good, assuming they didn't send in a blank-faced guard to keep an eye on her. This close to lunch, though, it was unlikely. She had to be back for the lunchtime roll call. Their adherence to the rules made them predictable, and predictability was a weakness, as Julian would have said.

Coffee it was.

Lifting it off the ground, so as not to scrape it, Mila moved a chair to the far wall, where the clock hung. She climbed up. The clock came off the wall easily, hanging, as it was, on a short nail. This surprised Mila a little; she'd expected some kind of over-engineered fixing tech. Magno-Grip perhaps, or newly patented Wall-Suck. It seemed even the Isles-dwellers still knew the value of good old-fashioned nails.

Mila stepped off the chair and took the clock to the table, laying it face down. She smiled with relief to see the back plate was fitted into a groove, rather than held on with screws. She slid it out and examined the insides.

In the center there was a rectangular block, which held the timing mechanism. That was no use to her, but next to it was a larger, sealed block made of plastic with wires attached. The battery. She'd seen this sort of battery before, in Frankfurt. She knew that a tiny fusion power plant nestled inside. The end result of thousands of years of human endeavor. Unlimited, free energy, packed into an object she could hold in her palm. And what did the Isles-dwellers use it for? To run an old-fashioned clock they didn't even need except to annoy Applicants.

Mila eased the block out of its casing. Turning it over, she smiled again as she saw a keypad and display screen. A lot of the newer tech didn't bother with these. Since everyone on the Isles had a phone capable of accessing the bios and adjusting the settings, strictly speaking keypads were virtually obsolete, as everything was connected via the Web.

She disconnected the wires from the timing mechanism with a sharp tug. Then she unzipped her all-in-one and tucked the battery into her underwear.

Next she eased the timing mechanism out and laid it on the table beside the clock. Using her fingernails, she pulled the thin face of the clock up and off the central pin. Underneath were the hands themselves. She yanked them off and slid them down the leg of her overalls and into her sock.

Mila zipped herself up and began replacing the components.

Suddenly she heard a noise outside in the corridor. She stopped, holding her breath, her heart pumping. Nothing. Someone passing, perhaps. She returned to the clock, jamming the face back over the pin, then the powerless timing mechanism over that. She replaced the back panel, finding it trickier than it had been to remove. This was always this way. It always took longer to put things back together than to take them apart.

But finally she'd done it. The clock reassembled, she wiped the dripping sweat from her forehead and stepped back onto the chair. Still over a minute to spare, she judged, though she no longer had a functioning clock to confirm it. She rested the clock back on the nail and stepped down again.

Immediately the clock dropped off the nail and fell toward the floor.

Mila shot out a hand, jamming it against the wall, arresting the slide. You are a cat, she heard Julian say. You are young, quick with your mind and your hands. This is your most valuable attribute. She breathed hard. If she were caught trying to steal the clock components, they wouldn't bother talking to her anymore. She'd be categorized as a criminal element and put on the first Hulk. She'd end up enslaved in some South American canning factory, or in a sub-continental sweatshop, dead by thirty from a thousand emission-zone cancers. Once we're in, Julian had said, do what you must to stay there. For me, it's not so bad. I'm an ugly old man. I will survive. You are a beautiful young girl. You have so much to gain by staying on the Isles; so much to lose by leaving.

Mila examined the nail. Broken. Only a stub remained. So much for old tech. What wouldn't she give now for some Magno-Grip. What would Julian do? He'd probably yank off a table leg and fight his way out. No. She remembered his words. You can always do something to improve your position. You can always score a point. Try to win the set, even if you can't win the match. It might not be obvious at first, but there will always be a way.

She calculated she had less than half a minute.

Then it came to her. A way to turn this to her advantage. Setting the clock on the table, facedown, she used a fingernail to pick at the soft plastic lip, sharpening it until it stood proud. She stood on the chair again and carefully, oh so carefully, she rested the sharpened lip on the stub of nail still protruding from the wall. It held, just. Slowly, cautiously, she stepped down off the chair, watching the clock all the time, looking for a quiver, a flicker of movement, ready to catch it. She replaced the chair and shuffled on tiptoe around the desk.

She heard footsteps outside. She sat and held her breath.

The door opened. Adam walked in, smiling brightly. Rebecca following, a scowl on her face. Mila tried not to watch the door slam shut, the walls shake. She looked away as the clock fell again from its precarious perch and she tried to look surprised as it shattered on the floor, plastic and Perspex flying across the room.

"Jesus Christ," Rebecca said, kicking a piece of plastic that had had the temerity to end up near her foot. "Stupid old tech."

Mila tried not to grin.

2

They weren't prisoners or inmates. They were known officially as Applicants. Once captured, they were made to sign a form, which, in theory, allowed them to apply for temporary residency, the right to stay and work, or Contribute, as they called it here. According to Julian, and the brief discussions she'd had with other Applicants, Citizens also Contributed, but they didn't have to do much if they didn't want to. There was no shortage of anything in the First. Production, distribution and services were largely automated, SEMINTs did the really unpleasant work: cleaning and maintenance, farming, laboring, wiping the arses of the infirm.

The form, in reality, was a legal nicety, giving the State the power to deport anyone it didn't like the look of, or to hold them indefinitely if it saw some advantage in doing so. Signing the form meant sacrificing any right to privacy, something they took seriously here. They could watch you twenty-four seven once you'd signed. The toughest, most troublesome Applicants were fitted with a dumb-phone so they could be monitored more easily.

"Why do they bother interviewing us at all?" asked Maya over lunch. They ate in a huge hall, at long tables, in shifts monitored by a dozen or so guards. The food was basic, but to Mila, who'd never had enough to eat before in her life, each meal was a feast. She had already noticed she was filling out a little, after just eight days in the Center. That was fine though. It wasn't going to be a problem. Not after tonight.

"This is what they do," Juno replied. "They love to find out about other people. They hate that we have no phones. They can't find out everything about us so they have to ask questions."

Maya and Juno had arrived at the Center with Mila. They had all been subjected to lengthy, regular interviews, though it had become clear over the last few days that Mila was getting more attention than the others.

All three had been caught on the same morning, close to the town known as Bridgehead. They'd all come over the bridge. Maya and Juno had come on a vehicle, Mila guessed, though they hadn't discussed it for fear of being overheard by a guard or a spy. Maya and Juno probably assumed Mila had crossed the same way, helped by a trafficking gang, or just stowing away. As far as Mila was aware, only she had ever successfully crossed using the cables. It seemed important she didn't give the information away, at least not without something in return.

They had been kept overnight in a small cell, somewhere unidentified. A prison van had brought them to the Center the next day. Mila had no idea where it was within the Isles. They had driven on featureless motorways for two hours or so, before turning off the highway and winding their way along country roads to arrive finally at this giant white box. There had been no signs on the roads, no signals. The vehicles were all SEMINT, with a human operator as a fail-safe. Julian had told her some vehicles didn't have a human operator at all. If the vehicle's sat nav failed, the operator, assuming there was one, could always use his or her phone for directions. No one needed street signs on the Isles.

"Mila?" Maya asked, raising an eyebrow.

Mila shrugged. "I guess she's right. They want to find out where we come from, how we traveled so far. How we got onto the Isles."

"I heard that they don't care where we come from, they'll just put us on any old Hulk, going anywhere," Juno said, clearly miffed that Maya had asked Mila for clarification. "Or else they send you to places where workers are needed. Horrible places."

"That's true, mostly," Mila said, hoping she didn't sound like she knew it all. "But it's not that simple. Look, sometimes they do let people stay. People who have special skills, people prepared to do the really awful jobs that can't be done by machines."

Juno was shaking her head. "Don't get your hopes up. I've never heard of anyone allowed to stay in any First-World state."

"I'm not saying that many get in," Mila said patiently, aware that Maya was staring, wide-eyed with hope. "And they don't advertise it. But I know for a fact that some are allowed to stay."

Their conversation was interrupted by a screeching of chairs and a chorus of shouts. A fight had broken out. A ring formed quickly around the two women involved. Juno stood on a table to get a better view.

"That big girl's got hold of the one with the frizzy hair," she reported.

Mila closed her eyes. She'd seen enough fighting. The Center wasn't nearly as violent as some she'd been in. In an overcrowded camp outside Prague, she'd seen a woman's eyes gouged out by another for stealing food. She was left, crawling and mewling, blood pouring from her eye sockets for more than an hour before the blank-faced guards came and took her away. Mila, like all the others, had been too scared to offer help, unwilling to show solidarity with a thief. She thought of that incident often, wondering where the poor woman was now. Probably dead. That might be for the best.

As she opened her eyes, the guards arrived and the circle opened up to let them in. A red-headed girl, overweight, was smashing a smaller girl's head into the ground. She had a curiously detached look on her face, as though she were pounding corn, thinking about supper.

One of the guards pulled a long strip from his belt and whipped it down onto the redhead's wrist, where it coiled around of its own accord, and dropping the free end, which flailed about for an instant, searching for the other wrist. The redhead seemed hardly aware of what was happening. She kept pounding the corn until she found both of her wrists seized. The strip tightened of its own accord and the guard shoved her to the ground with his boot.

"Fun's over." Juno sat down again and pulled her plate closer.

Maya turned back to Mila. "So, you know someone?" she asked, eagerly.

Mila blinked at her.

"You said you knew someone who was allowed to stay?"

Mila nodded. She'd said too much, but it was nice just to chat, to have friends. She couldn't help herself.

"That's right," she said.

Juno narrowed her eyes doubtfully.

"Who? Can she help us? Or he?"

"He. And no, he can't help us; he's dead."

"This the guy you were blubbing about yesterday?" Juno shot. "Your boyfriend?"

Mila fixed her with a stare. "He was a friend."

Juno didn't reply, perhaps realizing she'd overstepped.

Mila returned to Maya. "Also, we know that sometimes, they do send you back home, but they . . . employ you. They give you money to act as an Agent."

Maya frowned. "I heard that. But why? Why would they need Agents?"

"The Agents run things. Factories, farms, distribution. First-World companies own assets everywhere. They get local people to run them, as proxies."

"I don't know anything about running factories," Maya sniffed, disappointed. "Do they need cleaners?"

Mila shrugged. "They don't just recruit managers. They also recruit people just to mix and see what's going on. They want information, about trafficking gangs maybe, or opposition groups, but also general stuff—the economy, the emissions, that sort of thing. They give them a phone, send them back and they observe what the Agent sees."

"Why don't they just send their own people?"

Juno snorted. "Citizens don't set foot outside the First World. There ain't many tourist attractions in Zone G. No five-star hotels. No golf resorts."

Mila nodded. "There's no reason for a Citizen to go overseas. Not when you can live through the eyes and ears of someone already there."

"There were four swans," Mila said. "Maybe five. They wouldn't tell me their names."

It was hot in the interview room. She was bored. Adam looked bored. Rebecca looked bored. Maybe she could bore her way out of this. Dinner was in two hours.

"Cooperating with us can't hurt you," Adam said. "In fact—"

"Where did you meet Julian?" Rebecca interrupted suddenly.

Mila was caught by surprise. She glanced up quickly. Rebecca smiled.

"That look tells me you know who I'm talking about," she said.

Mila said nothing, just stared at her spot, hoping her face wouldn't reveal her inner turmoil. They must have found Julian's body. She imagined him, bloated and gray, being pulled from the Channel.

"Where did you meet him?" Rebecca repeated. "Was it in Köls? Somewhere else in the Eastern U?"

Mila kept her mouth firmly shut.

"Is he your father? Your lover?"

Mila was aware of the two of them watching her intently, trying to glean information from her reactions. She kept her face impassive, but her breathing had sped up.

"Julian was one of our Agents," Rebecca said. "But you knew that, didn't you?"

"I don't know who you're talking about," Mila said. Julian, an Agent? It couldn't be true. He told her he worked for the Corporation. That he had to work with Agents from the Ministry of Third Development. That he hated them.

"We have CCTV footage of the two of you in Calais," Rebecca said.

When Mila made no reply, Adam spoke up. "He's an interesting man. Had we known he was returning to the Isles, we would very much have liked to speak with him. We find it . . . unusual that he was trying to slip onto the Isles unnoticed, and with an illegal. Now why would he do that?"

Mila said nothing. She breathed deeply through her nose, trying to calm herself as her mind raced. She felt her heart rate slowing gradually.

"Did Julian have harmful intentions toward the Isles?" Adam asked. "He must have discussed his plans with you?"

She didn't believe Julian had had "harmful intentions." But why had he lied to her? If he had lied to her . . . perhaps she was being lied to now? She knew Julian had lived on the Isles before and had made some powerful enemies.

"What was his mission?" Rebecca snapped, losing patience. "And what was your part in it?"

Mila looked up at her in affected surprise. "He was your Agent. Why are you asking me?"

There was an embarrassed pause.

"Julian went rogue some time ago," Adam said, finally.

"Rogue?" Mila asked, putting on a puzzled expression.

"We lost contact with him," Adam said. "We thought he must be dead. Now we find him floating in the North Sea."

"I didn't know he was an Agent," Mila said quietly. "And there was no mission. Or none that he told me about."

"We want to believe you," Adam said, gently. "But you need to come clean with us. Why did you come to the Isles?"

Mila looked up at him, glaring. "Well, wouldn't you?" she asked. "Wouldn't you?"

"You're not seriously telling me you believe her?"

Adam shrugged. He was in the canteen, eating lunch. Rebecca was elsewhere in the building, her location set to private.

"I'm good at reading people," he said.

Rebecca snorted. "So you're saying she didn't come over the bridge with Julian?"

"No, I think she did. I saw the pictures of them together in Calais. I just don't think she is involved in a plot against the Isles."

He took a bite of his sandwich while he waited for Rebecca to reply.

"Did you know Julian?" she asked.

"No. Before my time," he said.

"Well, I knew him," she said. "He's capable of anything. And when he went rogue, he became a threat."

"But you have no proof he was planning an attack."

"Not yet," she said.

"So what do you want me to do?" Adam asked. A SEMINT waiter hummed by and swiped his empty coffee cup off the table.

"Monitor her," Rebecca replied. "Give her a slave phone and Watch her closely."

"You think it's best if I do it, and not you?"

"She's more likely to slip up if you're Watching her. You're the good cop, after all." Rebecca ended the call.

After dinner the Applicants were allowed to watch the Channels. The brainless dramas and impossibly fast action shows brought distraction and a release from the dull anxiety they all felt. But at the same time they brought an exquisite pain of their own. It was as if the Isle-dwellers were displaying to the Third-Worlders just what had been missing all their lives, just what would remain outside their grasp.

Four giant screens showed different programs, though all were pretty much the same, Mila thought. Some clever tech ensured that you heard only the soundtrack of the screen you were watching. Short, punchy episodes, just a few minutes long, followed each other in quick succession. First a hilarious dog who seemed to be singing along to a music track, then a hospital scene in a drama series Maya had already become obsessed by, then a documentary piece about a nature reserve somewhere Mila had never heard of. It must have been in the First, to judge by the clear running water, the untouched forests, the thousands of birds. There were few birds in the Third. Those tough specimens that did manage to scratch out an existence tended to end up in the pot, valuable protein for starving people.

The Channels were just a taste of what the Citizens, those with phones, could access day or night. One of the screens kept jumping to follow the live Feed of a man in an office. Mila tried to make sense of the display on the upper right-hand side of the screen. They were Watching a real, live person, going about his daily business. His colleagues in the office seemed to find him hilarious and he had them in fits most of the time. But his speech was so fast and full of breezy references, Mila couldn't understand much of what he was saying.

Juno must have seen her puzzled expression.

"His name's Brandon Judd. He's in Focus at the moment," she said.

Mila raised an eyebrow. "Focus?"

"It means attention is Focused on him," Maya added, helpfully.

"Everyone Watches him," Juno said. "See the number in the top right-hand corner? That's how many people are Watching right now. 1,330,568."

Mila blinked. "Over a million people Watching him? He's that funny?"

Juno shrugged. "I can't understand what he's saying, but they seem to like him."

"They might not be actually Watching him all the time," Maya said. "They just have the Feed open."

"They can Watch more than one thing at once?" Mila asked.

Juno nodded. "Yeah, they have all these little screens pop up showing what all their friends are doing. If something interesting happens, they get a signal."

"Something interesting? Like what, they sneeze? They go to the bathroom?"

Juno grunted by way of response.

Mila was exaggerating the extent of her ignorance. There were Channels where she was from. Limited, heavily censored. Electricity was sporadic, at least in the Eastern U where Mila had grown up. She'd seen it, at richer friends' houses, and during the brief period when she was employed. She'd seen the Web too, in the same partial fashion. But she wanted more. Knowing that such a wealth of knowledge and information was available, but inaccessible, drove her mad with frustration. Part of her wondered if the real reason she'd finally made the decision to leave hadn't been hunger, or fear for her future, but simply a determination to find a way to access the Web and the Channels. To be free to explore their boundless content. It infuriated her to be shown this shallow drivel when she knew such depths lay just beyond reach.

Mila noticed the guard before the others. She watched him out of the corner of her eye, ready, calculating. She could see he was coming for her. Had they discovered the missing pieces of the clock? Or was it something else?

"Could you come with me please, miss?"

Maya and Juno looked up in surprise.

"Again?" Juno asked. "What's going on?" Whether this was directed at the guard, or at Mila, it was hard to say.

The guard didn't take Mila to the interrogation room. He made a left turn, not the right she was expecting. Her heart pounded and she took a deep breath or two to calm herself. If she wasn't going to the interview room, that suggested a decision had already been made about her fate. They wouldn't be sending her to a Hulk, would they? The Applicants being Hulked were collected early in the morning and taken away in a van. She'd heard the screams. But if it wasn't that, then what?

Security doors opened for them as they approached, the guard merely sending a signal via his phone.

"Where are we going?" Mila asked, trying to keep the tremble out of her voice. The guard said nothing. Another door hissed open.

He stopped by a door in the corridor and waited. Mila realized he must be phoning someone. Or texting. That way he didn't have to speak out loud. Julian had told her how, through some insanely sophisticated tech, Citizens could send each other text-based messages simply by thinking the words. She hadn't properly grasped his explanation. But it was clear that the guard didn't have security access to this door. He had to wait for someone to let them in, which meant there was something important inside.

The door swung open and they entered, passing down a short hallway and through another door into a large white room. Mila's eyes hurt from the glare. In the center of the room was a chair, comfortably padded and clearly designed to be moved into various positions and inclinations. Mila took in the straps and the restraining belts. To the left of the chair stood Adam. To the right, a young woman in a lab coat. The woman was pretty, like most women seemed to be in the First. This one didn't seem the sort to pay much attention to her appearance; her hair was tied back casually with a simple band and, contrary to the current fashions, she wore no makeup.

Adam smiled. The young woman was busy inspecting a monitor. You didn't often see monitors on the Isles. Everyone used their phone. Was this for Mila's benefit?

"I'm not getting in there," she said, indicating the chair.

Adam looked regretful. "I'm afraid you are," he said. He held up a stubby, pistol-like device. "You know what this is, don't you?"

Mila's mouth went dry. It was a dummy gun. She'd seen them used in camps, but was surprised and sickened to see one here. The effect of being hit was to render the victim insensible. Incapable of any form of decision-making. It directly acted on the cortex, rather than the nervous system: effectively, the higher-functioning part of the brain stopped telling the body what to do. The victim stood about looking vacant and drooling. The effects wore off after a day or so, but from the evidence Mila had seen, the luckless recipients never properly recovered. Some part of the brain damage was permanent.

"You won't be hurt," Adam said, quietly. "We haven't brought you here to hurt you."

"So why am I here?"

Adam looked down at his feet, then back up at her. "I'll be brutally honest with you," he said. "You are here because . . . we do not trust you. And because we want to trust you. We want you to help us. You have skills. You have experience. We know you were associated with a former Agent gone rogue." He paused, looking serious. "We have our suspicions about you, but some of us aren't convinced you mean us harm. It's possible that at some point there may be a role for you here on the Isles, but there are some . . . procedures we need to go through first."

"What sort of procedures?" Mila asked, eyes narrowing. "Do they involve rubber gloves? Because I can tell you I went through one of those procedures when I first arrived. They didn't find anything." She was acutely aware of the uncomfortable lump of nuclear-fusion clock battery in her underwear.

"Not that sort of procedure, no," Adam said, with what Mila judged might be the first genuine grin she'd seen on his face.

"What if I refuse?" Mila said, eyeing the chair. "What if I don't want to be part of your gang?"

"Then you go on a Hulk," Adam said. "But even then you'll still have to go into the chair. You're not leaving this room until we've completed the . . . procedure." He waved the dummy gun again and smiled apologetically.

There was no choice. But Mila took her time before stepping forward. Adam waited. The technician continued to ignore them both, standing and looking into the middle distance. Mila had noticed this before on the faces of the guards, technicians and Agents. When concentrating on their Internal Display Screens, or IDSs, they took on a curiously vacant expression, like they'd been hypnotized.

Mila tried to figure out what was happening. It seemed unlikely they were going to torture or kill her. They'd have just gone ahead and done it, not sent Smiling Adam to ease her into it. But clearly they weren't just going to hand her a phone and her freedom. They wanted something from her. Which meant she had something they wanted. She had something to negotiate with.

She got into the chair.

"What was all that about how lovely you were here on the Isles?" Mila asked, as she made herself as comfortable as her flip-flopping stomach would allow. "So much more civilized than the U? You know what, the only difference between the Isles and the U is that here you're given a square meal before you get lobotomized."

The lab-coated woman ignored her and began strapping her down. Mila's heart fluttered like a trapped bird in her chest.

"No one's going to lobotomize you," Adam said. He held up the dummy gun to his head and squeezed the trigger. Fake. He crossed his eyes and stuck out his tongue in a parody of an imbecile.

"Hilarious," Mila said. "You should be in Focus. You'd have a billion Watchers."

"Look," Adam said. "Don't be mad at me. If you knew what I knew, then you'd understand why we're doing this."

"Then why don't you tell me?"

Adam shrugged. "It's easier just to do it like this."

"Where's Rebecca?" Mila asked, her questions distracting her from what was coming next.

"She's Watching," Adam said.

"Is she your girlfriend?" Mila asked. Maybe he'd give her something she could use. Did she see a flush of red high on his cheekbones?

"No, she's my boss," he said.

Mila nodded, affecting relief. "Glad to hear it. She's just about old enough to be your mother."

Adam was silent a moment and Mila imagined the choice words Rebecca would be pouring into his phone. Whether it was a good idea to needle them like this she wasn't sure, but somehow it made her feel better.

The technician finished strapping her down and stood back. The seat reshaped itself around Mila, aligning with her contours and clamping her body and head firmly until she couldn't move. She was breathing shallowly now, feeling as though she might throw up. The technician passed a small glass vial to Adam. There was something moving about inside. Mila tried to get a closer look, but Adam's hand obscured the contents.

"Now, this might hurt a little," he said. "But it'll only be for a second."

And he twisted the top off the vial and upended it onto Mila's torso. Something dropped out and Mila sucked in both her belly and her breath.

A tiny metallic creature sat on her stomach, just to the right of the zipper of her jumpsuit. It spun, got its bearings and shot up along her body, between her breasts, over her chin and onto her face. It stopped there for a second, whipping thin sensory whiskers across her skin. It resembled a tiny crustacean, silvery and slick, its dozens of long, threadlike tentacles flying in all directions, probing, examining her.

Mila suddenly lost her composure. She screamed, tried to twist her head, shake off the creature. The headpiece of the chair—a SEMINT, Mila realized—clamped her hard. The robotic crustacean scrambled up her face, and though her eyes were tightly shut, she felt a tiny, tickling tentacle insinuate itself under her eyelid. Light flooded in as the creature tore her eyelids open and there followed a brief, sharp pain, as the thing crawled under the lid. It slid around her eyeball, greasy and slick, thrusting itself deep into the socket, squeezing in between her eyeball and the side of her nasal bone. She felt an urge to sneeze as it clambered deeper inside her head, the trailing tentacles sliding in, dragging against her eyelid. Then it was over. She felt nothing. The whole thing had taken a second or two.

"What. The Hell. Was that?" she asked, struggling to cap the rising hysteria.

"That was your new phone," Adam said. "It's installing itself. Nothing to worry about."

"Through my eye?"

Adam laughed. "Get over it."

Mila paused for a moment, her breath gradually slowing, taking it in. "Hang on, you're giving me a phone?" she asked. "Why?"

"So we can Watch you," he replied. Out of the corner of her eye, Mila could see the technician studying her monitor. On the screen was a cross-section image of what she imagined must be her own skull. Something was moving inside.

Adam followed her gaze. "The tentacles will implant themselves into your brain, deep in your cortex. One will attach itself to your optic nerve, receiving Visual signals directly. Another, tuned to pick up sound waves, will burrow inside the bone next to your ears. The tech is not yet sophisticated enough to translate touch, taste or smells."

The headrest relaxed, allowing Mila to move her head again. Suddenly lights flickered in front of Mila's eyes and her vision became blurred, as though a thin gauze had been thrown over her face. The gauze faded, leaving behind characters, machine code, visible. She moved her head, rolled her eyes; the machine code followed her line of sight, overlaying everything she saw.

Adam was watching as she blinked and squinted.

"I can see what you can see," he said. "Via my own phone. I've established a permanent link. Neither of us can switch it off, though I can send it to sleep if I get bored with Watching what you're up to."

"Kind of creepy, no?" Mila said.

"Tiny bit," he admitted. "At this stage only I have access to your Feed. Though of course I can open that up to others to Watch via my phone."

"Yeah, who wouldn't want to Watch me go to the loo? You could charge." She was talking too much, jangled nerves loosening her tongue.

"What you're now seeing is your IDS," he said. "Your Internal Display Screen. It's a direct Feed into your brain. It's not like a HUD, which stands for Heads-Up Display. That would be projected inside a helmet or windscreen, as and when you want it. You can't switch the IDS off."

Mila knew what an IDS was, and an HUD for that matter, but Adam didn't need to know that. Better to play ignorant and let him keep talking until he gave away something she didn't already know.

The code scrolled and flicked across Mila's vision. She closed her eyes. It remained. Her stomach was knotted, filled with a sense of dread. She tried to sound casual. "Do I have to look at these stupid numbers the whole time?"

"No, this is just the start-up sequence," Adam replied. "I'm going to fire up your Applications now."

The machine code disappeared and a row of icons popped up at the bottom of her vision. Most had a padlock symbol overlaid.

"Those are your Apps," Adam said. "Not many are functional, I'm afraid. You have a calculator, a telescope, a notepad. Basic stuff. I'm going to turn off your passepartout. The key that opens doors." An icon bearing a key symbol flashed and turned gray. "Infrared too," he said, flicking off another icon.

"You won't be able to see in the dark, like we can. And this is the Go App," he said as an icon with a tick mark on it flashed and grayed. "That's the one we use to make things work. Can't let you have that."

"Sat nav off. Internet off. Video record off. Audio record off. Games off."

Up until this moment, Mila hadn't been aware such augmentations were possible, and via a phone. Now suddenly she wanted them, all of them. Even the games.

"You can keep the clock and the music player," Adam said, chummily. "I'll scoot you some tracks."

"Thanks, bud," Mila said.

"This one is your Feed," he said, indicating with a cursor an icon featuring a human head with concentric circles around it. "That stays on. It's how we'll be monitoring you." Mila felt a little sick. It was disorienting to watch what was happening on the IDS as well as looking out into the room. She could see her IDS twice, through her own eyes and projected on the monitor.

The scene on the monitor suddenly shifted slightly so it was out of sync with what Mila could see herself. She winced.

"Sorry," Adam said. "There's a delay on your Feed. Default setting. What I see, what is on the monitor, actually happened seven seconds ago."

The technician turned the monitor off. It wasn't necessary now that Mila's phone was installed. She had figured out how to select the various icons and drop-downs on the IDS. She could do it just by thinking about it, or even without really thinking about it. As though her subconscious was operating it before being asked.

A drop-down menu appeared at the top of her IDS and Adam began clicking option buttons, turning off all her rights and privileges. No access to the Web, no external calls, no Quiet Time, no Idle.

"Your phone is slaved to mine," Adam explained. "Once I've set the options, they are locked and cannot be changed without a physical shunt. It's to stop people hacking into the phone's software and messing about with it."

"What's that?" Mila asked, focusing on a button marked 7SD.

"Ah," Adam said. "That's the seven-second delay I mentioned. When you're, you know, Showing yourself on the Web—when your Feed is on—there is always this delay built in. So if you say something dumb, or offensive, or you walk past a mirror naked or something, then you have seven seconds to cut the Feed. Then you Watch yourself on your own Feed, which stays on for you, and wait until the embarrassing incident is over. Then you reconnect."

Adam clicked on the button, graying it out.

"Can I keep that?" Mila asked.

"What's the point?" Adam said. "I'm gonna turn off your ability to cut your own Feed, so it won't make any difference. You'll just have to wear a towel when you get out of the shower."

Mila's heart was pounding again. She wanted to scream and kick, yank off the restraints and smash the machines. She forced herself to calm down. Look for the best outcome. Julian whispered. Improve your odds. "I don't know, I just think . . . It's just that if there's a delay, then it's less invasive," she said. "You know? You won't be watching the real me, you'll be watching a past me."

It sounded silly when she put it like that. Why should he give in to such a pointless request? But Adam regarded her solemnly for a moment. Then something in his usually cheery countenance seemed to give, and a brief impression of sadness seemed to come over him. He nodded.

"Sure," he said. He hit the button again, turning the delay back on.

"So what's this little picture of you doing on my screen?" Mila asked, changing the subject before he changed his mind.

"That's my Avatar. All your Contacts will have one. You have to set people up as Contacts before you get their Avatar, otherwise they are just Watchers."

"What's the difference?"

"Contacts are like your friends, those close to you. You keep them in that little address book there."

A little box popped up with three entries. Adam, Maddie and someone called Jason.

"Who's Jason?" she asked.

"He's a Tech," Adam replied, "Like Maddie here."

A baleful glance from Maddie suggested this comparison had not gone down well.

Adam's entry had a star next to it.

"There'll be an animated picture of each Contact," he said. "The picture will display the emotions the Contact is feeling at any time. So if I'm in a good mood, the Avatar will smile at you. If I'm feeling grumpy, the Avatar will scowl."

"And Watchers?"

"They are just random people who have found your Feed over the Web and are following you, Watching what you do. They don't have your phone number so they can't phone you or text you, unless you're dumb enough to make it public. But they can send you brief messages in the chat box."

Another box opened on the other side of Mila's IDS. A header at the top read WATCHERS: 0. It quickly changed to WATCHERS: 1 and a message popped into the box.

Adam: UR now being Watched.

"As your phone is slaved to mine," he went on, "Watchers won't be able to find you. Unless I direct them to you."

"Okay," Mila said.

"You can open and close the chat box," he said. "It's not really important. If I need to talk to you, I'll phone or text."

Simply by willing it, Mila selected the box and clicked the close button. It winked out. She also closed the Contacts box. Adam's Avatar remained in the bottom right of her screen.

"You can't turn me off, I'm afraid," Adam said. "I've opened a Permalink between your phone and mine. We won't open any more Permalinks—there's no need—but anyone who has access to my Feed will automatically be able to Watch you as well."

"Great," Mila said.

"We're in this together, for better or for worse."

"Does this mean I have to look at your face twenty-four seven?" Mila asked. "What if you're, you know? At your personal business?"

"I can Sleep the connection without breaking it," Adam said. "If either of us needs the loo, then I'll do that of course. But I don't expect I'll need to be connected to you all the time. I have other clients to look after, and a personal life, of sorts. If I'm not Watching you, someone else will be. I can make your Feed public over the Web so the whole world could Watch you, but there's no need for that."

"Really? I have so much to say," Mila protested.

"Now, I can hear anything you say over your Feed, of course," Adam continued, ignoring her sarcasm. "But only with a seven-second delay. If I want to talk to you in real time I'll phone you. That's a different tech entirely."

A gentle chime sounded inside Mila's head and a see-through keypad appeared on her IDS, the green "Answer" button flashing.

"I'm not home," Mila said.

Adam sighed. "It's been a long day, Mila."

"Okay, OKAY," she said, and clicked on the green button.

"So now we're connected." Mila could hear Adam's voice in stereo; in the room, but also in her head. "Can you hear me through the phone?" he said.

She nodded.

"Now, I should point out," Adam said, "that as your phone is slaved to mine, I can simply force the call through if I want to. Unless it's urgent, I'll ring before I start speaking. But you won't actually be able to pretend you're not at home." He hung up.

"That call was in real time," Adam said. "The Audio-Visual strands of your Feed are the only things delayed."

"So if I say something when you're calling me, will you hear it again seven seconds later?"

"No. When you're on the phone, the Audio Feed cuts out."

"So Watchers can't hear my phone calls?"

"No. If you make a call, all sound is muted for anyone except the person you're phoning. Phone calls are private. The law is very particular about that."

"And can my phone be traced?" she asked.

Adam shrugged. "The tech exists. But privacy laws forbid phone tracing. In any case, I'm not sure it would work with a slaved phone. We don't need to trace you anyway. We can just Watch your Feed and figure out where you are in the Center."

Mila felt encouraged that Adam was going to so much trouble to explain. They wouldn't take this much time over someone they were just going to throw onto a Hulk, surely?

"Okay," Adam said, yawning and stretching. "I think we're done. Maddie here is just going to perform a scan, make sure everything's tight in there. Then we can let you up and about."

"You're going to let me leave?" Mila asked, her heart surging.

"Not leave the Center, no," Adam replied, shaking his head. "But you can go back into the common room."

"Can I tell them I have a phone?"

He shrugged. "Tell 'em what you like."

A low hum and a gentle throbbing started up in the headrest. It was surprisingly soothing and Mila found herself relaxing, despite everything. She had a phone now. It was a means of monitoring her, true, but they wouldn't give her a phone unless they needed her. Wanted her. Perhaps they were going to make her an Agent. For the first time since Julian's foot had slipped on that damn bridge, Mila allowed herself a little sip of hope.

"What's that?" Adam said suddenly.

He looked bemused, staring into space, clearly examining something on his internal screen. Mila focused on his icon and it expanded to fill her screen. It was remarkable just how quickly she'd picked up the functions of the IDS. Everything was intuitive. She could make things happen just by thinking about them.

She could see exactly what Adam was looking at. A three-dimensional image of the inside of her own head. She saw her brain, pink and faded out. A more solid layer of gray skull surrounded it. Buried in the upper rear part of her head was a small black lump, the metallic crustacean. As Adam zoomed in for a better look, she saw the whiskers spidering through her brain matter. She shuddered slightly. But as he zoomed in further, she realized he wasn't focusing on the phone, but going deeper, further, toward the lower portion of her brain.

And then she saw what he was looking at.

A second lump. Smaller. Lighter in shade.

"What is that?" Maddie breathed. The first words Mila had heard her say.

"Can you increase the resolution?" Adam asked.

The angle changed, swiveled and shifted, and suddenly the image grew sharper. The lump was clearer now. A small cylinder, maybe the size of the top section of a pinkie finger. It was feature-less, apart from a tiny protrusion from one end.

"Is it an old phone?" Adam asked.

A new Avatar popped into being on Mila's IDS. It expanded into the unwelcome visage of Rebecca. She looked furious. Slightly scared too.

"What the hell is that?" she demanded.

Then suddenly they were all shouting. Rebecca via the phone. Adam in the room. Maddie doing both. Somewhere, an alarm was going off. Mila shrunk within herself, out of her depth now, sudden-ly terrified.

What the hell is going on? she thought.

"It's a bomb!" someone shouted. "She's got a damn bomb in her head."

Panic rose again, restricting her breathing. Adam backed slowly away from her, a look of horror and fear on his face.

"No," she said, trying to shake her head. "No."

3

A mountain of old, broken tech towers over the truck, teetering, looking like it might collapse any minute and swamp them under a thousand tons of motherboards, batteries, and monitors. There are eight of them. Besides Julian, Mila knows the names of three. There is the other woman, Hester, the one who'd been there yesterday. There is a grizzled old drunk called Gilbert, and finally, Jay, a boy of around her age who keeps watching her, looking away when she meets his stare. The others she hasn't seen before. There are new ones every day. Some, it turns out, have lied about their ability to read or to use tools; they don't come back. There are always more waiting to take their places, willing to shift old junk, cut their hands on the sharp wires, taste the acrid tang of battery acid. The money is pitiful, but as Julian explains, they aren't there so much for the money, but the knowledge.

"Learn the tech," he says. "Particularly the newer stuff. You'll need to know how it works."

They are given ancient, creaking tablets, reconditioned so many times there is nothing original in them. Mila learns to find the right connector to hook the tech to the device to analyze its bios and figure out if it is worth salvaging. Sometimes, if she can find the right software through the limited Web connection, the devices can connect to the tablet without a cable. Usually it's easier and quicker just to plug the damn thing in.

Along with the others, she clambers up the mountainside, looking for the shinier pieces of circuitry or complete-looking machinery. Sometimes SEMINT machine arms or cleaning bots move feebly as she passes, her proximity waking them from android sleep, half-corrupted programming demanding they help her or get out of her way.

Beyond the factory she hears the dull booming of artillery as a distant city is besieged. Julian had told her the guns are fifty miles away or more. But they seem nearer. She is struck by the fact that life continues as normal, regardless of the warfare on the horizon. That is how things are in the U. So many battles, so many armies. The people here have learned that they can't stop every time a troop of soldiers comes marching across the front lawn.

Mila often finds herself watching the hover ships gliding miles up in the burnt-orange sky—huge, rust-brown tangles of metal, pitted with battle scars. They occasionally meet with enemy ships and conduct lazy, long-range dog-fights, firing silent, jagged bolts of energy until one collapses, slowly, untidily, to the ground, breaking into pieces as it drops.

"ECM blast first," Julian tells her as they watch one such battle.

"ECM?" Mila asks.

"Electronic Counter Measures," Julian replies. "Used to shut down electrical systems in the vicinity. If a ship can take out another's electronics, then it's left defenseless. It can be finished off with a few hits from an energy beam."

"How come the ECM doesn't affect both ships?"

"Every time the attacker lets off a volley, its own systems are shut down for an instant so they're not damaged."

"Like shutting your eyes before firing a gun?"

"Yes. Something like that."

Julian had thought it a good idea to hole up in Frankfurt for a month or so while this current siege raged. He is vague about exactly who is fighting whom. Maybe the armies don't know either.

Mila and Julian had arrived gaunt, stinking and half dead from malnutrition. But they found work, food, shelter and knowledge. Julian knows the man who runs this operation and managed to get them both jobs in the warehouse, reclaiming and reconditioning tech.

Occasionally, Mila has a few minutes in which to search the few sites on the Web they are allowed access to, talk sites about tech reclamation or illegal software downloads. But there is information there about the First World too, and other parts of the Third. It is on that old tablet that she learns about the oil, about how there is still plenty of it. Just not for them. It is here that she learns about the wars, and how the emissions hadn't been too bad before. It is here she first hears about the Corporations and their connection with the Agency.

This is when she gets angry.

Mila sat on the edge of her bed, trying to slow her breathing, trying to think. She'd been dragged out of the lab, marched back to her cell and thrown roughly inside. She figured they'd put her here to keep her secure while they decided what to do.

"I don't know how it got there. I don't know what it is!" she'd cried as they took her away. They hadn't listened. She wouldn't have in their position. How had that . . . thing gotten into her head? Her mind wheeled with the enormity of the question. Had it crawled in through her eye, like the phone? She'd remember that, she thought. It must have been when she was asleep or unconscious.

Adam's Avatar was grayed out. He'd Slept the connection. She opened the Watcher box and saw she was being Watched by Maddie, Jason and Frank, who was presumably another Tech. She clicked on the Audio-Visual drop-down and selected her own Feed, which appeared on the lower left of her IDS. It seemed disjointed and off-kilter to her, until she remembered the seven-second delay. She lifted an arm, waited seven seconds and Watched the mini Mila raise an arm too. This was what the Watchers could see.

Mila clicked on Adam's Avatar, bringing up the Contact box. She had to explain to him. She had no more idea about the thing in her head than he did. She had to make him understand. She clicked on the "call" button, but a pop-up told her he had rejected the call. Desperately she wondered what to do next.

Focus, Julian said in her ear. Use the anger. Use the fear. Don't let it take over. Control it.

Easier said than done. She was in a hole. She had a bomb in her head, planted by persons unknown. Her captors would never believe she knew nothing about it. What would she do, in their shoes? Eliminate the threat, probably. Evacuate the building and explode the bomb.

An alarm shrieked angrily. An evacuation. It was almost as though the Agents had been waiting for her to reach this conclusion herself before they acted. Once the evac was completed, they'd come for her. Destroy her. How would it happen? A compression grenade dropped through the food slot in the door? Gas? She looked up at the air filters. The Isle-Dwellers were resource-rich and obsessed with safety. Maybe they'd flatten the entire building, just to be sure.

The klaxons wailed and a red light on the wall flashed insistently, making it difficult to think. But Julian's voice came through once more, calm, collected, humorless.

What have you got at your disposal? What tools? What knowledge? What advantage do you have? What cards are in your hand?

Her new phone? That was worthless. No functionality apart from a calculator and a telescope. And the delay. That was all Adam had left her. Seven seconds.

Mila looked up at the door. Beside it was a card slot but no keypad. She guessed the card slot was old tech to the Isle-Dwellers. Obsolete and never used now that everyone had a phone. Old security, old codes.

Suddenly she was back in Frankfurt.

"Everything is multifunctional," Julian says. "Everything is designed to work with everything else. These devices read cards, but they will read other things too. If you can jam something in it which will fire a pulse, you can talk to the door."

"Yes, but what do you say?" Mila asks. "How do you get it to, y'know, open up?"

"You'd be surprised," Julian says, ignoring the joke, as he always does. "If you can convince the door there's a fire, then it'll open automatically."

"So I just type 'fire, help'?"

"You type in this code. It means fire, at least on the Isles."

The mechanism clicks. Mila smiles.

"And that will always work?" she asks.

Julian shrugs. "Maybe not always. They can override the code. If they want to capture you, they can shut everything down. If they're Watching you, they'll block it."

"But the first time I try it? If they don't know I'm doing it?"

He shrugs. "It's worth a try."

She had seven seconds before they realized what she was up to and acted to stop her. Was that enough time? They'd be Watching through her Feed, seeing everything she saw. She stood up and walked calmly to the door. Without looking down, she unzipped her coverall, slipped a hand inside and extracted the clock battery, warm from her body. Still without looking, she tapped the battery's keypad and felt a murmur inside the device as it sprang into life. She closed her eyes and visualized the display as she'd seen it before in the interview room. A basic bios. It was a simple matter to adjust the functions so that the battery would send pulses through the wires, rather than AC/DC current. But she'd have to be quick.

She reached down and fished the clock hands out of her sock, and twisted the wires of the battery around them. The alarm carried on. Would they silence it when the evacuation was complete? When it was time to come for her?

"What are you doing?" a voice sounded.

Startled, she turned around, expecting to see someone in the room. But of course it was Adam, speaking through her phone. Clearly the Permalink meant he didn't have to wait for her to pick up, but not the other way around.

"What are you doing?" he repeated.

Mila ignored him and returned her attention to the door. Working steadily, she carefully fed the clock hands into the card reader. For this she had to look directly at the device. They'd see what she was doing, but she had little choice. She had to hope seven seconds would be enough.

"What's that? What the hell is that?" Rebecca shouted.

Adam enlarged Mila's Feed, zooming in, trying to make sense of it.

"It's a battery," he said. "Where did she get that?"

"She's trying to open the door!" cried Frank.

"Can she?" Rebecca snapped.

She wasn't in the building. She was at the Ministry, in London, trying to explain things to the Minister. Adam was in an emergency control room in the gatehouse, two hundred meters from the Center, which by now was nearly empty.

"Not in theory," Frank replied, gruffly.

"Tell me there are guards outside her room," Rebecca said.

"There's no one in the building," Adam told her. "Your instructions were to carry out a complete evac."

"Well, get some guards back in there!"

Frank had thought things over. "She might be able to open the door, if she were to—"

"Override it," Adam interrupted. "Lock it down—now."

The Tech's fingers skittered madly across his keyboard. Some jobs were too complex to manage via IDS drop-downs.

"Too late," he said. "She's out."

None of the other things Julian had showed her proved necessary. The door meekly accepted the fire code and opened without a fuss. She slipped from the room and shut the door behind her. The alarm was just as loud out here, the lights red and flashing. She'd need to be quick. They would send guards, of course. She looked up and down the corridor. Fire doors at either end.

She ran lightly down the passage, past a dozen cells just like her own. At the end was a fire door with no keypad. She stood, confused for a moment, before realizing that this was the oldest tech of all. She turned the handle and the door opened, revealing a stairwell.

Acutely conscious that her every move was being Watched, Mila blocked the Feed by the simple expedient of closing her eyes. She shuffled forward until she found the rail and went up the steps, three at a time. Her Watchers could still hear her, of course, but without visual clues, she figured they'd most likely guess she'd go down, try to exit the building. Instead she climbed as high as she could, eyes tight shut, gripping the banister for support, trying not to pant with the effort and dropping back to two steps at a time. She'd grown softer as well as fatter in the last few days.

As she reached the top of the stairs, she heard a door open down below and the clatter of guards bursting through. She had no choice but to open her eyes. In front of her was a door. A heavy fire door again, with a keypad. She pulled out the battery and slid the hands in. The clatter of guards had faded a little as they headed downstairs. In seven seconds they would realize their mistake and come back up. Someone, somewhere, would be cursing the lack of CCTV, she was sure. No delay on CCTV.

The display asked for an input and Mila punched in the fire code. A red light and an angry bleep told her the code had been blocked. Dammit. According to the clock display at the top of her IDS, her seven seconds were up.

They knew where she was.

Using base code she'd learned in Frankfurt, she logged into the door's bios and tried to make sense of what she saw. The sound of another door crashing open and heavy footsteps a couple of floors down caused her a moment's distraction.

Focus, she heard Julian whisper in her ear.

Suddenly she saw it. The signifier code. The sequence of numerals that told her this was a Cobalt system. As every tech-geek knew, the code for resetting a Cobalt was 45-32-65. She punched the numbers in and a new window popped open on the battery display, asking for a new door code. Mila tapped in Julian's birthday, clicking the "No override" option. The door blinked green. The thud of the guards' boots was close now. Mila slid the clock hands out of the keypad and was through the door in an instant, shutting it behind her. She was safe until they worked out what she'd done and reset the code.

But if they caught her, they'd kill her. She was certain of that.

Mila was now outside, the final door having opened onto the roof. She stopped to scan her surroundings, the cool night breeze flicking her hair against her forehead.

The Center was huge and the roof largely featureless; just a few stairwell doors she'd need to watch, and an array of satellite dishes and aerials.

She skipped lightly over to the edge, where a low wall ran along the roof line. Peering over, she was disappointed to see no drain-pipes. There were gutters, but it looked as though the rainwater must be drained through pipes concealed within the building itself, probably feeding the Center's water supply. Whoever designed it had done their utmost to prevent the inmates from escaping.

Then Mila saw something that might be of use. Her heart lifted. If she could just find—

But hope tore rapidly apart as a meaty hand clapped on her shoulder. Mila's heart exploded in panic. Where had he come from? Check your six, she heard Julian's voice hiss angrily.

Now you remind me.

She slipped the guard's grip, rolled away and sprang to her feet again. There were two of them. Soft, overweight Center guards, not Agency, thankfully.

"Stay calm," one of them said. "Don't do anything stupid."

Did they know about the bomb? They'd clearly been told she was dangerous.

In the distance she heard the rumble of an aircraft. She risked a glance. A drone, probably with a belly full of bombs. She'd seen them enough times in skies above the U, usually in formation, on their way to obliterate some hapless town. Was this one coming to level the Center?

She stood for a moment, frowning. Then she nodded and stepped toward them. One of the guards held out a hand to grab her arm. Mila guessed he was in his fifties. Both guards seemed mild, kind even. She felt bad about what she was going to do.

The closest guard, the one holding out his hand, she temporarily disabled by a flat-handed blow to the solar plexus. Even through his flexi-armor, the surprise punch was enough to wind him. He fell on his backside in an ungainly heap, blinking and gulping like a fish. Mila bent down and, with a light-fingered swipe, plucked an item from his belt. Then she turned her attention to the second guard.

He had reacted quickly, pulling out a stun baton, which he was raising as Mila knocked him off his feet with a low sweep with her right leg. He crashed to the ground and in a second she was on his back. As he tried to push himself up, she slapped the SEMINT lock-whip she'd taken from the first guard onto his wrist, the free end flying out of her hand and flailing about, seeking its target. The guard cried out in anger as the lock-whip found his other wrist and snapped tightly around it. His arms secured, Mila easily shoved him over with her foot.

The first guard had recovered slightly. He was upright now, wheezing. He pulled out his stun baton. Mila couldn't let him discharge it; that would be the end. She stepped in toward him, then leapt up into the air. Lashing out with a foot, she caught him in the chest and he fell sprawling to the ground, dropping the baton, which clattered across the rooftop. Mila picked it up and pointed it at him.

"Sorry," she said, and meaning it. She had felt the agony of a stun baton on a number of occasions; a hideous, nauseating sensation, as though every nerve had been dipped in an acid bath.

She clicked the trigger just as a door burst open and a stream of guards ran out.

Mila heard, rather than saw, the new arrivals. At the same time, the low rumbling of the drone was much closer. Her stomach flipped as she heard a whistling sound. She looked up to see something fall from its belly, a canister, dropping impossibly slowly, spinning hypnotically.

"My god," she breathed, her heart thrashing, threatening to break out of its cage. She forced herself to move. There was a way out, possibly. She reached down, unhooked the belt of the spasming guard and pulled it through the keepers with a flourish. Then she was away, sprinting across the gray rooftop to the escape route she'd spotted earlier: a thin, taut cable, tethered to a stout pole atop the wall and running off into the tall trees surrounding the Center. Some form of back-up Web connection, she guessed. She whipped the guard's belt over the cable, grabbed the free end with her left hand and jumped, zip-lining down the length of the wire into the trees.

Behind her, the world ended.

"What the hell just happened?" Rebecca cried inside Adam's head.

He stood in the temporary control room, surrounded by monitors. The three Techs, Maddie, Jason and Frank, sat around the room in easy chairs, casually dressed and carrying the slightly vacant look that suggested they were concentrating hard on their IDSs. Jason retched suddenly, and ran for the toilets. Adam was busy viewing replays of the incident, from the perspective of various guards. He switched back and forth between the Feeds, Watching the fleeing girl. Each replay ended the same way. With a flare of white as the bomb hit, ending the transmission. Ending the guard whose Feed they'd been Watching.

Rebecca pinged Adam to get his attention. "What's happening there?" she snapped.

Adam gulped, fighting back nausea. It hadn't been his decision to bomb the Center. He'd expected the mission to be aborted when they sent the guards back in.

"We just killed fourteen of our own security guards," he said quietly. "We just blew up a Detention Center. The prisoner escaped. Anything else you need to know?"

He closed his eyes, blocking the Feed without cutting it, a gesture of retreat, sadness, guilt.

"But how was she able to escape?" Rebecca asked, apparently unconcerned about the deaths of the guards. She was going to have to explain the failure, he knew. Explain why the fourteen were dead.

"Security sucks here," he said. "You know that. We've got no CCTV. The guards get no exercise, no training. No one knows what the hell they're doing. How could we know she had a battery?"

He was ranting now. This had got very serious, very fast.

Maddie and Frank looked over at him nervously, the implicit criticism clear.

Rebecca's white-tipped Avatar invaded his screen space. "What are you going to do about this, Adam?"

"She won't get far," Adam said, trying to unscramble his thoughts. "Guards are already out looking and we have the drone. I'm Permalinked to her."

"She was your case," Rebecca hissed. "You didn't identify her as a flight risk, you didn't even rate her as a potential threat . . ."

Adam sighed. "How was I to know? She's just a girl."

"A girl with martial arts training, tech skills and a clear disregard for her own safety. Not to mention the company she keeps. She's a terrorist, Adam."

Adam shook his head. "She's not a terrorist. . . . I mean, I don't think she's a terrorist. . . ."

"She's got a bomb in her head!" Adam noticed Rebecca had kept her Feed open to the Techs as well as him. They could hear the dressing-down he was getting.

He tried to open a private dialogue but she'd closed off to him, preferring to act out her aggression in front of an audience. Her Avatar grayed out as she hung up on him. He had never seen Rebecca so angry.

Adam sighed. He left the room and went into an empty office, taking deep breaths, trying to calm himself. He flicked through the recordings and found another Visual of Mila's death-defying flight taken from the Feed of a guard at ground level. Her lithe body stayed perfectly still as she flew down the wire, disappearing into the trees. The guard began to run after her. Just a second later the Center disappeared in a ball of fire. The blast knocked him off his feet and by the time he'd regained his footing, she was gone.

Adam switched off the replay and archived it. He maximized

the real-time Feed from Mila's phone. Mostly black, with blurred bushes and trees sliding by the periphery. He could hear her panting.

Just what was he dealing with here? Who was he dealing with?

Mila ran. She had no more idea what was going on than Adam had, but running as fast and as far as she could seemed a no-brainer. Huge black trees loomed at her out of the darkness like craggy monsters, interspersed with the occasional pale and ghostly silver birch. Branches whipped at her face. Punishing, but not stopping her.

Had they really just blown up their own Center? They'd killed their own guards. That had been no accident. The thought made her sick. Who were these people?

Julian wouldn't have been surprised, she suspected. According to him, the Isle-Dwellers were not nearly as ethical as they proclaimed themselves to be. Not when their interests were threatened. "We can be your best friend, or your worst enemy. That's what they say," he had told her. "They use carrots or sticks, whatever gets them what they want."

Would this be on the Channels? she wondered. Probably not. If it was, it would be blamed on her. The Isle-Dwellers were liberal and open to a fault, until the point National Security was threatened. Then the Emergency Protocols came into force and all bets were off.

She'd quickly become accustomed to the grayed-out Apps framing her field of vision, and it wasn't until one blinked into color and motion that she remembered the new phone in her head. Along with something else, something she was trying not to think about.

Adam's Avatar popped up. Distracted, she tripped over a root, sprawling on all fours. She stopped for a moment to collect her thoughts and listen for the approach of pursuers.

"You can't get away," Adam said.

"I think I just did," she replied. She got to her feet and brushed the clagging soil off her jumpsuit before running on, slower now, watching for more tree roots.

"You forget I can see everything you see," he said. "I can hear everything you hear. You can't escape us."

"Is that right?" Mila said, stopping again. She wanted to shake herself like a dog, losing the dirt and the objects in her skull at the same time. In the distance she thought she could hear the cracking of branches as guards searched for her. She started to move again, walking now, picking up her feet, trying to make no sound.

"That's right," Adam replied.

"You can see everything I can see?"

"I can."

"So you can see this tree?" she asked, looking at an oak dimly visible in the moonlight.

"Yes," Adam replied, seven seconds later, when he'd caught up with her Feed. "In fact, I can see it better than you, because I have an App that can boost the visible portion of the spectrum."

"So you know the individual location of every goddamn tree in this forest?"

Adam made no answer. His Avatar stared straight ahead, watching her intently.

Mila fought to control her anger. She took a deep breath and increased her pace to a steady trot.

"I don't know much about your country, Adam," she said. "But where I come from, all trees look pretty much the same."

Again he did not respond.

"So unless you have a tree-recognition App," Mila went on, "then you have no idea where I am right now."

Adam's Avatar rolled its eyes.

"Do you?"

"No, Mila," he replied. "I don't have one of those."

"Okay," she said. "In that case, good luck finding me."

She allowed herself a little smile, flushed by her small victory.

"The forest isn't that big," he said, quietly.

"So come and get me," she said.

And again, she ran.

4

The Minister had kept Rebecca waiting for nearly a half-hour while he read the report and watched a monitor on his desk. She needed the lavatory desperately. His elbows rested on the desk, thin fingertips and thumbs pressed lightly together, forming an inverted love heart. He was the only Citizen she knew of who didn't have an implanted phone. The idea was extraordinary and she wouldn't have believed it had she not seen it firsthand. He used an impossibly antique handset which sat on his desk. He picked up one part with one hand and held it to his mouth and ear, while using his other hand to punch the buttons on the half that remained on the desk. She'd seen such phones in old films, of course, but to watch one in real life was an unnerving experience.

Finally the Minister sat back and opened his eyes. His expression hadn't changed. He had one of those ageless faces. He looked like he was in his mid-fifties, had always looked like he was in his mid-fifties. He had probably been born looking like he was in his mid-fifties. As far as Rebecca could tell, the Minister had never had work done, either reconstructive surgery, which almost everyone had done at some point, or gene therapy, which everybody who was anybody had. Rebecca herself had had three surgical procedures. She'd also undergone a period of gene therapy, which had kept her confined to the clinic for six months but had taken nearly two decades off her appearance.

"And what's your next step?" the Minister asked coldly. He didn't look directly at her. He never looked at anyone. It was as if the sight of other humans made his skin crawl.

"We are confident she will be killed or captured within twenty-four hours."

"Is that so?" the Minister said.

"Yes. She has no food or water. If she finds her way to a road or village we'll be able to locate her using Visual and Audio indicators."

"You're reliant on the Audio-Visual Feed from her phone?"

"Well, we have guards out looking for her, and drones . . ." It sounded weak.

"Why doesn't the phone have a tracking device?"

"I . . . It isn't standard procedure. . . ."

The Minister stared through her, waiting for her to continue.

"Since the new privacy regulations came into force," Rebecca said, "it has been difficult to utilize tracking systems. We have no satellite coverage. We cannot use invasive procedures anymore. . . ."

"Are you suggesting," the Minister interrupted, "that this is somehow the fault of the government? My fault? For passing laws which stop you doing your job?"

"No, sir. Not at all," Rebecca stammered. Her bladder tugged urgently at the pull cord. She didn't need this. She didn't need to work. Like most of her colleagues, she was a volunteer. She could turn around, pee on the sofa in the waiting room and walk out of the building right now if she wanted to. She could do that and still live a long, comfortable life.

But that would mean failure. The end of her career. The end of her useful Contribution and the privileges that came with it.

"It's just that we're not authorized to install tracking devices," she said weakly.

"You are when the security of the Isles is under threat."

Rebecca opened her mouth to explain, but the Minister held up a gray hand. He tapped a few keys on the PC on his desk.

"I've given you Level Three Authority under the Emergency Protocols. The resources you need to finish this are available to you now. I am also activating three Special Agents who will act independently of you. They will report to me, but you are to offer them assistance should they request it. I would like to see you fix this problem yourself rather than rely on them."

"I understand," Rebecca said.

"I'm not sure you do," the Minister said, finally looking directly at her, a look of cold contempt on his face. "So let me explain myself as clearly as I can. This girl, this escapee, is a clear and present danger to our state. If she is not captured or killed soon, if she explodes her device, or delivers it into the hands of domestic terrorists who do so, then my career will be over."

The words hung in the air, looking for the next sentence to connect with.

"You will not allow that to happen," he continued, softly. "Because you know that if you do, I will initiate, as my last act in office, some Emergency Protocols of my own. I am a vengeful man, do you understand?"

Rebecca nodded, dry-mouthed.

"Go," he said, and as she walked awkwardly to the door, her bladder protesting with every step, he picked up his desk phone, stabbed a series of buttons and made a call.

Mila walked and ran, ran and walked, trying to put distance between herself and her pursuers. She could hear planes close by, slow-moving drones. The heavy tree cover kept her hidden and she was careful to avoid clearings. The planes seemed to be concentrating their attention to the south, though one or two came nearer from time to time. At one point she doubled back, disguising her change of direction by closing her eyes, turning, then opening them again. Eventually, when the sound of her pursuers had faded sufficiently, she decided she'd traveled enough, and finding a fallen tree, she curled up in the hollow beneath its tangled roots and shut her eyes, exhausted.

"Wake up, Mila," Adam said. His Avatar waved. She couldn't even shut off the IDS when her eyes were closed. That was tiresome.

"Go to hell," she said quietly.

"We won't let you sleep," he said. "You need to give yourself up. Then you can sleep all you like."

"You'll send me to sleep permanently," she replied. "Like you did to those poor guards."

There was a pause. Mila wondered how Adam felt about the deaths of the guards. He'd seemed so much more . . . normal than the others. Did he feel any regret? She considered it a mercy she was linked to Adam's phone rather than Rebecca's. Nonetheless, he was one of them and, it seemed, not such a good cop after all.

"Their deaths are your fault, Mila," he said. "If you hadn't brought a bomb into our country, if you hadn't tried to escape, we wouldn't have had to take such measures."

Something in his voice suggested these weren't his own words, that he was reading from a script.

"I didn't bring a bomb into your country," she said. "I don't know how that thing got into my head."

"I'm afraid I don't believe you, Mila."

"I know," she said. "That's why I ran."

"We'll find you."

"So you keep saying. Can I ask you a question?"

"Go on."

"Was it your idea to destroy the building?"

Adam didn't answer.

"Did you order the strike? Knowing that the guards would be killed?"

She waited for his response.

"No," he said eventually. "It wasn't my call."

There was genuine pain in his voice. Mila felt oddly relieved. It wasn't that she trusted him or thought he was a good guy, but she was pleased that her instincts hadn't been entirely wrong. He was at least human. That made him easier to deal with.

"Now, I have a question for you," Adam said.

"Okay, shoot," she said. "In a metaphorical sense, obviously."

"How did that bomb get into your head?"

"You don't know it's a bomb!" she said.

"How did it get there?"

A plane droned in the distance. Mila got to her feet and began to hurry through the trees again.

"Mila?"

"I have no idea," she lied.

A white light, so bright it must be heaven. Mila can't see. She is blinded by angels.

"Am I dead?" she asks.

"Not yet," Julian says. A dark shape moves into her field of vision. Her eyelids are heavy and it's hard to keep them open. "You had a close shave, but you're still here."

"Is this a hospital?"

Julian is swimming back into focus. He smiles down at her, concerned, scared, but relieved.

"Sort of. It's a clinic."

"What happened?" she asks, but as she speaks the memories come flooding back. The tech mountain. She'd found an intact motherboard, recent tech, useful. She was examining it carefully, crouching, when she heard someone approaching. She'd looked up with a grin, expecting it to be Julian.

It wasn't. It was the young boy with the wide-set eyes. Jay, the pretty one. He'd smiled back at her, then lifted a lump of metal and brought it down on her head.

Later, in the hospital, Julian explains how another worker had raised the alarm. The warehouse owner didn't seem to care. He left it to the workers themselves to sort out.

"What happened to the boy?" she asks.

"He won't trouble you again," Julian says, coldly.

"And my head?"

"You suffered serious injuries and I had to find a surgeon quickly. I have some contacts. He's not registered but he's good."

"Thank you," she says, taking his hand.

"Mila, when you agreed to come with me to the Isles, I promised to look after you and keep you safe."

"I knew the risks," Mila says. "I'm not sorry I came."

"I'm taking steps," Julian says, "To make sure nothing like this can ever happen again."

Mila sighs. "I can take care of myself."

"I'm going to give you something, Mila," Julian says. She looks back at him intently, her vision now clear, and notices a faint hint of moisture in his eyes. Julian, crying? "Something that will get you out of trouble. Something that you can use as a last resort."

"What is it?"

He shook his head. "Not now," he said. "I'll explain more when—if—we get to the Isles. When we get you a phone."

Mila walked all night, resting occasionally in a gully, or under a fallen tree. Despite what Adam had said, the forest was big. Occasionally she heard the sound of motorbikes crashing through the undergrowth, and once she waited under a tree while a plane roared overhead. It seemed they'd realized their mistake in concentrating on the south and were expanding the search.

She'd traveled a long way in the meantime. Now and again, Adam told her to give herself up, but she ignored him and eventually his Avatar grayed out. There were always the Watchers, of course. But at least they weren't in her ear the whole time.

Adam's question kept returning to Mila's mind. An obvious answer presented itself. Julian could have implanted the device while she was in the clinic in Frankfurt. Even as she thought about it, the scar at the back of her head itched.

But it was impossible. She refused to believe it. Julian would never have done such a thing. If he had betrayed her, she might as well give herself up now. No, there must be another explanation.

She forced the question from her head. Mental discipline is the deadliest weapon any soldier can have, Julian had said many times.

I'm not a soldier, she had replied. But now it was time to show that mental discipline. She needed to focus on the situation she was in right now. The bomb, and the specter of Julian's betrayal, could wait.

Eventually the trees around her started to become more defined and she realized dawn was not far away. She looked about cagily. Were there searchers hidden in the forest, waiting for first light? If she'd been running the operation, that's what she would have ordered. These guys were amateurs. She guessed they didn't get many runners. She shouldn't underestimate them though. What they lacked in guile they made up for in firepower, and they'd shown they were willing to kill their own in their attempt to bring her down.

She was distracted by Adam's Avatar blinking into life.

"Morning," she said, brightly, trying not to reveal just how cold and exhausted she really was. "What's for breakfast?"

"There's bacon and eggs here," Adam replied. "Just give yourself up and they're yours."

"I'm on a diet," she said.

In the distance, she thought she heard the rustling of the trees, and behind this a more regular, mechanical sound. Was there a road up ahead? She had to be careful. If she came within view of a road, Adam would be able to identify it. She checked her Apps again. Still grayed out. The cursor light came to rest on the ID App icon.

Mila had seen enough on the Channels to know what the ID App could do. When activated, everything suddenly had a nametag. At least, anything with an ID chip, which was most things on the Isles, as far as Mila could tell. You looked at a building, and the App gave you the address and the name of the occupants. You looked at a pie in the supermarket; it told you what was in it. You looked at a bus; it told you the destination. Clicking again on the tag would reveal further information, a side panel popping up with text, a video-based dictionary or encyclopedia entries. Phone users—Citizens—could find out everything they needed to know about an object simply by selecting a few options on an internal drop-down menu.

This was why there were no signposts on the Isles. No menus, no nameplates, no labels.

The question was, if she couldn't ID things, could Adam? If she managed to get to a car, or truck, or maybe even a bus, would he be able to ID it, knowing instantly her destination? He claimed to be able to see things better than she could because of his vision-booster App. Did that mean he could use his Apps on everything she saw? Julian would have known. But Julian wasn't here.

She stopped for a moment and stretched, ignoring the hunger and the pain from the ankle she'd twisted slightly while flying down the zip-wire. Then she ran lightly across the dewy grass through the woods and toward the sound of the road.

Frank's Avatar gurned urgently at Adam via his open Comms App.

"Look where she is," Frank said.

"I'm Watching, Frank. I can see," Adam replied, tetchily. He hadn't had much more sleep than Mila, having had to field calls from Rebecca, representatives from the Minister's office and four different press officers asking for details on the explosion at the Center. The official story was that one of the Applicants had started a fire.

He put it all out of his head and concentrated again on Mila's Feed. She had come to a road. Adam pulled up the map of the area he'd become familiar with lately. The Center sat within a forest bordered on three sides by roads large enough to be this one. To the south were moors and wetlands, which was where he'd expected Mila to head. Instead she was here, to the north, west or east. If only he knew which.

"Which road is it?" he asked, directing a query signal to Frank. Maddie's and Jason's Avatars popped into life too. Thankfully, Rebecca was offline for now.

"We're checking that," Frank replied. "Comparing the visuals with archive images."

Adam shrank Mila's Feed and moved it to the top left-hand side of his IDS, dragging the map to sit alongside it. She was trotting along the side of the road, up a hill. Ahead, the road hairpinned sharply as it ran around the spur. There was little traffic at this early hour. No leisure vehicles, just slow-moving SEMINT trucks. Larger or faster trucks carried a human "driver" ready to take over should the tech fail, which, somewhere, once or twice a year, it did. But many trucks had no driver, controlled instead by SEMINT brains and monitored by remote drivers via phones. These were required by law to drive extremely slowly, to minimize the possibility of injury to other road users should the tech fail. Three Citizens had died this way in the last five years, when driverless vehicles had made sudden, erratic decisions and plowed into leisure vehicles. According to the forensic inquests, two of the deaths could have been prevented had a human driver been in the driverless truck. Two preventable deaths was a manageable risk. Realistically, driverless trucks were here to stay, as it was hard to get human drivers. Few people were prepared to Contribute by sitting in a truck cab for twenty-four hours a week.

Mila stopped to look back the way she'd come, toward the oncoming traffic. A slow-moving articulated truck was heading up the hill. Driverless.

Adam suddenly felt uneasy.

"Why aren't I getting ID on this truck?"

"ID App not activated on the girl's phone," Frank replied, dryly.

"So I can't ID via her Feed?"

"No. That tech does not exist."

Adam hated Techs. They seemed to know everything, yet tended to go missing when things got messy. But they were a necessary evil. However good a phone was at providing information, nothing could compete with the speed and accuracy of the replies given by a team of geeks.

"What's she doing?" he asked.

"Crossing the road?" Maddie suggested.

Adam shook his head.

Mila turned and ran further up the hill, toward the switchback where the bank overhung the road.

"Got it," Jason said. "It's the M51. Drone is on its way." He sent Adam an archived image of the road in question, showing its construction. The switchback was clearly identifiable.

"Get some cars there."

"Two on their way," Jason replied. "The first should be there in twelve minutes."

"And the plane?"

"Three minutes tops."

Mila had reached the switchback. She stopped on the overhanging bank, peering down at the road below. Via her phone, Adam could hear the distant whine of the sluggish drone plane, increasing power in an effort to reach the runaway before she could escape again. He maximized her Feed so it filled his field of vision. It was a strange experience, immersing oneself so completely in someone else's point of view, one which most wouldn't undertake willingly. Other people's Feeds tended to be kept small, tucked away, or cascading down one side of the display.

But Adam wanted detail. He wanted to see everything, miss nothing. He saw the truck approaching, laboring up the steep slope, slowing, ready to turn. Freight trucks ran on electricity, collected through solar or wave energy. Even if they'd been authorized to drive faster, they lacked the power for high speeds, especially up hills.

As the truck passed under the grassy bank where Mila stood, he saw her leap. The world twisted and flipped, and he felt a sudden wave of nausea as his confused brain, locked on the Feed, told him he too was falling. Then he saw Mila's hands slap down on the roof of the truck. She slipped and scrabbled for purchase, sliding toward the edge.

"Hold on," he found himself thinking, involuntarily. Mercifully he kept the thought to himself. It was all too easy to broadcast one's thoughts without meaning to.

In the last few seconds before the truck plunged into the darkness of the tunnel ahead, Adam saw that Mila had gained a hold. She was clinging grimly to a slender ventilator casing. Then everything went black.

Adam minimized the Feed. "Frank," he said, "keep Watching her. Amp the light in case you can see anything useful."

"Yes, boss," Frank replied.

"Where does the tunnel come out?" Adam asked the world at large.

Maddie responded by sending him an aerial cam shot of the other end of the tunnel. "Three point two K away. She's a long one."

"What speed's that truck doing?"

"Went in at twenty-five kph, but will speed up a bit. Hard to judge exactly, but should emerge in 450 seconds."

Adam considered his options. Traffic was light, but there were drivers in some of the trucks, and the odd leisure vehicle. He could contact the trucking company and ask them to override the SEMINT driver, bringing the truck to a stop. But then what? At least while Mila was on the truck he would know where she was. He could wait for a clear space and bomb the hillside, causing a landslide which would stop the truck, then his cars could wait at either end for Mila to emerge. Or go cautiously into the tunnel, should it be necessary.

Rebecca's Avatar popped up at the bottom of his display.

"Have you been Watching?" he asked her.

She nodded. Rebecca was able to Watch via the Feed.

"You must stop her," she said. "Use the plane."

"To block the tunnel?"

Rebecca blinked in surprise. "No, wait for the truck to emerge, then destroy it."

"Is that necessary?" he asked quickly. "There's more risk that way. There are other vehicles. . . ."

"Damn the other vehicles," she snapped. "You still don't seem to have any idea how serious this is. I know you have a soft spot for the girl, but for God's sake, Adam—"

"Okay," he said, feeling queasy. "I get the message. Do we have clearance?"

Rebecca sent him an eDoc with the Minister's signature on. Level Three Authority. He could do whatever he liked, effectively.

He took a deep breath and flicked his attention back to Mila's Feed. The screen was totally black. But he could hear the low rumble of its wheels and the hiss of its engine echoing off the tunnel's tiled walls.

"Can you get anything at all?" he asked the Techs.

"I think she has her eyes closed," Jason replied. "The truck should have been passed by two leisure vehicles by now. We'd expect to see their headlights, but there's nothing, even on max amplification, light or Infrared."

Adam switched to the Feed from the drone and watched another white truck enter the tunnel from the other end. He could see a leisure vehicle approaching at high speed, but, other than that, nothing else for a couple of kilometers. There should be just enough time. . . .

"There, she looked up," Jason said.

Adam quickly replayed the VT. A brief fragment in which he saw the dim glow of an emergency light, the safety lights of the second truck, the tunnel mouth beyond that.

Get off, he wanted to shout to her. *Get off the truck.* But of course he couldn't. Everything was being recorded now. If she escaped, there'd be an inquest.

Anyway, did he really want her to escape? She carried a bomb. What was wrong with him?

Instead he contacted the pilot of the bomber, located remotely, in some comfortable facility miles away. He now had five Avatars stretching across the lower part of his display: the three Techs, the drone pilot and Mila. All except Mila watched him expectantly. Why, he wondered briefly, had he been put in charge? Rebecca could just as easily have handled this from wherever she was. He suspected it had a lot to do with the matter of who would take the blame should there be a cock-up.

"Sir?" the pilot said, answering Adam's ping.

"The truck should be emerging in under a minute. When it comes, if you have a clear shot, with no occupied vehicles within a hundred meters . . ."

"Take out the fugitive, sir?"

"Take out the truck," Adam heard himself saying. "Use something big."

"Roger," the pilot replied, cold, professional.

You shouldn't have run, Mila, Adam thought sadly. You shouldn't have run.

"She'll open her eyes in a second," Frank said. "She'll have to."

"How long til she appears?" Adam asked.

Silence.

"How long?" he repeated.

"Maybe fifteen seconds?" Frank replied.

The rumble-hiss of the truck continued through Mila's Audio, but still there was blackness. She must be clinging on, eyes tight shut, hoping desperately that she'd lost her pursuers. Adam felt a stab of something. Regret? Pity?

"Jeez, open your eyes," Frank said. "I wanna see this from her perspective. . . ."

"Frank, watch the tunnel mouth!" Adam snapped. "Jason, you watch the Feed from the plane. Maddie, watch the road. I'll watch the girl."

The attention of the Techs now firmly elsewhere, Adam maximized Mila's Feed and amped up the AV.

In the lower right-hand corner of his display he had the view from the hovering drone, fast-scrolling text IDing everything: distance, wind speed, material density.

"Leisure vehicle approaching fast, sir," Maddie said. "I can't warn the driver, phone on Sleep. We'll need to take the shot as soon as that truck appears."

"Do it," Adam said.

And then he heard the sound of the plane through Mila's Feed and saw, ahead, the bright glare of the tunnel mouth. She had finally opened her eyes. Adam switched his attention to the Feed from the plane, unwilling to follow her Feed into the mouth of hell. Sooner than he'd expected, the truck rumbled out of the tunnel.

"Ordnance released," said the pilot, and in the same instant all their feeds went white.

Adam didn't ask what was used. A battlefield clean nuke perhaps.

A thermo-bomb. High-yield conventional explosive missile. It didn't matter. The truck was obliterated, along with the tunnel mouth and a good portion of the hillside.

When the screens finally cleared, Adam watched the smoking devastation, trying to find something recognizable. Here, a mangled wheel. There, a torn-up section of trailer roof.

The leisure vehicle was now frantically reversing down the road away from the tunnel as a wave-front of smoke rolled toward it.

The Techs were whooping and high-fiving each other.

"Is it done?" Rebecca asked, popping into view.

"It's done."

"Good," she said, and winked out.

It was only then that Adam realized Mila's Feed was still running. Blackness again, but still there. He'd never Watched a dead person before. He wasn't sure what was supposed to happen, but surely the Feed should have ended? Or given him an error message or something? He watched for a moment longer, then his heart flipped as he saw light. He ramped up the signal again. The headlights of an approaching vehicle. In the distance the dim glow of a tunnel mouth. She was still alive? How could she be? He'd seen her, still on the truck, just a few seconds before.

He made his excuses from the victory party and retired to a private room, where he rewound the Feed and Watched again, full-screen, everything amped up to maximum. If he vomited, so be it.

As Mila's truck entered the tunnel she clocked her escape route immediately. She had no intention of emerging from the other end, but she stood a better chance of confusing her pursuers if she left it until the last minute. An old sign painted on the concrete entrance, pre-dating ID software, gave her the tunnel's length, the speed limit and most crucially, the clearance. She knew how long she had and she knew what she needed to do.

She was acutely aware of the one advantage she had: the seven seconds Adam had graciously, and foolishly, allowed her.

Once she'd established how the tunnel was constructed, she

shut her eyes tight and counted down the seconds. The only sounds were the hiss of the engine and the low hum of the wheels bouncing off the walls.

A couple of minutes in, she heard the rumble of an approaching truck. She risked a look up and saw the headlights. Could she? Worth a try, she decided. She stood and walked quickly, nimbly, up the front of the trailer. Then she turned and sprinted back down. She hadn't timed it perfectly and would have to leap before she'd reached full speed. She was running, she guessed, at around twenty kph, and the truck was traveling at thirty. Ten kph difference. This was going to sting.

She leapt.

Her forearms slapped into the hanging clearance sign and she clutched the top edge, pulling the heavy board violently as her backward momentum was arrested. The sign hung from stiff old chains, which jangled and creaked with the extra load. She looked quickly behind her to see where the second truck was. She had four or five seconds, she judged; more time than she needed. Quickly she swung from one end of the sign to the other until she was hanging on the other side of the road.

She sensed, rather than saw, the second truck passing underneath. She pushed away from the sign with her hands and feet and dropped, face down, hoping to land on all fours. But the sign twisted slightly as she pushed, and her body twisted with it. She landed heavily on her side, the wind knocked out of her. Lacking the truck's momentum, she tumbled and rolled backward along the trailer's long roof.

She scrabbled for purchase but found none on the well-maintained, shiny vehicle. Horribly, sickeningly, she felt her legs flip over the back and in a second she was gone.

But her fingertips finally caught on the lip where the back met the roof and somehow, impossibly, she hung there, trying to catch her breath. She squeezed her eyes shut and clung on as the truck rumbled along through the tunnel.

A few seconds later she heard the sound of a massive explosion behind her, followed by a hot blast of compressed air as the blast wave hit, funneled by the tunnel walls. The truck swayed and she felt a stab of pain as one of her fingernails tore off. Still she held on. But her heart sank as the vehicle slowed. Please don't stop, she pleaded. The truck was her only chance of escape. If it followed some emergency safety protocol and pulled over, she was finished.

Then she felt a shudder through the trailer as the truck changed gear and sped up again, its SEMINT brain presumably deciding that it was better to clear the area.

Mila knew she wouldn't be able to hold on much longer. Her fingers burned, her wrists ached. She lacked the strength to pull herself up onto the roof. She opened her eyes, looking for a foothold and saw she was hanging against the left rear door. It was too dark to see much, but she could just make out the bolt which held the doors closed. There was no lock. Nothing in this country was locked. Nothing outside the Center, at least.

She kicked at the bolt, without success. She kicked again and this time she felt it move slightly. The light was growing brighter; she needed to do this before they came out of the tunnel. Once they realized what she'd done, they'd send the plane to the other end.

She kicked again and this time the bolt slid right across. The door opened outward slightly and she was able to shift her grip to the top of the door, giving her greater purchase and instantly relieving the shrieking pain in her fingernails.

The door swung open further and Mila shimmied along it and around to the inside. It was fully open now. Daylight was fast approaching. She kicked backward with her feet and found something solid. The door outward swung wider still, and she tightened her grip in anticipation.

As she expected, the door hit something on the side of the tunnel, and flew back violently, swinging her into the open trailer. If she hadn't let go of the top before it slammed shut, she would have lost her fingers.

Mila bounced off something hard within the trailer and fell forward. The door threatened to open again as she teetered against it, but quickly she slammed her left hand against the closed right-hand door, grabbed the bolt of the swinging door and pulled it tight, just as the truck emerged from the tunnel and daylight stabbed briefly through the closing gap.

She crouched against the door, eyes tight shut, heart pounding, waiting for the strike from the drone plane. Would she feel it? The searing heat? Would she hear the rending shriek of metal tearing? Or would she be vaporized immediately?

The explosion didn't come. The truck rumbled on down the road.

She was still alive. For now.

5

Adam watched all this in replay, shaking his head in astonishment and admiration. On the first viewing he'd been unable to keep up with what was happening, Mila was so fast, and the images so jerky. But he slowed it down and watched it again until he understood.

It had taken him a while to figure how Mila had managed to escape the bombing of the first truck. Counting down the seconds from the moment she opened her eyes, he knew she didn't have enough time to perform the maneuver before the truck emerged from the tunnel mouth. The second truck should already have passed.

Then he remembered the seven-second delay and almost laughed out loud. What a fool he was. Rebecca would be furious. She'd be doubly so when she found out he'd neglected to order a plane to cover the other end of the tunnel as soon as he realized Mila was still alive.

Why hadn't he ordered the plane to destroy the second truck? He wasn't entirely sure about that. He admired Mila, it was true. And despite the presence of the bomb in her head, he couldn't quite bring himself to believe she was a terrorist. The look in her eyes when they'd discovered it, the confusion and fear, had been genuine. She'd had no idea it was there. If there was a terrorist, it had been Julian, with Mila the unwitting mule.

The confusion and then the celebrations when the first truck was destroyed provided a plausible excuse for letting her escape. He'd get dragged over the coals for incompetence, possibly told to go home. But at least he hadn't had to kill her. And she could be collected easily enough, quietly, without fuss, when the truck reached its destination or stopped to charge up. Maybe they could get that thing out of her head. Maybe she'd be allowed to stay. . . .

Adam switched to Mila's live Feed. He could see she was trying to open a cardboard box. The only light source was from a few rivet holes in the trailer's bodywork.

"What are you hoping to find?"

His voice caused Mila to jump.

"Oh, god!" she said. "I'd forgotten about you. You've been quiet."

"I've been busy," he said.

"Yeah," Mila replied as she scratched at the seal on the carton with her bleeding fingernails. "Busy trying to kill me."

"I have my orders."

"Where have we heard that before?"

Adam ignored the jibe. "What are you looking for, anyway?" He had called up the truck's manifest earlier, and knew it carried nothing but clothing.

"Food," Mila replied.

"This is not a food truck."

"What sort of truck is it?"

"Clothing."

"Great," Mila said. "I could use some new threads."

"You can't escape, you know?"

"You said that before. Just before I escaped."

"I could have ordered a second strike," Adam pointed out. "I could do it now, hit this truck."

"So what's stopping you?"

There was a brief pause before Adam responded. "I would prefer to bring you in alive. I'm on your side, Mila."

She laughed.

"I mean it, Mila. Other Agents wouldn't be so reticent. And I can't protect you for long. Next time they . . . we'll obliterate you."

"At least I'll look fabulous when I die," she said out loud. She had managed to get the carton open, and held up a spangly cocktail dress. "Too much?"

After the delay, Mila saw Adam's Avatar smile quickly, before regaining its customary staid countenance.

"Give yourself up quietly, Mila," he said. "We can remove the device. There may be a future for you here."

Mila snorted by way of response.

"You may have a chance to wear that dress someday."

She began to open another box.

"We know where the truck is going, Mila," Adam said. "It'll arrive at its destination in six hours. Or we could stop it remotely if we choose. Wherever you stop, we'll have people there waiting. There'll be security guards. There'll be Agents. There'll be the military. You won't be able to escape. The only question is how you choose to end it. Peacefully and easily . . . or . . . messily."

"I'm getting changed now. You gonna Watch?"

She unzipped the coverall.

"No," he replied quietly.

Adam had momentarily forgotten Mila couldn't block the Feed. He didn't Sleep the connection, he continued monitoring her by Audio, but minimized the window showing the Visual Feed. He needed to call Rebecca.

Time for a quick mocha first, though, he thought.

"She's still alive."

"She . . . what?"

"She got off the truck we bombed."

"How the hell did she do that?"

Adam shrugged. His Avatar would follow suit. "She's . . . resourceful."

"Where is she now?" Rebecca snapped.

Adam linked Rebecca to Mila's Feed. Blackness. A low rumble on the Audio Feed.

"Why can't I see anything?"

"She's asleep. In the back of a truck."

"So destroy it!"

"This isn't some crappy old road she's on," Adam explained patiently. "She's on the M2. There are human-operated vehicles all over the place. Anyway, we don't need to destroy her. We can pick her up quietly when the truck reaches its destination."

"Where's it going?"

"North," Adam said. "Around London on the M25 and up the M1 to a depot near Leeds. We can have a team waiting for her there."

"You think she's going to let you take her without a fuss?"

"Look," Adam said. "We tried it your way, and we have fourteen dead security guards, and smoking craters all over Kent. Let me deal with this."

"Easy for you to say," Rebecca snapped. "You're not the one who has to explain this to the Minister."

"You can trust me," Adam said.

"Prove it," she said, before hanging up abruptly.

"What are you doing?" Adam asked.

"Art," Mila said. She had opened the back door of the truck and was throwing cartons out onto the road behind. An oncoming car, tiny and sleek, slowed suddenly as the boxes bounced across its path. She carried on hurling boxes until the truck slowed and pulled into the emergency lane. An alarm sounded, a thin, piercing whine. The truck had registered that there was a problem with the rear door and it had lost part of its load, and called for assistance. Mila had surmised, correctly, that the vehicle would be programmed to stop in such a circumstance.

"Not clever," Adam sighed, as she hopped down onto the tarmac and looked around. The road ran through a shallow valley cut into the terrain. Grassy banks obscured her sight lines on either side. "A plane is tailing you. We have other assets in the area as well."

Even as he said this, a small black car pulled off the road and aimed itself directly at her.

But Mila was off, running at a right angle to the road. She leapt a small safety fence and sprinted up the hillside. It had been a risk staying in the truck for so long, but she felt a little better after her brief nap. She'd figured that if they were going to bomb the truck, or stop it, they would have done it sooner rather than later. Something had made her believe Adam when he told her they were intending to pick her up at the depot.

Her ribs ached from where she had slammed into the hanging sign in the tunnel. Her fingers and lower arms were bruised and she had twisted her knee slightly, but there was no significant damage as far as she could tell. She'd chosen bland, functional clothes from the cartons in the truck. A brown top, leggings and a loose skirt which wouldn't get in her way. There had been no shoes. The shoes she had been given at the Center were still serviceable enough, though decidedly grubby now. At least she wouldn't attract too much attention in this get-up. She would lose herself in a crowd, should she be lucky enough to find one.

She slowed briefly to allow herself a glance behind. A man had emerged from the black car and was following her up the hill, running fast. He wore a navy suit and carried something in his left hand. A gun, perhaps? Behind him another larger car pulled up and a group of uniformed officers got out. Agents? A rare sighting of actual police officers? None of them would be friendly, she figured. She turned back to the serious business of running.

"He's not one of ours," Adam said in her head. "The guy in the black car, I mean. Special Agent to judge by his phone signature. Probably sent by the Ministry."

Mila didn't answer.

The terrain was flat and the going was firm. Farmlands, fields. The grass was cropped and she saw sheep in the far corner, looking over at her in dumb amazement.

"Stop, Mila. Please," Adam said.

"Can't talk now," she replied. "Bit busy." Her breath was becoming ragged. Just as well she'd had some sleep.

"I'm telling you," Adam said. "The man behind you is a Special Agent. He will kill you if you don't give yourself up."

"He'll kill me if I do give myself up," she said, and carried on running. Her legs burned with the effort. The aches and pains had gone though, blasted away by sheer exertion.

She came to a fence with a gate and hurled herself over. Then she was off again, sprinting up a dusty track skirting a field. It seemed to head up a slight rise, toward a small wood. If she could get some distance between herself and her pursuer, perhaps she could lose herself in there.

Mila knew how to run. She'd had enough practice, fleeing from the police or soldiers in various towns and cities across the U. Caught, with Julian, stealing food or clothes. Or just finding herself in the wrong place. You didn't last long as a refugee if you couldn't get up some speed.

And even before that, back on the shattered streets of Köls, she'd run with her friends—from security guards or shopkeepers, stealing food or clothes from the decrepit stalls in the ever-shrinking market. She and her friend Vaclav would run after the white Land Rovers of the Corporation, waiting for a plump employee to throw them a bottle of water or half a doughnut. The employees would watch them through the back window, wait until the pursuing group of kids thinned out, until only one or two remained, then throw the rewards to those with the staying power. Mila and Vaclav won often enough, but it had been Mila who'd had the revolutionary idea of sharing the wins out equitably.

"We all start off running," she said. "And if it's not your turn, you drop out quickly. That way the winners don't have to run so far. Then next time it's someone else's turn to win."

The system had worked for a while, until gaunt Alex Gregor cheated, and kept on running when it wasn't his turn, unable to sacrifice short-term personal gain for long-term mutual benefit. The Prisoner's Dilemma. Mila couldn't blame Alex. He was starving. He couldn't wait for his turn.

The next time, Mila outran him, outran them all, and won the prize. Water and a wrapped tuna sandwich.

She did what she needed to do to survive.

It became clear after a minute or so that the man was gaining on her. He was fit and strong. Mila was still a little out of shape and hadn't eaten for twenty-four hours. She could hear him now, the heavy thump of his feet on the dry track behind her.

"When he's close enough," Adam told her. "He will stop, take aim and shoot. He's a trained assassin. He's unlikely to miss."

"If you're trying to cheer me up," Mila panted. "It's not working."

"Stop, Mila," he said. "Turn, raise your hands. He will escort you back to the road where you will be put into a vehicle and taken to a high-security prison."

"You make it sound so tempting."

"There we can assess the . . . device in your head," he said. "To see if it can be removed safely."

"And then you'll kill me."

"No. You've got us all wrong, Mila."

"Adam?"

"Yes?"

"Shut up."

There was a crack and a whining ricochet off to her left as the man fired a projectile weapon and missed.

"Ha," Mila muttered. "Trained assassin, my arse."

The fear of the next shot, though, gave her a burst of speed and she flew off the track, in among the trees at the top of the hill. Tall bracken fronds whipping at her face, she plunged deep into the ancient wood, leaping over fallen trees, ducking and twisting through the oaks and the ashes. In these conditions, her small size and nimbleness gave her the advantage.

This, and the extra time she'd gained when the Special Agent had paused to take his shot, gave her enough of a lead that, once she'd run a couple of hundred meters into the wood, Mila judged she could safely stop to listen.

She looked around quickly. She could hear the crashing of her pursuer some distance behind. Julian would have told her to hide in a tree, but Adam would simply inform the Special Agent to look upward. She found a thick oak and cowered behind it, chest heaving. Adam would report whatever she did, but he'd be seven seconds behind. She had to make that time count.

The sounds of the Special Agent charging through the bracken had stopped. Adam too had gone quiet, perhaps talking to the Agent, telling him where she would be found. The only sounds now were some crows out in the field and the distant drone of what she thought might be a hover plane. She didn't have much time. Even if she eluded the Special Agent, it was possible they'd firebomb the woods. Maybe she should take Adam's advice, give herself up. Take her chances with these strange people, however slim those chances might be. Then maybe she'd find out what the device in her head was, whether it was Julian who'd put it there, and why.

She could hear the crack of snapping foliage as her pursuer came toward her. Her ankle ached. Her wrists burned. She lacked the energy to run.

"Come out, girlie."

Girlie? Mila's eyes narrowed. Well, that settled it. Let them kill her, let them put an end to this. She would not give herself up to people who called her "girlie."

There's always a way. Julian's voice came to her. Look for the best option. The one that gives you the best odds. What's your strength?

Snap. The Special Agent was close now, a few meters away. Too close for her to run, even if she had the strength. Giving up was not an option. What was her strength? The delay. It had been at least seven seconds and Adam would have told the Special Agent she was hidden behind a large oak. As if to confirm, she heard him again, moving toward her. It was time.

Mila stood, bent her knees and sprang upward, grabbing a low, thick branch. She swung herself up and began to count the seconds down. 1 . . . 2 . . .

She leapt nimbly onto a higher branch and ran up the sloping trunk til she was three meters off the ground. 3 . . . 4 . . . 5 . . .

She looked down. The Agent crept around the base of the tree, gun in hand, looking backward and forward. The Feed Adam was seeing would still show her crouching down by the trunk.

. . . 6 . . . 7 . . .

She leapt. And as she did, the Agent looked up suddenly, either hearing the movement, or having been warned by Adam. He raised his gun and fired a micro-second before her feet slammed into his right shoulder.

Mila felt something crunch as she connected. The Agent went down heavily. And then she too was on the ground, earth in her mouth, rolling away to cushion the fall. The Agent was on his feet quickly, his right arm hanging uselessly, the shoulder clearly dislocated. His face was contorted in pain and anger. He lifted his left arm, still holding the gun, and pointed it toward her. But Mila was already in the air, kicking, anticipating this next move. She felt his wrist snap, and the gun flew from his grasp, landing in the dead leaves a few meters away.

Mila ignored it and backed off. Adam was silent in her head, presumably screaming instructions at the Special Agent. Grow a new arm, perhaps?

"I don't want to have to kill you," Mila said, blood pounding in her temples, her voice shaking with the adrenaline.

The Agent stared at her for a few moments, then laughed. With his broken left wrist, he reached across and, using his forearm, wrenched the right shoulder back into place with a crunching pop.

"Gene tech," he said, his voice gravelly. "I can switch off my pain receptors."

"Can you repair a broken wrist?" Mila replied. She felt sick.

"I have a spare," he said waving with his right.

Then he strode toward her. Her heart sunk. He was fifty centimeters taller than her; forty kilograms heavier. Even with one wrist out of action, she figured she was in trouble. But she stood and waited, assuming the stance Julian had shown her.

He stopped close and raised his fists, leading with his good right hand. He edged forward. She waited.

"Take a swing, girlie," he said.

Mila watched, still waiting.

Then he punched, explosively, with impossible speed, using his injured left hand. She hadn't expected that. She leaned back just in time, avoiding the blow, and returned a left jab which he blocked. He followed up with a series of stabbing attacks with his wrists and elbows, some Far Eastern martial art, by the look of it. Mila was forced back, unable to get in a return punch, unable to do anything but deflect blows, each of them jarring her slight body, firing bursts of pain through her own injured wrists. Then he got one through, and her head snapped back, filling with pain and a flash of light. She fell backward and kept going, her feet flipping over her head in a backward somersault, then stumbling as she landed and falling onto her bottom.

And that was when the Agent made his mistake. He grinned and ran toward her. She knew exactly what he intended. He was going to leap at her, feet first, as she tried to get up. But the move was telegraphed and she stayed down, rolling toward and under his body as he flew over her, landing with a grunt of surprise in a pile of leaves. Already on her feet as he raised his head, she kicked him as hard as she could in the jaw.

If Mila had been wearing heavy boots, she might well have killed him. She had a good kick. She'd knocked Julian out once, during a sparring match. But the Special Agent was a tough veteran, his body artificially enhanced, capable of withstanding enormous damage. His head snapped back, but almost immediately his right hand shot out and grabbed her leg. He yanked hard and she fell. He was still dazed from the kick, though, and was reacting slowly. She pulled up her knees and pinned him to the ground. Before he had the chance to flip her over with his greater weight, she slammed her fist into his face.

Once you've hit them, don't stop to admire the result, Julian would have said. Hit them again. And keep hitting until they can't hurt you anymore.

Mila complied. Screaming in anger and adrenaline-fueled hatred, she pounded and pounded the Special Agent's face, smashing his nose, his cheeks, his jaw, splintering bone and cartilage.

She kept punching long after he'd stopped moving, then she slumped forward and rolled away from the corpse, sobbing, a river of emotions coursing through her. She could hear the crows, and a weak rustling in a nearby bush. In the distance she could hear a plane and the shouts of men, searching for her. Dusk was approaching.

"Mila?" Adam said, after a while. After the delay.

She didn't answer. Instead she stood, blinked away the tears, and again she ran.

"You just killed a man, Mila," Adam said, inside her head.

"Shut up!" she replied, knowing she should ignore him, but unable to do so.

"A Special Agent," he went on. "You just killed a Special Agent. They won't rest now until they've got you."

"He would have killed me!" she screamed. She could hear the drone plane again. It seemed to be coming closer.

She walked along the muddy edge of an empty field. It was getting dark and the sounds of her pursuers had faded for the time being. The plane was a worry. It would probably have infrared cameras. Her body heat would appear bright white against the cooling earth.

"He wouldn't have killed you had you given yourself up," Adam said calmly.

"Really?" Mila said. She stopped walking for a moment and turned in a slow 360-degree sweep, speaking to the surrounding dusk. "You seriously believe that? After what happened at the Center? You killed your own people. In cold blood. It was no accident. There was no self-defense involved."

Adam didn't reply.

"Don't you judge me, Adam," she spat. "You have no right."

Adam said nothing and Mila walked on.

Mila knew she didn't have time to sit and watch the truck stop for long, as her instincts told her to do. And as Julian would have insisted. Cresting the hill, she had seen and recognized it immediately, and she knew she had to move quickly. It was dark, and she guessed all these truck stops looked much the same, but there couldn't be that many in the vicinity. Adam and his Techs would easily figure out where she was and either storm it or drop a tactical nuke, depending on how angry they were about losing their Special Agent.

Mila was trying not to think about that. About what she'd done. She knew she'd had no choice, but, still, she'd killed a man. She'd killed before, once. And she'd put plenty of men in the hospital, some of whom may have died. But this was different. She shook her head, trying to clear the image of his face, the crushed purple mess. Where had that violence come from? Where had she found the stomach to do it? Was she a monster? A murderer?

She turned her thoughts to the present situation. She needed to go inside the truck stop. There would be food, and she was weak with hunger. Her body needed to heal itself; she needed to feed it. She also needed sleep, but that would have to wait.

She trotted toward the small collection of buildings, hurdled a low fence and identified the refectory. There were a few people about: a party of laughing teenagers, pushing and shoving each other as they came out of the sliding doors; an elderly couple in evening wear, entering just ahead of her. She made straight for the toilets.

Once inside, she stopped, astonished by the luxury, the cleanliness. She could happily have lived in these toilets. Everything was marble, or an approximation so exact as to make no difference. Dark mirrors reflected a million Milas. She was surprised by how normal she looked. Her clothes were immaculate, she was puzzled to see. Even under close inspection, her top seemed perfectly clean. Her face, though, was pale and she had leaves in her hair. In the reflection behind her she saw a water fountain and suddenly realized how thirsty she was. She drank deeply, the water sweet and cool.

"Dirt-repellent fabric," Adam said out of nowhere. He must have just caught up with her looking in the mirror seven seconds ago.

He'd been quiet for the last hour or so, presumably occupied with something else. Wincing, Mila washed her bruised, bloodied hands. She shook out her ponytail and ran wet fingers through her straight black hair, frowning.

"There'll be a toiletries kit somewhere," Adam said, "in a vending machine."

She paused, then looked around. He was right. She went over to the machine, punched a button and a small vinyl bag dropped into the vending slot. Inside were a comb and a disposable toothbrush. She used them quickly and, satisfied, left the toilets.

"You didn't need to tell me that," she said.

"Agreed," Adam said. "I just thought you needed to feel . . ."

"Human again."

The Special Agent's face came back to her, anger turning to surprise, then to bloodied fear as she punched and punched and kept punching. A comb and some soap wouldn't make that image go away, but at least she felt slightly less like . . . an animal.

"How long have I got?" she asked, knowing Adam would be listening. There was probably a reason he had told her about the toiletries. He wanted to delay her, until they could figure out where she was, get some Agents there.

He didn't reply.

"You know where I am? Which truck stop?"

She didn't expect an answer, but she guessed he'd figure it out soon enough. Despite the lack of signage, and the bland, mass-produced design of the stop, there would be visual clues. A code printed on a fire-extinguisher, a wall picture unique to this stop maybe. How many truck stops could there be in walking distance of where she'd killed the Agent? Four? Five maybe. They'd probably send Agents to all of them. Or planes.

She checked her exits, then walked over to the food counter. An elderly couple was standing there, looking vacant. Checking the menu on their phones, no doubt. She walked up, confidently, and spoke to the woman.

"Can you get the menu? I can't call it up."

The woman looked surprised. "You can't call it up?"

"I think there's something wrong with my phone," she said.

The couple stared as though she'd told them she was a gibbon with a shoe fetish. Who'd ever heard of a phone that didn't work?

Mila smiled winningly at them.

"This isn't going to work," Adam said, sighing. "They'll be suspicious."

"I can order something for you, if you like," the man said. His wife looked at him with slight disapproval.

"Oh, for heaven's sake..." Adam muttered.

"Thanks!" Mila said.

"Would you like me to read off the menu?" the man said.

"Do they have lasagna?"

After a brief pause, he nodded. "Yes."

"I'll have that," she said. "And ice cream for dessert."

He laughed. "Okay, one thing at a time." He made the order. "Would you like to sit with us?"

Mila blinked. She hadn't expected this.

"Yes, please," she replied. No point arousing any more suspicion than necessary, and sitting near civilians would reduce the chances of a long-range blitz.

"See what I told you, Mila?" Adam said in her ear. "People are nice here. They don't deserve to be blown up."

"Tell that to the pilot," she muttered.

"What's that?" the man asked, turning.

"Just talking to myself," Mila replied hurriedly.

Their food arrived almost instantly, the serving hatch hissing open and revealing three platefuls of food. The man had also ordered lasagna for himself; the woman was having a salad.

"I'm Joe," he said. "This is my wife, Darcie."

"Hello, Joe," Mila replied, as they moved to a nearby table and sat down. The seat molded itself immediately to her backside. She flinched, unused to the sensation. "Hello, Darcie," she said, recovering her wits. "I'm Mila."

"I've never heard of a phone malfunctioning before," the woman said, eyeing her coolly.

"Overuse, I think," Mila said, playing the dappy teenager. The lasagna was hot but she tucked in regardless, burning her tongue.

"Looks like I should have gone ahead and ordered that ice cream after all," Joe said. He stood to return to the counter.

"Starving," Mila said, through a full mouth. "You couldn't order me a sandwich, maybe a wrap, to take with me? I'm not going to be able to get this phone fixed until tomorrow."

"It's quiet tonight," Darcie said, when Joe had gone. "We always stop here on the way back from the city. There are usually more people."

"What city?"

"Leeds. We've been to the theater."

"It's almost empty," Joe said, returning with the ice cream. "Where is everybody?"

Mila stopped chewing. She looked out through the cafeteria doors, toward the main concourse. It was deserted. She looked up at Joe, holding a wrap in one hand and the bowl of ice cream in the other. He made as if to say something else, then stopped, focusing internally. Darcie was doing the same. The elderly woman's face suddenly dropped. She looked over at her husband. Together they spoke.

"We have to go."

They had been warned.

Joe slapped down the wrap and the two of them hurried for the door, the old man shooting a scared glance at Mila.

"Thanks for the food," she called. She stood, picked up the wrap, then made her way to the emergency exit she'd seen set into one of the panel windows. It opened easily and she slipped through. Emerging into the cold night air, she heard the drone of a hover plane. They wouldn't bomb the building with civilians in, would they? They must surely give them time to get clear.

Then she heard something else. The whistling sound. A canister dropping from the gaping maw of the plane. Her first thought was for Joe and Darcie. They couldn't possibly have gotten away in time. Then she was sprinting away from the building and the road, back into the darkened fields.

A brilliant white light illuminated the wooded surroundings. A second later she felt the blast. It knocked her from her feet and she landed with a heavy thud on the grassy verge. She flipped onto her back and looked toward the cafeteria, feeling the blistering, blinding heat from the firestorm, then began to crawl backward, desperate to get away, like a scuttling bug escaping a forest fire. A section of roof crashed down a few meters away, and glowing cinders rained down around her. One hit her shoulder, burning her flesh. She hurried to brush it off.

Then she was up again and running, into the darkness. Mercifully cool, mercifully black.

It was a good few minutes before she realized Adam's Avatar had disappeared. In the bottom right of her screen, some tiny text read, CONNECTION LOST.

The drone hovered over the burning building, most of its cameras blinded by the flash of the firebomb. Only one camera managed to record the arrival of a small black car, which hissed to a stop in the staff car park close to the burning cafeteria. A tall man got out and, without pausing, ran across the grass to the rear of the building and disappeared into the darkness, following Mila.

"Who gave that order?!" Adam shouted.

Rebecca sighed and looked out the window.

For once, they were in the same room. Adam had left the Center and come to London, bringing his three Techs with him. They were in the Ministry building, overlooking the Thames. The walls were covered with screens showing various Feeds, which they ignored most of the time, their phones giving them more immediate access to whatever they needed to see.

"There were Citizens inside," he snapped.

"They were given the order to evacuate," Rebecca replied. "They had a good chance. We could have just bombed the building as soon as we knew she was in it."

"You didn't give them enough time. Some of them were old. Infirm."

"The fugitive moved. We had to strike. We got her, didn't we?"

Adam checked again for Mila's signal. Connection lost. He sat down, suddenly feeling lost himself.

"I don't want to do this anymore," he said.

"There's nothing more to do," Rebecca said. "She's dead. It's just the clean-up now."

Adam's head sank down and he covered his face with his hands.

Don't judge me, Mila had said. You have no right.

How could he argue? Mila had asked if it had been him who'd ordered the air strike on the Center. It might as well have been. He was part of this. A cog in the machinery that did nothing but smash and destroy.

"Look," Rebecca said. "You've had a tough time. Seen some things . . . difficult things."

He grunted.

"Go home. Take a week off. Gardening leave. You'll still get your credits."

Adam looked up at her. He knew what this meant. He wouldn't be welcomed back.

He nodded.

"I think that's a very good idea," he said.

Then he shut down his Feed, closing himself off from the world.

Mila knew she had triggered the release of the bomb. Seven seconds after she'd stood from the table. She had calculated they'd wait for everyone to leave the building before striking. But it seemed they were willing to kill civilians in order to stop her. Citizens this time, not just security guards. Her instinct had been right in the Center. Running was her only chance. They would kill her, whatever Adam said.

Mila limped as she skirted a field of tall grass. She considered her options. She needed sleep, but she should take advantage of the broken phone connection. Even if they suspected she'd survived the explosion, they couldn't follow her right now. She had no way of knowing how long it would be down. Presumably, the explosion had caused the problem, bringing down a mast, interrupting the satellite uplink. Would the signal come back if she moved away from the fire? Maybe if she stayed in the countryside, away from civilization, she would remain untraceable? But this was a short-term solution. She needed to travel to London. Julian had told her about people there who could help her. Where to find them or whether they'd be willing, she had no idea.

Her fingers ached. Her ankle felt hot and swollen. She was cold and tired, had dozens of bruises, scrapes and grazes. Even her ever-clean top was damaged, the falling ember having left a black singe mark. On the plus side, she had a chicken wrap, slightly squashed. And for now she was alive, and free.

Up ahead she heard a car on a road and she stopped. The phone signal was still out. Perhaps now was her chance. What other choice did she have, really?

✳ ✳ ✳

It nearly kills her but she pedals all the way to the top. It's the first time she's done it without having to get off and push. Father is there already, tinkering with the antique mountain bike. There are no spare parts to be had anymore so he makes them all himself, grinding and twisting scrap metal in the workshop at the back of the barn.

She gets off the bike and rests it carefully on its side before turning, still puffing, to look at the view. In the old days, before the collapse of the U, this had been a busy mountain pass with a café, tourist shop, car park and viewing area. You can see all the way to the Ural Mountains in the east, and to the west, the valley of the Gul River, winding a silvery path through patchwork fields. She looks for their farm and spots it there below, guarding a fold of the river. Beyond, halfway up a gentler mountain range which forms the other side of the valley, she can see the tumbledown city of Köls. It had once been a thriving, small city, the administrative center for the region, and famous for steel, refined from the iron ore that was plentiful in the surrounding mountains.

But then there was a war, and another one. Köls changed hands each time. The workers fled or were conscripted. The mines and refineries were blown up to deny the resources to the enemy. Everyone said they'd be reopened when things calmed down. But they weren't. Köls was left to slide into decay, worthless without its infrastructure, forgotten even by the warlords.

"You're getting stronger," her father grunts as he tightens a bolt.

Mila smiles as she looks up and drinks in the hazy, russet sky. She knows her father loves her, but he isn't much given to praising her. The occasional gruff acknowledgement means a great deal. And it's true she is getting stronger. She's always been a thin, slight girl. She often wonders if her father had been disappointed she wasn't a strapping boy, to help out on the farm. She does her best, mucking out the pigs, helping with the meager harvest. It is hard to grow much here. The sun punches only weakly through the emission-laden sky. There is no chemical fertilizer to be bought; they rely on animal manure and last year's compost. And taxes are high. The army needs to be fed, after all, and the war machines need fuel. It is a tough life, especially since Mila's mother died giving birth to her stillborn younger brother. But they manage. They are luckier than many farmers, as they can draw usable, slightly tainted water from the river. Water is scarce in other parts of the country. Rain is infrequent and often acidic.

Mila's father stands beside her in silence as they look down into the valley. The wind whips around them and Mila wishes she'd brought a sweater. She shuffles closer to her father and he puts an arm around her.

"We got a letter yesterday," he says. "From the government."

"What did it say?" Mila asks, resting her head against his shoulder.

"Some stupid proposal to build a dam here."

"A dam?" Her eyes blink open.

"Yes, they said there's potential to flood the valley; said they could irrigate a thousand farms with the water. Some Corporation from the Isles is investigating."

Mila pulls away from her father, looking at him in alarm. "But we live here!" she says.

He laughs. "It won't happen, Mila," he says. "It's a crazy idea. Even the First hasn't enough money to waste on a mad project like this."

"Do you promise?" she asks, knowing she sounds like a frightened child.

He nods. "I promise."

Mila stepped confidently out into the middle of the road where she was sure to be seen in the darkness and waved as the car headlights approached. The vehicle slowed rapidly and hissed to a stop a few meters away. A window sighed open and the head of a young girl popped out.

"Are you okay?" the girl asked, concerned.

Mila had been crying. The tears were self-inflicted, but no less real for that.

"My boyfriend dumped me," she said, wiping her eyes.

"What? He just left you here?"

"Well, sort of. We had an argument and I made him stop. Then I ran off, in there," she said, indicating the small wood to the side of the road.

"And he drove off? At night?"

"Yes. Eventually," Mila said. "He waited a long time. I blocked his calls. Everyone's calls."

"The bastard!"

"Yeah. Could you please give me a lift?"

"Of course. Where are you going?"

"London," Mila said, smiling brightly.

"Oh, I'm going the other way, to Leeds. But I can drop you at a coach stop?"

"That would be perfect, thanks."

"You have an interesting accent," the girl said. "Are you from the West Country?"

"East," Mila replied, without thinking.

The girl paused. "East, really?"

"Um, east part of the West Country," Mila said, glancing over at her new companion, who raised an eyebrow but didn't reply.

The girl's name was Holly. She was at college, studying the Third. She liked cats and loud, discordant music. She also liked to talk.

"Did you know they don't have phones in the Third?" Holly asked loudly over the entertainment system. She'd wanted to know more about Mila's boyfriend and the fight, but Mila had shut that conversation down immediately. Instead, to forestall further questions, she had got Holly talking about herself.

"Really? How do they manage to communicate?" Mila asked absently.

"I suppose they just shout," Holly said. "Seriously though, they have old-fashioned phones. Landlines, they call them."

It was warm inside the car. Mila's seat was ridiculously comfortable. She felt safe, and despite the music, she wanted to sleep. Of course, she reminded herself, she wasn't safe. She wasn't safe anywhere on the Isles.

"Development's stalled in most of the Third; gone backward often," Holly continued. "Pollution is a terrible problem. They say the sky is a dark purple over most of Asia now. Dust storms, fog, emissions. Those poor people."

"Most people don't think much about the Third, I suppose," Mila said.

"No," Holly said. "I find it fascinating though."

"Would you ever consider visiting?"

"Visiting?" Holly asked, as if the idea had never occurred to her.

"Some parts are very beautiful," Mila said. "I hear."

"Maybe one day," Holly replied. "When things have improved. When the development programs really start to get moving. I've wondered about making my Contribution at the Ministry of Third Development."

Holly was actually driving the car, Mila noticed. The onboard computer could have driven it if required, but in order to travel at a higher speed, Holly gripped the wheel herself and applied the accelerator. The car wasn't so different in design from the entirely manual models Mila had learned to drive on the farm, just much cleaner.

"I remember when I was a girl," Holly said, "there was a lot on the news Feeds about the war in the U. Or the EU as we called it then. Everyone was worried about whether it would slip back into the Third. Everyone was sure there'd be waves of immigrants escaping their countries, swamping the Isles."

"Mm-hmm," Mila said, drowsily. She wished Holly would let her sleep.

"And they did come, at first. But then we put up the Watchtowers, remember those?" Mila saw Holly was watching her closely.

Suddenly uneasy, Mila nodded. She vaguely remembered reading about the Watchtowers. The Corporation in Köls had made sure the warnings went out. Giant towers dotted around the Isles' coastline, bristling with cameras and guns. If you're thinking about smuggling yourself over, think again. The Isles operated a shoot-to-kill policy in those days, for reasons of National Security, they said. It seemed the towers were gone, but the shoot-to-kill policy remained.

"We don't need them anymore," Holly went on. "Not now everyone has a phone. Oh, what's your number? I'll ping you mine."

Mila froze. If Holly had been suspicious before, soon she would be doubly so.

"What's wrong?" Holly asked. Mila could see it was not the done thing to refuse to swap numbers.

"It's just . . . since the fight with Mark, I've felt I want to . . . hide away. Do you know what I mean?"

The car slowed. Holly took her eyes off the road and peered curiously at Mila.

"Not really, no."

"Sorry," Mila said and turned to look out the window. It was awkward, but what else could she do?

Holly said nothing, but the car sped up again.

"Tell me more about your studies," Mila said, feeling the block of ice which had suddenly formed between them. "Any other fields you might Contribute to?"

Holly paused for a moment before answering.

"I'll probably join the Agency," she said. "Homeland Security. Immigration Control. Somewhere my studies might help."

Another one, Mila thought to herself in bemusement. Everyone's an Agent on this damn island. "Are there that many immigrants these days?" she asked.

"Oh, yes, loads," Holly said. She turned again to look at Mila, who stared out of the window, hiding her flushed face.

"Do any sneak in, evade capture?" Milas asked, trying to keep her voice level.

Holly shook her head. "Yes, but not for long. The Security Ministry employs Special Agents to capture illegals and deport them. Did you know, many of the Special Agents were once immigrants themselves?"

"No, I didn't know that," Mila said. "What happens when they catch them? The escapees?"

"They put them on ships which take them to parts of the world where labor is needed."

"The Hulks."

"Yes, that's what they're called by the immigrants."

"What happens when they get there?"

"They're given housing, food and jobs," Holly said. "They're supported until they can look after themselves. It's all part of the Third Development Program."

Julian had told Mila that the Hulk deportees were, in fact, sold to the highest bidder, be that a warlord in South-East Asia looking for cannon-fodder, or a factory owner in Central Africa looking for workers to extract acid from batteries. She'd met a few illegals on her travels, who'd been Hulked and had escaped. But only a few. Life for most deportees was nasty, short and brutish.

"I heard sometimes they're used as slave labor," Mila said. "Or as soldiers in civil wars."

Holly shifted uncomfortably. "That's what some people on my course say. But the lecturer says it's just propaganda."

"From whom?"

"Our enemies."

"Do you believe that?"

Holly quickly turned her head, this time catching Mila's eye. "I don't know. I like to keep an open mind."

"Okay," Mila said, her heart pounding. She sensed Holly knew there was something odd about her. But why was she hiding her suspicions?

"So the Special Agents are immigrants?" Mila asked.

"Yes, sometimes."

"Then some immigrants are allowed to stay?"

"Mostly they're foreign nationals who've worked for us in their home countries. They are given Agency status, and those foreign Agents who offer loyalty over an extended period are sometimes granted Citizenship."

"Like a reward for services rendered?" Mila said.

"Yes. Veteran Agents who've served overseas are often more effective than volunteer guards from the Isles. That's why they are called in to hunt down dangerous illegals."

Tell me about it, Mila thought.

Julian had provided an alternate view of the relationship between the First and Third Worlds. "The Third World," he'd said, "consists of Africa, most of South America and Central Asia. It is caught in a desperate cycle of poverty. The First controls the economies of these countries via proxy, using Agents, who are constantly monitored and guided via phone. The bugger of it is that the Third isn't really poor. Or shouldn't be. The Third has most of the world's raw materials. It also has thriving manufacturing industries. But ultimately it's all owned by First-World corporations, linked to First-World governments. Most of the profits and much of the best products are taken by the First as payment for 'administrative services.'"

"Why do they put up with it?" she'd asked. "The Third-World governments?"

Julian had laughed at the question. "The governments and elites of the Third-World countries are kept in check by a combination of bribery, blackmail and military threat. Everyone wants to live in the First, and dangling the carrot of Citizenship is one way that the governments of the West coerce the leaders of the poorer nations. Basically, any Third-World politician who wants to get into power has to get into bed with the First-World corporations. Once there, there's no incentive for them to rock the boat. There are plenty of benefits in going along with the status quo."

Mila found herself wishing she could sit across a kitchen table with Holly, mugs of coffee between them, debating the issue into the small hours. She wanted to go to college with her and the other students, talk about her experiences, make them see the truth.

But it was a dream, a fantasy. Something that could never happen.

"Here we are," Holly said, slowing down and pulling into a truck stop identical to the one blown to smithereens an hour earlier.

As Holly looked for a parking space, Mila said, "Did you hear about that explosion up the road earlier?"

"What? An explosion?"

"Yeah, it was on the news."

Holly went silent for a moment as she focused on her Internal Display. The car maneuvered itself into a tight spot between two others.

"I can't find anything about it," Holly said.

"That's odd," Mila said, thinking it was anything but odd. In this land of liberty, the news Channels were tightly controlled.

She got out of the car, scanning the area.

To her left was a long row of coaches, great white monsters, sleekly identical. Groups of people were boarding or getting off. One of the vehicles pulled out as she watched and another two came in, heading for empty spaces. None of them had destination boards. To her right she saw a security guard half asleep in a booth. Behind her was a low building with the toilets, shops and cafeteria, and beyond this, another building, which she guessed was a hotel. Why didn't they signpost anything in this damn country?

"Look, thanks for everything," she said.

"Wait," Holly said. She walked around the car and stood in front of Mila. She had light brown hair, freckles and a sideways smile.

"Where are you really from?" Holly asked.

Mila's mouth went dry. This was where Holly revealed she'd called the Agency, and the drone plane was on its way.

"Your English is perfect, but you have an accent," Holly said. "It's not from the West Country, even the east part."

"Have you reported me?" Mila asked quietly.

"No," Holly said. "I haven't."

"Thank you."

"Not ideal behavior for someone thinking of joining the Agency, I guess," Holly said. "But I'm a good judge of character. I don't think you're a threat."

"I'm not," Mila said quickly. "I just want to be left alone. I need to get to London."

Holly thought for a moment. "Look, I don't have to be back at uni for another couple of days. I'll drive you to London," she said.

Mila shook her head vigorously. "No, no way. You've done enough for me already. You could get into trouble. It could be dangerous."

"Really, I want to help..." Holly began.

"Thank you, but no," Mila said firmly. It was just too risky. Holly seemed to be on her side, but what if the full truth came out? That she was a fugitive and a suspected terrorist? Holly would change her mind soon enough. And besides, the Agency had bombed the truck stop with civilians inside; they wouldn't think twice about bombing Holly's car.

"There must be something I can do," Holly said. "Hold on!" She ran around to the back of the car where the boot hatch hummed as it opened, and started digging around.

It was then that Mila realized Adam's Avatar was back. The connection had been reset. Whatever hiatus had been caused by the explosion had been resolved. It—he—seemed to be asleep. Odd, thought Mila.

"Here it is. I knew I had one," Holly said, holding up a pen triumphantly. "It's old, but I think it works. Now, paper."

"Here." Mila pulled out the chicken wrap, removing the paper cover and handing it to Holly before taking an enormous bite. She grinned contentedly.

"You are so odd," Holly said, laughing. She scribbled something on the scrap of paper then handed it back.

It was a phone number. Fifteen digits.

"You don't want to give me your number, that's fine," Holly said. "But I want to give you mine. Just in case you need . . . well, anything."

Mila couldn't speak for a moment. The gulf between the genuine kindness of the Isle-Dwellers and the casual cruelty of their government snatched her words away.

"Thank you," she said.

Holly watched her closely for a moment.

"You escaped from the Center, didn't you?"

"What makes you think that?" Mila said, backing away.

"It's okay," Holly said. "I told you, I'm not going to report you."

Mila considered for a moment before shrugging. "What gave me away?"

"It was when you mentioned the explosion. It reminded me of

another explosion a couple of days ago in Kent. An Immigration Center building."

"That was on the Channels?" Mila asked, surprised.

"The Agency said it was a fire that had got out of control, but there were pictures. It looked like the place had been nuked."

"They dropped a bomb on it. Not a nuke, some kind of thermo-bomb."

"Who did?" Holly asked.

"The Agency."

"Why would they do that?" Holly asked, sceptically.

"They were trying to stop me escaping." Mila said. "I don't expect you to believe me, but ask yourself this: if they're telling the truth, why would they have pretended it was just a fire?"

Holly looked thoughtful.

"Look," Mila said, "I've said too much. Forget you ever met me, okay? Thanks for the lift."

She turned to go.

"Wait," said Holly.

Mila froze. Was Holly going to give her away after all? She regretted telling her about the bomb. She should have just kept her mouth shut for once.

"Take this," Holly said. She held out a soft navy sweater. Mila grinned and pulled it on.

"I don't know what your real story is," she continued. "But I don't think you're a bad person. I hope it works out for you." She moved forward and gave Mila a quick hug before getting back into her car.

Part of Mila was desperate to go with her. Adam might wake at any moment and realized she was still alive. She waited until Holly's car had reversed slowly out of the forecourt, finished chewing her wrap, then turned and walked toward the coach stop.

On the one hand, thought Mila, having the ID App would be useful right now. She had no idea which of these buses was going to London. On the other, she knew that anything she IDed would also be visible to Adam. She wouldn't be able get on a coach without him being able to tell the destination.

The trick would be to find out where a coach was going and get on it without revealing the destination to Adam. Easier said than done, but she had an idea.

Mila was glad to have the new sweater. Not just because it covered up the burn mark on her shoulder, but the late-night air was cooling quickly. She mingled with the groups of travelers as they laughed, joked and messed around with their luggage. Most of them were young, too young to have their own cars, young enough to be excited about a coach trip. She listened to the chatter, filtering for information, hoping to get a clue as to the destinations.

". . . when we get to Solihull . . ."

". . . how long does it take to get to Edinburgh?"

". . . ages since I've been to Barrow . . ."

She paused, frowned. She knew enough about Isles geography to know that these were northerly destinations, heading away from London. Walking out to the rear of the parked coaches, she peered out toward the road. On the other side of the motorway was the harsh yellow glow of a matching set of floodlights. Of course, there were two stops, one on either side of the road. London coaches stopped on the other side.

She wandered down the row of coaches again, wondering how she was going to get across to the other side, when she overheard something that made her stop.

" . . . you're going to love Beverley . . ."

She froze, momentarily confused, and peered at the girl who was speaking. She and the friend she was chatting to were young. Both had mountain bikes.

"There's this amazing old cathedral there. Good shopping. Loads of great rides around the Yorkshire countryside. And so pretty. Old-fashioned, like it hasn't changed for a hundred years."

Beverley was a place? Is this what Julian had meant? He'd told her he'd had a farm in Yorkshire. But who, or what, was a Minster?

She walked up to the girls. "Excuse me?"

"Yes," the girl said, smiling, no trace of suspicion or concern.

"Did you say you were going to Beverley?"

"Yes, that's right."

"Could you tell me, is there a . . . Minster there?"

"Err, yeah. Beverley Minster."

"And what, exactly, is a Minster?"

"Is this a joke?" Mila realized the girl was wondering why she didn't just search the Web. But she answered anyway.

"A Minster is a big church, like a cathedral."

"I think I might have been there once, when I was little," Mila said. She was remembering something Julian had said, a long time ago.

The girl raised an eyebrow, but seemed to accept this.

"Thanks," Mila said and stepped away. She waited in the shadows for a few minutes until the girls got on the coach, followed by more passengers. The coach started up. Mila rubbed her chin, uncertain.

"Mila?" It was Adam.

Mila's heart lurched and she ran forward, stung into action. The door was just beginning to close.

"Have a nice sleep?" she asked as she ran lightly up the stairs.

The driver winked at her. "Plenty of seats down the back."

"So you're alive," Adam said.

"So it would seem, Sherlock." Mila slumped into a seat, across the aisle and a couple of rows back from the mountain bike girls. The coach pulled out of the forecourt and swung heavily to the left, heading toward the motorway. She risked a quick look out the window. The plump security guard was still sleeping in his little booth. Then she closed her eyes. If she kept them closed, Adam wouldn't be able to tell where she was heading.

"Where are you going, Mila?" he said after a while.

"Just let me sleep," she replied. Was he going to keep bothering her? If only she could block him out.

But Adam didn't speak further and within half a minute, sleep overtook her.

7

Adam froze the picture of the sleeping security guard, zooming in on his lapel, where his number was displayed. He had seen the same thing as Mila as she looked out the window, seven seconds behind.

Though there were few signposts on the Isles, certain things were labeled manually. Low-tech or no-tech objects, which didn't contain ID chips, for example. But also security guards, police, Agents and the military. Anyone whose job put them in danger. In a combat situation, or a tactical theatre, phone signals might be lost or scrambled. And it would be hard to ID a headless corpse using a phone.

All such personnel were required to wear their number prominently displayed on the outside of their uniform. It was this number that Adam read on the replay. He called it immediately, using a hi-urgency ping to let the guard know he'd better answer, dammit.

"Sir?"

Adam switched immediately to the guard's POV.

"Look at the coach leaving," he snapped.

"What?"

"Turn around and look at the exit. There's a coach leaving."

The guard turned. There were three coaches lining up to pull out into the traffic on the motorway.

As was standard procedure, the guard's ID function was turned on. Three nameplates appeared on the guard's Feed, visible to Adam, superimposed over the three coaches. One was headed to Edinburgh, a second to Barrow-in-Furness, the third to Leeds in Yorkshire.

Adam clicked on the drop-downs. Each coach had a number of stops on the way. In seconds he had collated a list and stored it on his phone.

"Do you want me to stop them, sir?" the guard asked.

Adam hesitated for a moment before replying. "No, officer. Thanks for your help." He hung up.

Adam stood in his own sitting room, having left the Ministry once it seemed Mila had been killed at the service station. He'd got most of the way home, dozing in his car, when he'd been woken by an alert informing him that Mila was back online.

He hadn't yet informed Rebecca. He knew he'd need to at some point. Even if he kept Mila's reappearance to himself, some-one would figure it out eventually. Perhaps when no body was found; perhaps when they analyzed his recordings. There'd be a full inquiry. If Adam could have broken the connection with Mila there and then, let someone else deal with the problem, he would have.

Or would he? He was trying not to admit to himself that part of him wanted the Permalink.

But the question was academic. He was tied to Mila, and she to him. The responsible, dutiful part within him accepted that he needed to resolve this situation.

But before he told Rebecca, he phoned Maddie.

"Yes, boss?" she answered.

"I'm sending you three lists of towns and villages. I want you to cross-check these with everything we know about Julian."

"Yes, sir. Can I ask why?"

"No. Just do it. If any of the towns on that list have any connec-tion with him, tell me immediately, okay?"

"Yes, sir. But is it necessary now? The girl is dead."

"Just tying up some loose ends, Maddie," he said.

Rebecca heard the chime of an incoming phone call. It was Frank. She rolled her eyes and wondered if she could ignore it. She was about to go into the Minister's office to confirm the good news.

She sighed and accepted the call. "What is it, Frank?"

"Watch this," he responded, gruffly.

No formality, no respect, these Techs, Rebecca thought.

"What am I looking at?" she asked.

Frank had scooted her a video recording. It was the Feed from the hover plane over the burning cafeteria.

"Watch the little car that drives up," he replied.

Rebecca saw the tall man leap out and run into the fields until he was lost from view.

"Who is he?" she asked.

"Looks like a Special Agent," Frank said.

"And where's he going?"

"That's what I wanted to know," he said.

He clearly had some information for her, but was going to make her tease it out slowly, for effect. She tried to stay patient.

Frank sent a second video, which Rebecca opened quickly. This showed an Infrared Feed from the plane. The cafeteria roof was a dull gray, surrounded by black. Then the screen went white as the canister exploded.

"What am I supposed to be seeing?" Rebecca asked, tetchily.

Frank rewound a little to just before the explosion, and she saw he'd added a graphic, showing an expanded section of the image. On the far side of the building, a white blob moved away from the cafeteria, out into the blackness. Then the building exploded again.

"What was that? A person?"

"I think that was the girl," Frank said.

"And the Special Agent was following her?"

"Yes. I think he must have seen her and took off after her."

"So why wouldn't he share that information?" Rebecca cried

as realization sank in—the hideous prospect of telling the Minister she'd failed again.

Frank's Avatar shrugged. "Special Agents play by their own rules."

"Thank you, Frank," Rebecca said, dry-mouthed. "Call me if you get any more information. In the meantime, get Adam and force him to open his damn Feed. It's the only way we have of tracking the girl."

"I've called him three times already," Frank said. "He won't answer."

"Keep trying. If necessary go over there and hammer on his door."

"Okay," Frank said, and hung up.

Rebecca looked at the Minister's door and swallowed hard.

The bathrooms in the coach were amazing. Not quite as amazing as the toilets in the truck stop, but most definitely the second-nicest lavatories Mila had ever visited. There were only about thirty seats on the coach, and downstairs four complete bathroom suites, each with a shower, toilet, sink and a selection of toiletries.

Mila had allowed herself to sleep for three hours. Julian had taught her the technique of setting an internal alarm clock.

"Adam, you there?"

"Yes, Mila?"

"I'm going to have a shower now, okay? Can you give me some privacy?"

"No, Mila, I can't do that."

"You let me get changed in the truck."

"I knew where you were then. We were following the truck. I can't stop Watching you this time."

"Fine, well, enjoy the show," she said, pulling off her top.

She hadn't really expected him to turn off the Feed. Though he had told her about the toiletries bag at the truck stop. And of course, back in the Center he'd left her the seven second delay so crucial to her escape. He was on the wrong side, certainly, but he was an anomaly, Adam, not just a good cop by profession. He was genuinely a good person. Like Holly, and Joe and Darcie. The Citizens were good, Julian had often told her. They were helpful, kind, warm-hearted, generous. It was just the governments in the First. The monstrous corporations. They were the cancer in this society.

The water in the shower was deliciously hot. There must have been some clever suspension arrangement in the bathrooms because the swaying of the vehicle was hardly noticeable. She thought of Adam a hundred miles away. Had he minimized the Feed? Or was he Watching her? She was surprised to find it didn't bother her too much.

Mila could have stayed in there for an hour, but she was conscious of the time. Any minute the coach could be stopped by the Agency. She towelled herself dry and slid back into her clothes, delighted to find a dispenser that provided fresh underwear, comfortable and practical by design.

"Are you there, Adam?" she asked, though she knew he was.

"I'm here," he replied, his Avatar expressionless. "I wasn't Watching. I minimized the Video but kept the Audio on to monitor you."

"Oh," she said. "Why didn't you tell me you were going to do that?"

"I didn't want you to know," he said. "You might have taken advantage."

"You wouldn't be lying to me by any chance, would you?" she asked, mischievously.

"Scout's honor," he replied, and she laughed.

As subtly as she could, Mila scanned her environment, looking for anything that might help her. Remembering, testing, planning. The service hatch beside the sink did not pass her notice. She'd need a set of Allen keys to remove the bolts, though.

Returning upstairs she found a dispensing machine providing hot drinks and snacks. She found herself attracting a few glances and knew she must have presented a curiously comical figure, trying to figure out how it all worked. But eventually she got herself water, a coffee, and a large selection of pastries and pancakes, which she jammed into a paper bag.

She'd been trying to figure out how likely it was that the Agency would discover which coach she was on. First they'd have had to identify which service station she'd been at, which they could probably do by process of elimination; they knew she couldn't have gotten far. They could compare the pictures from her Feed with archive footage, or the Feeds of guards or employees at all the service stations in the area. They could also check the records of the coach company and find out which vehicles had left at around the time her link to Adam had been reconnected.

She reckoned they could then find the phone numbers of the drivers and monitor their Feeds. Did the coach contain some sort of tech that could ID each passenger? Was everyone onboard a potential spy for the Agency?

Mila wished she hadn't drawn attention to herself by making such a hash of getting the coffee. She hunkered as low in her seat as she could. What would they do if they found her? Drive to an Agency building? Stop to let a team of waiting Agents onto the coach?

Dawn was breaking. They'd pulled off the motorway while she'd been in the bathroom and were currently on a narrow back road. Mila reflected that it was a good thing there were no visual clues as to her whereabouts or destination. As long as she didn't know where she was, neither did anyone Watching her.

Once Mila had returned from the bathroom and he had checked she was safely back in her seat, Adam had gone to bed. But he had slept just half an hour before he was woken by the sound of an alert. Someone was at the door. Gentle lights came on automatically for him as he stumbled down the hall, IDing the visitor as he went. But whoever it was wouldn't ping back. Adam reverted to the more traditional method of peering through the old spy-hole. After a brief hesitation he used his phone to open the door.

"Good evening, sir."

The visitor was handsome, with blond hair, a fashionable suit and the look of a man who very much knew how to handle himself.

"Good evening. Identify yourself, please," Adam said.

"Special Agent Miles, sir. May I come in?"

Another hesitation. Then Adam nodded. He showed the man through to the sitting room and gestured to a sofa.

"A drink?"

"Thank you, no," Miles said. He perched himself lightly on the edge of the sofa and watched Adam carefully. He in turn was being comprehensively scanned, electronically poked, x-rayed and monitored by a sophisticated array of devices installed around the flat. He carried a handgun, but as far as Adam's phone told him, nothing else.

"What can I do for you, Special Agent?"

"It's not what you can do, sir. It's what you will do," Miles said, smiling.

"Oh?" Adam said, bristling a little. In theory, he outranked any Special Agent. Even if he was on gardening leave, Miles should not be speaking to him like this. "And what will I do for you, Special Agent?"

"You'll share your Feed with me. I need to see what you can see."

"And why would I do that?" Adam replied, trying not to show how irritated he was by the Agent's smug grin.

"Because I think your little terrorist friend is still alive," Miles said. "I think you're sheltering her."

Adam froze. How the hell . . . ?

"How do I know this?" Miles asked, reading Adam's mind. "I'm a Special Agent, asked to look into this matter. I have contacts with security companies and coach companies. I plan to use my phone, my brain, my wits to solve what is, in fact, a very simple puzzle, but seems to have been too much for you."

"You think Mila is still alive?" Adam asked, stalling for time.

"I know she is still alive," the Special Agent said. "And you are going to let me view your Feed, which will confirm it."

"As far as I'm concerned," Adam said, trying not to let his nervousness show, "Mila is dead and the matter is closed. I have been temporarily relieved of my duties and have all the rights of a private Citizen. You have no authority to force me to share my Feed with you."

"But why would you deny me this simple request, if you have nothing to hide?"

"Ah, the argument of all those who seek to take away our liberties. . . ." Adam began.

"Spare me the student debate," Miles said, waving a hand airily. "Just open your Feed to me and if what you say is right, then I'll leave with an apology."

"No," Adam replied.

"Why not?"

"Because," he said, sitting down opposite the Special Agent and returning his gaze levelly, "I don't like you."

Miles laughed. "I can get the Minister to authorize a tap on your phone, if you prefer. We can force entry, and if we do, then we'll look at everything. Every message you've ever sent, every adult film you've watched, every affair you've conducted. We'll strip you bare."

"Why would that concern me, if I have nothing to hide?" Adam shrugged. "Go ahead."

Suddenly Miles stopped smiling, struggling to control his temper. "We don't have a lot of time here," he said quietly. "We have a terrorist on the run. She has a bomb in her head and could set it off at any moment."

"How do you know that apprehending her won't cause her to set the bomb off?" Adam said. "Maybe she'll blow the coach to smithereens."

"So she is on a coach?" Miles said, smiling again. "I thought you said she was dead."

Adam said nothing, cursing himself for the slip. If only he'd had more sleep over the last few days. This was exactly why the Agent had chosen 3:45 a.m. for his visit, when Adam's wits would be most scattered.

"What does she mean to you, this girl?" Miles asked. "Why are you protecting her?"

"I'd like you to leave now," Adam said. "Go get your warrant from the Minister."

"Do you know her? Or the people she works for?"

"Do I have to call the police?" Adam asked.

The Special Agent watched him carefully for a few moments,

then stood and walked to the front door. He stopped on the threshold and turned to Adam.

"Ask yourself why you are doing this, sir. Ask yourself whether it's worth it. Whether she's worth it."

"Good evening, Special Agent," Adam said, not meeting his gaze, one hand on the door, ready to slam it shut.

Miles shook his head briefly and was gone.

Adam put his back to the door and slid down it, holding his head in his hands. Why was he protecting Mila? It wasn't through fear of being discovered that he'd delayed passing on the fact that she had survived the explosion. He knew that holding onto the information carried a far higher risk. What did he hope to gain? He'd told himself he wanted to solve the case himself. Bring her in peacefully and prove his point. But if he was honest with himself, there was more to it than that.

There was something about her. The way she thumbed her nose at authority. The way she never gave up. She reminded him of a younger Clara, except with a sense of humor. Mila was no terrorist, he was sure of it. He couldn't just let them kill her. He had to find out what the object was in her head. Neutralize it and remove the threat. Show the Agency that he knew what he was doing. Thumb his nose at those like Rebecca and the Minister who wanted to throw out the Privacy Laws and smother the country in CCTV cameras.

Adam asked his servitor to make him a coffee. It was too early to make the call he needed to make. He Watched Mila instead. She also had a coffee in front of her, but was apparently finding sleep easier to come by than he was. Her eyelids were drooping wearily and the comforting hum of the coach engine seemed to be lulling her to sleep.

He pinged Maddie.

"Yes, sir?"

"Any updates on Julian's connection with the list of destinations?"

"Not yet, sir. Still working on it."

Adam sighed. "What else do we know about Julian?" he asked.

"What do you mean?"

"He used to be an Agent, I know, but in what field?"

"The Ministry of Third Development."

"He worked in the field?"

"Yes, mostly in the U, I think."

"He never worked on the Isles?"

"I don't know, his record is heavily redacted. He stopped working for the Ministry around eight years ago. What he got up to after that I have no idea, except that around two years ago he went rogue and there are no further entries."

"That part of the report has been blacked out?"

"Yes, that's right," Maddie replied.

"So someone knows what he's been up to."

"I would say so, yes," Maddie said. "I'll send you the link to the report."

"Don't bother," Adam said. He knew his access had been cut, the documents rendered unreadable to him.

Something else occurred to him.

"Julian would have had a phone, as an agent?"

"Yes. But the connection would have been severed once he went rogue. It would have had limited functionality."

"And was the phone recovered from the body? Was the data accessible?"

"I'm not sure I can say. . . ." she said, after a pause. "It's just— Rebecca told me you've been sent home."

"Maddie, I'm on gardening leave," Adam said. "I'm not suspended. You can tell me what was found."

"Frank said he's been trying to call you," she said, cautiously.

"I don't want to talk to Frank," Adam said, shortly. "I want to talk to you. Look, Julian's body was found in the Channel. Has it been autopsied?"

"Yes, they carved him up."

"And the phone?"

"The phone was damaged," she said. "Most recordings were lost. . . ."

"Was it Julian who implanted this device in her skull?"

"We don't know. The records are incomplete, as I—"

"Do you know what the device is?"

"No, we don't. . . ."

"Is there anything you do know?" he snapped, then felt bad. None of this was Maddie's fault.

"We're assuming it's some kind of bomb," she continued patiently.

"You have anything else on the device? Anything you picked up when we scanned Mila?"

"Not really. It has no ID panel. The casing is impervious to ultrasound, so we couldn't see inside it. The projection at the lower end is probably a receiver, so it can communicate with a phone."

"So it could be activated by a phone call?"

"That is likely, yes."

"Thanks, Maddie. Sorry I snapped," he said. "If anything comes up, let me know, okay?"

"Sure," Maddie said. "And Adam . . ."

"Yes?"

"I know what Frank wanted to talk to you about."

"Yes?"

"He wants you to reopen your Feed to us. To Rebecca."

Adam said nothing.

"What should I tell her?"

"Tell her I'll think about it," he said, finally, then hung up. He walked into the kitchen and looked out the back window into the gloom of an overcast morning. He needed sleep, but there were too many questions floating around in his head.

He sat with his mocha before him and watched the milk swirl, smelling the sweet warmth, remembering when he was happy. It was some time before he realized that he'd already made his decision.

He called Rebecca.

She answered immediately.

"What the hell do you think you're doing?" she said. "We've

been trying to contact you for hours. The girl is alive. You knew and said nothing."

"I'm on leave," he replied. "I was catching up on my soaps."

"You think this is funny?" she spat. "Open your Feed to me now!"

"I'm not going to do that, Rebecca," he said quietly.

"Adam," Rebecca said, with ice in her voice. "You need to think this through."

"I've been doing nothing else," he said. "Thinking about those guards you had killed. Thinking about those poor civilians in the cafeteria. Thinking about how many more people you'll kill with your aggression and your paranoia. I won't be part of it anymore."

"We can force you to open your Feed," she said. "We can insert a physical shunt. Insert a cable into your skull."

"Good luck getting the authority for that," he replied.

"I have Level Three clearance from the Minister," Rebecca told him.

"And I have recordings of you ordering a military strike on a building with civilians in it," he fired back.

She said nothing.

"I found out something else," Adam said. "Ten years ago Julian was working for the Ministry of Third Development," he said.

"And?"

"I looked up who was running that department at the time. It was our friend the Minister. He was only a Junior Minister at the time."

"What's your point?"

"I just think it's a strange coincidence that the Minister has taken such a personal interest in the associate of one of his former employees."

"Hundreds of people worked for that department," Rebecca snapped. "You're the one who's paranoid now."

"What's their connection?" Adam asked. "Why was Julian's record redacted?"

"Adam," she said, clearly trying to control her temper, "it doesn't need to be like this. Come in. We can talk about this face to face. Sort things out."

"I've had enough of talking," Adam said, and hung up.

He made another call to another number. The call was held. Either she was occupied and would answer soon, or she couldn't make up her mind whether to answer or not. He waited for a while, then hung up again.

He judged he had around fifteen minutes before they came for him.

Mila woke as the coach began to slow. They pulled off the road and stopped at an uncomfortable angle. Something felt wrong. Mila raised her head blearily and peered out of the window, half-blinded by the low-hanging sun, impossibly bright and golden, so different from the watery red orb that floated wearily across the sky of her homeland.

"Agents," said one of the cycle girls opposite. "There's a roadblock."

Mila's breath froze in her lungs. But why should she be surprised? Of course they were going to track the coach down. She should have gotten off it hours ago.

Always be one step ahead, Julian said. It was too late now.

Clearly roadblocks were not a common occurrence on the Isles. The girls, along with the other passengers, craned their necks to see what was going on. At least this meant she hadn't been identified publicly as the suspect. She remembered the frightened faces of Joe and Darcie just before the cafeteria was bombed.

While their attention was engaged by the scene outside, Mila reached up and grabbed a backpack belonging to one of the girls. Keeping low she headed for the steps down to the bathrooms, shoving her breakfast pastries into the backpack as she went. She entered the same cubicle she'd been in before, closed and locked the door behind her. In the corner of her vision, she could see Adam's Avatar, awake and observant.

"You're quiet," she said as she rummaged through the backpack.

"I'm just curious to see what you're going to do in the bathroom," he replied.

"Pervert."

"You know what I mean."

The backpack contained a whole load of useful items. Energy bars, a bottle of water, a raincoat, rolled up impossibly tight. Right at the bottom, Mila found what she was looking for, a cyclist's multitool. Holding it brought back memories of her father. Those precious few days when they'd had the time to cycle up the mountain, or along the river. She shook her head and concentrated on the here and now.

Seven seconds later, Adam spoke.

"Ah," he said. "Clever."

Mila had already unscrewed one of the bathroom panel bolts and was starting on the second. She could hear voices and heavy footsteps upstairs.

"I've managed to access the Feed from one of the passengers," Adam said. "There are six Agents on the upper deck. One is talking to the girl you stole the backpack from. She's noticed it's missing. The other has found your empty seat."

The second bolt dropped to the floor and she moved to the third.

"Why are you telling me this?" Mila asked. "I'm not giving myself up."

Adam didn't answer.

The third bolt was stiff. Oh hell, she thought, please don't let it be cross-threaded. The Allen key slipped and the tool clattered to the floor. The footsteps were coming down the steps.

"More haste, less speed," she muttered. Find the right key, slip it back into the third bolt and twist with everything you have, Mila.

She winced with the pain, her damaged hands protesting. But then it gave. She twisted hard twice then spun the multitool. The bolt came out easily.

One more.

There was a knock at the door of the cubicle next to hers.

"They're coming down the stairs," Adam informed her.

"Keep up," she replied, rolling her eyes.

"Oh, yeah, I keep forgetting the delay. Do you have company already?"

"No . . ." she said, then, "Yes," as someone banged on the door. The final bolt came out and the panel sagged toward her. She grabbed the backpack, shoved it through the gap and rolled through behind it, just as something heavy crunched against the cubicle door.

As she'd expected, she found herself in the luggage compartment under the coach. It was mostly empty, just a few heavy suitcases and, over in the corner near the door hatches, the two mountain bikes.

It was too low to stand. She scooted on her bottom across to the furthest hatch and looked for a means of opening it from the inside. Thuds echoed from the bathroom above.

"Ah, the luggage compartment," Adam said.

Dammit, she thought. He'd tip them off, of course. They'd have people waiting for her outside.

Tentatively she pressed a few visible parts of the lock mechanism, to no effect. Then a huge crash from behind spurred her into action. Sitting on her bottom, she kicked powerfully with both feet. The door didn't open, but she felt something give. She kicked again, then once more, and the hatch flew open. The morning sun flooded the space, momentarily blinding her. She smelt the sharp tang of cut grass, with a faint, earthy undertone of manure. The smells of the country. For an instant she was back on her father's farm.

Then she was deafened as someone fired a gun and she felt a burning in her hip. Adrenaline took control of her body and some-how she was outside, dragging one of the bikes with her. There was no one outside waiting for her, but she didn't question it, just jumped on the bike and cycled off down the road.

She tried to build up speed but the bike seemed incredibly slow. She twisted the gears and stood on the pedals, exerting her full force, ignoring the pain from her hip.

A shout came from behind, and further shots. But she was moving faster now. There was a track leading off the main road and she turned onto it, tires crunching gravel. Another gunshot split the air and a bullet whined as it ricocheted off a concrete guardrail.

They'd be after her in a car, she knew. She had to go where a car couldn't follow.

"You stole that girl's bike," Adam said. "You could get into trouble for that."

Adam was acting very strangely, Mila thought. Flippant, irreverent. But she had no time to analyze it just now. She needed to focus on getting away.

She raced down the dirt track, swooshing through puddles and bunny-hopping over tree roots that snaked across the path. The track was bounded on both sides by a hedge-fence combination that would take some getting over. The fields beyond didn't look conducive to cycling either. She could hear a vehicle behind her, engine racing as it strove to catch up. She looked anxiously for a turning point or a gap in the fence. Still nothing. Gentle bends in the track offered no real cover. The car was getting closer and she soon heard the sound of another shot. They obviously felt they were near enough to have a chance of hitting her.

There it was. A stile, over the fence. Mila braked sharply and skidded to a stop, almost losing control. Risking a quick glance back up the track, she saw the car was actually two cars, the first just a dozen meters away and approaching fast, an officer hanging out the window, a gun pointed straight at her. She threw the bike over the stile and leapt over after it. She caught her foot in her haste but got over just as the car came smashing into the fence. Metal screamed as it was gouged by the barbed wire. The stile was demolished.

Mila got back on the bike and flew off down the narrow path. Mercifully there was a bend after just a few meters and she was out of sight. She heard shouts and the slamming of car doors behind her. But they couldn't catch her now.

"Ouch," Adam said, a few seconds later. "That paintwork's going to need touching up."

"Why are you so cheerful?" Mila panted.

"Day off," Adam replied. "Well, actually a year. Possibly the rest of my life."

"They fired you?" Mila asked, swerving to avoid a low branch hanging over the path. "Nothing to do with me, I hope?"

Adam laughed.

The countryside was glorious in the morning sunshine. It was high summer and the woods were bursting with life. Scurrying animals bustled away through the undergrowth and panicky birds flitted off as she rode by. Mila took a deep breath and tried not to think about the warmth spreading around her midriff where her hip wound continued to bleed.

"So why are you still Watching me?" she asked.

"I don't have a choice," he replied. "It's a permanent connection, remember?"

"You could Sleep it. Or are you still feeding information to other Agents?'"

"No," he said. "Not for now."

Mila's heart lifted slightly.

"But don't you think I'm a terrorist threat, like everyone else does?"

"I'm not sure," he answered. "I don't entirely trust you, it's true. But I saw the look on your face when we found that bomb in your head. You were as surprised as the rest of us."

Mila cycled on in silence for a few moments. She was well clear of the Agents, but she'd need some time to look at her wound. She needed to put more distance between her and her pursuers before she stopped.

"I was surprised," she said. "I don't know what it is. I don't know how it got there."

"You have your suspicions though," Adam said. Not a question. A statement.

"It was probably Julian," she said.

"How could he have put it there without you knowing?"

So Mila told him about waking up in the hospital in Frankfurt. About the head wound which had itched like mad, the headaches she'd had ever since. About what Julian had told her. That he'd given her something to keep her safe.

"I guess this is what he was talking about," Mila said. "This gift. He had some dodgy back-street surgeon implant it when I was out cold." She pulled up and dismounted, the pain in her hip too much now. She pushed the bike behind a huge oak and kneeled down, gently pulling her top out of the waistband of her skirt. She was putting off removing the sweater, frightened of what she might find.

"Why didn't he tell you what he'd done?" Adam asked softly.

Mila shrugged, then winced with pain. "I suppose he thought I'd freak out. I might demand whatever it is be removed. Maybe he thought I'd leave him and refuse to go any further."

"Yes, of course," Adam said.

"It's a big deal, isn't it?" Mila said pointedly. "Implanting something into someone else's head without their permission?"

Adam sighed. "Maybe he had his reasons."

Mila lifted up the hem of her sweater. The self-cleaning fabric of her top couldn't cope with this much blood. It was drenched a rich crimson; bright vitality bursting through broken flesh. She touched the swollen, bloodied skin gingerly, wincing again. The wound was a gash in her hip, the bullet having ripped its way through and out the other side.

Adam was speaking. "So what's your plan now? Are you . . . Oh my god, you've been shot!"

"Welcome aboard," she breathed softly.

"You need to get to a hospital," he said.

"I can't go to hospital, Adam. They'll catch me."

"I'll smooth it for you," he said. "No one will ask any questions. We're a trusting lot, you know. Those of us who aren't Agents, anyway."

Mila felt weak. Her head swam. She pulled one of the pastries out of the backpack and ate it quickly, washing it down with the bottled water. She needed to move again. The Agents would be following, on foot. And was that the sound of another damn drone?

She took off her sweater and the burned top underneath, which she ripped, with difficulty, into two halves. She tied them together and around her waist in an attempt to stop the blood loss. Then she put her sweater back on. It was stained but not so badly it would be immediately visible.

"Come on, Mila," Adam said, urgently. "You need treatment."

But she stood for a moment, listening to the birds, breathing in the scent of the countryside. Across a field she could see an idyllic farmhouse, painted white, with roses around the door and a crooked chimney pot.

"Now, Mila," Adam said.

Slowly she turned, and bent painfully to lift the bike.

"I've checked the Web," Adam said. "There's a small community hospital in Beverley. Just walk in and ask for emergency triage."

"Won't they want to access my records?" she asked.

"They'll try to ping you, but just ignore them and keep asking for the triage. They'll do it."

"And then they'll call the Agency."

"I'll phone them beforehand, tell them you're a Special Agent and they're not to ask any questions."

"Will that work?"

"For a while," Adam said. "They'll check out my credentials, and when they find I'm suspended they'll contact my superiors. But all that will take a while."

"Okay," Mila said. The sound of the drone was clearer now, unmistakeable.

"I've got a map of the area," Adam said. "I'll guide you."

She hesitated.

"You have to trust me, Mila."

"Right."

How could she trust him? This could be a ruse. Even if he didn't want to kill her, he might have decided the best thing to do was get her to a hospital where she could be anaesthetised and brought to a secure facility.

But in the absence of other options, she got back on the bike and cycled off again, following Adam's directions.

So do they not have money in the First?" she asks. She is counting what's left of the cash they took from Köls. It hasn't lasted as long as they'd hoped. Everything is expensive in the U. No one has enough food, or petrol.

"Sort of," Julian says.

They are driving along a pitted tarmac road, running through endless white polytunnels. Thousands and thousands of them. "It works like this. Basic stuff is free. Decent food, bog-standard clothes, healthcare, schools, public transport, housing and that sort of thing. But if you want something special, then you have to pay extra for it."

"Like what, fancy food?"

"Yeah, or if you want to live in a nice house, with a big garden, rather than a block of flats. Or if you want the latest fashions."

"So how do you pay for those things?" she asks, looking out the window, wishing they could stop and walk into one of the poly-tunnels and gorge themselves. They haven't had a lot to eat lately, trying to conserve their money. Julian has told her that the polytun-nels have anti-intruder security systems, including gas. Breaking in would be a short-lived experience.

"You work," he says. "Or Contribute, as they call it. You don't have to lift a finger if you don't want to, and most people don't work very hard, but if you do a few hours here and there you can build up credits, which they store on your phone. You use those to buy extras."

"So it's like a normal economy?"

"Not really," he says, laughing. "It's all for show. Everything's subsidized. And because they don't let immigrants in, they end up paying a lot of credits for low-skilled jobs that no one wants to do. You can get a job as a nighttime security guard or a loo cleaner, work twenty hours a week and live like a queen. That's why it's such a great place once you get in and have a phone."

"So how does the economy function, if no one works hard and everything's free?"

Julian waves a hand out the window at the polytunnels.

"Because of this," he says.

"What do you mean?"

"You remember the spreadsheets I showed you back in Köls? All the wealth, all the resources traveling from the Third to the First? Well, here it is. You guys work so they can sit on their arses getting fat."

Mila is silent for a while as she watches the white tent-like structures whip past.

"That's not fair," she says.

"Life's not fair," Julian replies.

Rebecca had called a team meeting. She wanted her Techs physically present. They sat, she, Maddie, Jason and Frank, at a long table in a boardroom that was hardly ever used. A great bank of windows looked out over the river. South London beyond was a glowing mass of light under the dark night sky. Listening in on the meeting was an anonymous presence, appearing on their IDS screens as a grayed-out Avatar. Rebecca hadn't said so, but everyone knew this was the Minister.

"Here's the situation," Rebecca said. "We've lost contact with the target. Adam has been removed from the case and has denied us access to the Permalink he had with the girl. What are our options?"

"We need to shunt Adam," Frank said immediately. Of the three Techs he was the most analytical, the least human.

Rebecca eyed him coldly. "What if we can't find him?"

The Techs looked at her in surprise.

"He's disappeared?" Maddie asked. Rebecca watched the dark-haired girl carefully. She suspected Adam and Maddie had a history. Did Maddie know something?

Rebecca half-expected the Minister to speak at this point, but he remained silent. She'd be called back to his office down the hall after this strategy meeting.

"Is there another way?" she asked.

"We have the number, and the access code of the girl's phone," Maddie said.

"Yes, but it's slaved to Adam's phone," Rebecca said. "How does that help us?"

Maddie tried hard not to roll her eyes at the slow-wittedness of her boss.

"We can reset the phone. Give her a new number."

"You can do this remotely?"

"Yes."

Rebecca thought this through for a moment.

"That would break the link between her and Adam," Jason volunteered.

"And then we could Watch her," Frank said, nodding his head. "We'd be able to figure out where she is."

"But she'd just block us, wouldn't she?" Rebecca said. "If we give her her own number, she'll have all the functions of the phone available to her, including the privacy settings."

But Maddie was already shaking her head. "It'll be factory de-faults. And without the access code to the bios, she won't be able to change any settings."

"And the default settings are no privacy?" Rebecca asked, surprised.

"On the AV Feed, yes," Jason said. "For everything else, de-faults are set to private by law."

"So she won't be able to stop us Watching her Video Feed, but we can't listen to her phone calls?"

"That's right. You can phone her, but she doesn't have to answer."

"What about the delay?"

"Delay is default," Frank said flatly. "Can't change that."

"Dammit!" Rebecca spat. "But we can break her connection with Adam?"

"Yes," Maddie said. "It's possible they could get back in contact, though, if they manage find one another's numbers."

Rebecca waited for a moment, watching the Minister's featureless Avatar.

"Do it," he said. "And find and arrest Adam while you're at it. We need him out of the game."

"Erm, I don't want to panic you," Adam said, "but I think you might need to pick up the speed a little."

The going was difficult on this part of the path. It wound erratically through ancient oaks, was thick with leaves and uneven with roots and stones. Despite everything, Mila wondered at the beauty. Soft morning sun, filtered by the leaves, floodlit spores and dust mites floating through the still air.

"Why?" she asked. Her side was numb now and she was finding pedaling harder than ever. She'd engaged granny gear to make it easier.

"I'm still monitoring the coach passenger," Adam said. "A man I think might be a Special Agent arrived on the scene a few minutes ago."

"And?" she asked, turning sharply to avoid a tree root thrusting its way out onto the path.

"And there were two bikes, remember?"

"There's someone following me on a bike?"

"Yep. Watch out for that tree root!"

"Oh, for heaven's sake, Adam," she replied impatiently. "Get with the program. The tree root was seven seconds ago."

"Oh, yeah, sorry. Anyway, speed up."

She twisted into fourth gear and tried to stand on the pedals, which caused a sharp stab of pain. She sat down again. Flicked back into third, she found she could pedal fast enough. Each bump of the track was agony though, and she could feel the creeping slickness of blood on her lower back.

"You should reach a small road soon," Adam said. "Turn left, and it'll bring you toward Beverley."

Mila was about to answer when she heard the unmistakeable sound of bike tires on the stony track behind her. She turned but her pursuer was hidden by a bend in the path. Gritting her teeth, she moved up to seventh gear and stood on the pedals, ignoring the pain.

Then there was nothing but pain and pedaling for what seemed like forever. She reached the road and swung out, not even checking for traffic, not daring to lose the momentum she'd spent so much precious energy achieving. The day was still and quiet. Other than the distant hum of the drone plane she could hear nothing but the hiss of her tires on the tarmac and those of her unseen pursuer.

Crack.

Another gunshot. She flinched, but didn't hear the bullet hit.

"You're going to need to get away from him," Adam said in her ear. "You're not far from the town. You must lose him before you go to the hospital."

"Thanks," she panted. "Hadn't occurred to me."

But she knew what he was asking was impossible. A tired, hungry and injured girl, even one as fit as Mila, couldn't hope to out-cycle a Special Agent. She'd have to try something else. Up ahead was a tight bend in the road, skirting another oak. She stood on her pedals as another crack rang out behind her. He must have slowed down a little to take his hand off the handlebars. Now was her chance.

She slalomed around the bend, braked hard and leapt off the bike. She found her feet, just, and picked the bike up, swinging it violently in a wide arc as the Special Agent came around the corner at speed. He held his gun awkwardly against the handlebars, affecting his ability to steer, and he was unable to avoid the horizontal bike heaving toward him.

The Agent was knocked backward off the bike, which carried on and crashed into the bushes at the side of the road. He hit the tarmac hard but clung onto the gun. Mila danced forward, adrenaline pinching out the pain, and kicked the hand holding the gun.

The Agent grunted but still held on. His other hand grabbed Mila's ankle and he pulled it suddenly to one side. She landed heavily beside him, feeling a stab of pain as her elbow cracked onto the tarmac. She lashed out quickly with her foot, connecting with the Special Agent's jaw, dazing him, and reached over to grab his gun. She had to get it away from him. Even if the weapon were to be lost to both of them, she still had a chance in engaging him in hand-to-hand combat. The element of surprise and her powerful kicks would even the game a little. Up close Mila could see the man was a veteran, probably in his early sixties. Experienced and hardened, but probably past his peak.

The Agent clearly didn't fancy the idea of a fair fight, for he put all his efforts into keeping the gun. He was still winded, gasping for breath. But he got his free hand up and, grabbing the side of her face, twisted her to one side, trying to crack her head on the tarmac. Mila let go of his gun hand and rolled backward to escape the force of his sideways shove. She flipped over and was on her feet again.

"Wow!" Adam said, having just seen Mila's maneuver with the bike.

Without attempting to get up, the Agent raised the gun and fired. Mila was already ducking and rolling to one side. As she got to her feet she was struck with a surge of fear and could think of nothing but getting away from the man. She took two long strides and sprang over the fence to the side of the road. Through the trees she saw the back end of a small building, a stone barn or storehouse. She crashed through the undergrowth, hurdled another low fence and ran around the back of the building. The Agent came running through the bushes. Mila shucked off the backpack and plunged her hand inside. Where was it?

There.

She heard the Agent thump over the second fence and run

around the side of the building to get a clear shot. His gun was aimed but already she was ducking around the corner. Bullets skipped off the stone behind her as she carried on along the length of the barn, pulling the pocket knife out of the bag as she ran. She flipped open the first blade her fingers located, and rounded the next corner, dropping the backpack to free up her arms. The Agent had anticipated this move and was coming the other way to meet her. He hadn't expected her to have a weapon, but overcame his surprise and fired off a wild round as Mila ran at him, sprinting and snarling. Suddenly she launched herself forward, her lithe figure forming a spear, its tip the blade of the pocket knife.

Time slowed as she flew. She could see everything in exquisite detail. The deep lines on the Agent's face. Skin that had seen sunlight harsher than that of the Isles. His expensive, loose-fitting suit. The dull-gray sheen of the weapon, which he was raising to fire at her again.

And then she saw the blade her fumbling fingers had found wasn't a blade at all, but a corkscrew.

The Special Agent leaned backward, arching his neck to avoid the strike. But Mila was too fast. The twisted steel plunged deep into his throat. Mila felt herself bounce off the solidity of his shoulder, then she was sprawling in the thick grass of the field.

Looking up, she was expecting to see him pointing the gun at her again, but instead he was holding the handle of the knife. With both hands he ripped it out, the steel spiral pulling with it a cork of bloody flesh. A gout of blood shot out from the wound, then became a steady stream, running down his throat, instantly turning his white shirt a dark crimson.

He swayed, a look of surprise on his pale face as he saw Mila with the gun, standing a few meters away and pointing it at his face.

He said nothing, perhaps couldn't. But he jerked his head back as if to say, "Come on then, do it."

Mila waited.

"A corkscrew?!" Adam exploded, having just caught up. "You hit him with a corkscrew?"

"What are you waiting for?" the Agent said, speaking for the first time. His voice was a hoarse croak.

"Advice," Mila replied, holding the gun steady.

"Adam," she muttered. "You caught up?"

"Yes," he replied. "Don't shoot him unless you have to."

The Special Agent smiled. He was fiddling with the knife. One-handed, he closed the corkscrew and flipped open the main blade.

"Drop the knife," Mila said, nervously. She could hear the drone approaching, likely called by the Special Agent's signal, and in the distance, the shouts of men.

But the Special Agent ignored her. "He taught you to fight, did he?"

Mila raised an eyebrow.

"Julian. He taught you?"

She shifted uncomfortably. "Drop the knife," she repeated. A soft breeze shimmied through the woods behind the barn, tickling the oak leaves.

"Be careful, Mila," Adam said quietly.

"He was good, Julian," the Special Agent went on. "One of the best, before he went rogue. Turned traitor."

You're a liar, Mila wanted to shout. Julian was many things. But he was no traitor.

"I'll give you one more warning," she said. "Drop the knife or I will shoot you in the face."

The Special Agent shrugged. "I'm dead anyway," he said, gesturing to his throat. An artery had been severed, perhaps the jugular.

And then he launched himself toward her, his pale face contorted with pain, chest ablaze with claret blood.

Mila flinched but managed to fire, twice, before twisting away to avoid the charge. The Special Agent collapsed heavily into the grass and did not move again. Mila closed her eyes. She could hear the drone overhead now. There was no time to reflect. She saw the bloodied penknife lying among the nettles and picked it up, folding away the blade and stuffing it in the backpack, along with the gun. There were three bullets left.

"Are you okay?" Adam asked, after a moment.

She flipped herself over the fence and, her right side a mass of pain, her elbow stiffening in agony, made her way slowly back through the woods to her bike.

"Mila?"

"I'm fine," she said. "Which way?"

Beverley was as attractive as the girl on the coach had described. Mila limped down a winding street lined with old-fashioned shops, which, in the old days, would have sold everything from bread to shoes, but which now offered speciality goods. Hand-crafted pillow cases. Antique clocks. Custom furniture. But Mila was in no state for window shopping. A few people gave her odd looks, staring at her rolling gait, straggly hair and pale, sweating face. At least her wound escaped attention, hidden by the cyclist's raincoat.

Adam had brought her in on the north side of the town. Feeling woozy, she'd abandoned the bike in a public bike rack and walked unsteadily down the busy Lairgate to the community hospital at the other end. She felt faint with the blood loss. She stopped and opened the backpack to find her water, spying the gun at the bottom. She couldn't take that into the hospital. Not without regret she dropped it into a rubbish bin and carried on down the street, swigging from the water bottle, desperate to replace the fluids she'd lost. She could feel the telltale slickness of the bleeding wound. The makeshift bandage had slipped, but she could hardly stop and fix it here.

"I've contacted the hospital," Adam said, "Told them you're on your way. I've said you're a Special Agent with a damaged phone and they're not to question you. Just walk in and tell them you need emergency triage. If they ask for your phone number to check your records, tell them it's malfunctioning."

"Will they believe that?" Mila asked. She could hear herself slurring.

"It doesn't matter," he said eventually. "It's just something to say. They'll patch you up anyway."

"And call the Agency."

"Maybe. I think they'll probably wait until the nurse has finished.

Then have one of their security people talk to you. We'll cross that bridge when we come to it."

The hospital was in an old, brick, five-story building. Mila walked up some stone steps into a high-ceilinged waiting room with a reception desk at one side. A grand staircase led up to the next floor. She took off the raincoat and immediately caught the attention of an orderly.

"Are you okay?" he asked. He put an arm around her and she fell against his comforting solidity.

"My phone's broken," she said, then passed out.

Adam was rejecting all calls. He was in his car, heading toward Beverley. He couldn't allow himself to be caught. They'd shunt him for sure, an invasive and dangerous procedure that could cause irreparable damage. To his memories. To his personality.

The Agency had one other option. If they gave Mila a new number, one they had access to, they could tap her phone remotely. It was risky, for it would activate many useful functions on her phone. But the more he thought about it, the more likely it seemed that this would be their decision. If they couldn't find him, they'd reset her phone, breaking the Permalink.

Why hadn't he thought of this before he sent Mila into the hospital? He should have had her memorize his number in case the connection was lost. The thought of losing contact was hard to bear.

Adam knew he needed help. He made another call.

The phone rang for a long time. Adam's heart pounded.

Eventually the chime came that told him she'd answered.

"Adam?" she said.

"Hello, Clara," he replied.

"You have to run fast," Vaclav tells her. "Very fast, then jump right at the last moment, time it so your foot lands an inch before the edge of the roof."

Mila looks doubtfully at the roof opposite. It doesn't seem possible to leap that distance. But Vaclav tells her he's done it before and is about to do it again.

"Watch, then follow me, okay?" he says.

Mila nods dumbly. She is hungry, dirty. Part of her feels bad about what they are planning to do. But that part is overruled by other feelings. Her uncle's business is doing badly. There's barely any food on the table. The building opposite is well-maintained, one of few such buildings in Köls. It is the headquarters of the Corporation, which built the dam that destroyed her home. The Corporation which sent local Agents to their house in the middle of the night to "persuade" her father to sell the farm, beating him so badly he later died in the hospital. The Corporation which paid next to nothing for the farm, that little sum going to her Uncle Yuri, who kept it as payment for her upkeep.

So, on balance, Mila is prepared to steal food, money or whatever else she can get, from the Corporation.

But first she has to get into it.

Mila's school was hit by a mortar round fired by a rebel group from the mountains. It has been closed for the last three weeks. She has been spending her days running wild through the cratered streets of Köls with a pack of other half-starved teenagers. They have no football, no baseball bats or bikes; many have no shoes. So they have started free running. Running up walls, dancing along rooftops, swinging from broken pipes, back-flipping down flights of stairs. There is competition between the strongest of the children; the older ones; the ones who would be leaders. They perform more and more risky moves, leaping over greater distances, climbing higher walls, shimmying down ever more flimsy drainpipes. The city is a death-trap. The buildings are crumbling, the metalwork rusty and riddled with tetanus, the ground strewn with glass and nails. Among the children there have been many injuries and a few deaths in the past few months.

Just last week Mila had watched as Goran Asanic attempted a handstand on top of a multi-story car park, only for the chunk of concrete he was gripping to crack and break away. He plunged fifty feet, silently, to a messy death. Mila didn't go to look, but Vaclav told her excitedly how they'd found him crushed under the concrete block.

"There were blood splatters on a w-wall five meters away," Vaclav had said, getting the hiccups; he always did when he was excited. "W-we measured it."

They had been told not to play in the ruins, of course, but what else was there to do?

Now Mila watches as Vaclav sprints past her along the grimy, flat rooftop. He is indeed going fast. As he reaches the edge he leaps, his arms fly-wheeling, his left leg outstretched.

He isn't going to make it, she thinks.

But he does, somehow, his torso slamming into the wall, his arms slapping down on the flat top, sliding back, then holding fast. She hears him bark a nervous laugh. Then he swings a leg up and, with great difficulty, drags himself onto the rooftop. He is visibly shaking as he gets to his feet, but smiles at her confidently.

"Your t-turn," he calls.

"No way," she says.

"Come on, I did it."

She looks at him for a moment, then steps to the edge and peers over. The cratered road is at least twenty-five meters below. There's no chance she would survive, even if she fell the right way. The way the older kids did, and the way she'd copied.

"I can smell the food," Vaclav says. "I can smell doughnuts."

Everyone knows Corporation buildings are stuffed with doughnuts. Whenever the white four-wheel drives leave the compound and roar through the city, Agents and security men can be seen through the windows, eating doughnuts. Sometimes they throw scraps to the children who run alongside them.

Mila loves doughnuts.

She walks back to the position from which Vaclav started his run up. He whoops and claps his hands in encouragement. She ducks her head, her heart racing, wondering what the hell she thinks she is doing. A drop of sweat falls from her forehead and runs down her nose. Then she lifts her head and runs.

She doesn't time her run perfectly and has to leap half a meter short of the lip. But even so she clears the gap easily. Vaclav's face is a picture; his mouth an O of astonishment at just how far this stick of a girl can jump. She lands well enough, stumbles a little but keeps her footing as she slows and stops. Then she turns and gives a little curtsey, the gesture reminding her of her father, who'd taught her to do it, trying to instill in his daughter some vaguely remembered articles of femininity.

Vaclav doesn't say anything, just nods his head, before beckoning her over to a doorway leading to a staircase that will take them down into the building.

They don't find doughnuts, but in a deserted corridor they do find a vending machine. Vaclav shakes and kicks it before figuring out he's not going to be able to get in. Then Mila has the idea of going through the desk drawers looking for money. It is half an hour before Vaclav remembers that First Worlders don't have money. They operate machines telepathically. Mila is not sure she believes this, but it's a moot point; they fail to find money anyway. Instead they find other treasure. Chocolate bars hidden in drawers. Packets of potato chips stashed in the kitchenette. Here they also find a strange machine, which gives them a fright when it whirs and moves slightly. It freezes again when they move away.

Mila is munching a bag of chips. The packet is featureless other than a barcode. She had no idea what flavor the chips would be before opening it. She is pleased with her choice; they are salty and taste like heaven. Vaclav has chosen a pack with an odd, but not unpleasant flavor they don't recognize.

As he munches, he approaches the machine.

"I wonder if I can get it to make us some food," he says.

Mila raises her eyebrows.

"It's a robot chef," he says. "It cooks whatever you want."

"How do you know that?"

"I saw it on the Channels."

"Go on then, make it cook something."

"What do you fancy?"

Mila thinks for a moment. "Trout," she says. "Fried in a little oil, with lemon and salt."

"Any vegetables?"

"Lentils."

"Puy?" says a voice from behind them. Mila leaps, Vaclav squeals like a pig and they turn, realizing they are trapped in the narrow kitchen. A man stands there. Curly dark hair, a weathered face. Short and stocky build.

"Or red lentils? Green? Black?"

Mila swallows. "We're sorry. The door was open. We were hungry."

"Don't lie," the man says, still smiling. "I saw you leaping. Impressive. You still want that trout?"

Vaclav runs for the door. The man stands aside and lets him go. Then he looks quizzically at Mila, still standing to one side, offering her an exit if she wants it. But although Mila wants to run, something stops her. It's not just the thought she might actually get to eat trout; there is something in the man. Some quality. She instinctively feels she can trust him.

"Black," she says.

"Sorry, what's that?" he says.

"Black lentils, please."

He laughs loudly and holds out a calloused hand. "Julian," he says.

"Mila," she replies, taking his hand in hers.

Mila woke up alone.

Drowsiness. Faint nausea. Light. Something was different.

She tried to blink away the blurriness. Focus on something.

She was propped up on pillows in a white room. An open window let in a gentle breeze. A thin net curtain swayed languidly.

Turning her head, she saw flowers by her bed and a jug of water. She shifted slightly, expecting to feel a stab of pain from her hip, but there was nothing, only numbness. The door to the room was open and she saw a white-garbed figure walk briskly by. She could hear voices outside, but couldn't make them out.

She went to click on Adam's Avatar, to call him. But it wasn't there. That was what was different. She opened her Watcher box. Three Watchers lurked. Rebecca, Maddie and Jason.

She received a ping from Rebecca. There's no Permalink, she thought. She didn't need to answer.

But she did anyway.

"Hello?" she said, cautiously.

"How are you feeling?" Rebecca asked.

"Where's Adam?"

"He's having a little break," Rebecca said. "We talked it over and decided he was getting a little too personally involved in your case."

"What did you do to him?"

"I'm afraid that's classified," Rebecca said, smugly.

Mila felt a pang of fear. "I thought the connection was permanent?"

"We've reset your phone," Rebecca said. "There's nothing we can't do, Mila."

"So, you can see what I can see?"

"Yes."

"Hear what I hear?"

"Oh, yes."

"But with a seven-second delay?"

Rebecca paused momentarily before answering.

"Yes."

That's something, Mila thought. I still have the delay. There was something else different, Mila noticed. The row of Apps at the bottom of her screen were lit up now. They were functioning. Even in her befuddled state, she could flick between the various Apps and controls on her IDS. As her gaze alighted on a piece of medical machinery against the far wall, a small purple label superimposed itself over the equipment, reading ECG Machine—Obsolete.

"So where am I?"

Rebecca hesitated. "You're in a secure hospital."

Mila looked through the open door again. She could hear a nurse chatting to someone on her phone. The curtains waved again at the window.

"There's nothing secure about this hospital," Mila said. "I don't think you know where I am."

Rebecca's Avatar smirked. "Oh, we know enough. There aren't that many hospitals around the area. We have them all surrounded. All Channels are broadcasting a bulletin with video of you and a full report of your crimes. It won't be long before you're identified by one of the hospital staff and our Agents will storm the building if necessary. I suggest you give yourself up quietly. We don't want to risk injuring anyone this time, do we?"

"I'll give it some thought," Mila said. She ended the call.

Rebecca instantly phoned back. Mila rejected the call and began limply to get out from under the bedclothes. Lifting the sheets, she slowly swung her legs off the bed, testing her side as she sat up. Still no pain. No sensation at all. But she still felt awful; weak and woozy. She blinked furiously, trying to clear her spinning head. No time for this, Mila, she told herself.

She stood, shuffled to the window and peered out. The pretty row of shops and a bustling market lay to her right. Turning to the left she saw the huge old church she'd seen before.

Beverley Minster, a pop-up informed her. If the Agency had been in any doubt as to which hospital she was in, they weren't now. Everything she saw could be seen by Rebecca and the Techs. Call Beverley Minster, Julian had said. She clicked on the pop-up. More information appeared: the history of the church, images and video. But no phone number.

She hadn't really expected it to be so easy.

She walked slowly over to the door. The brown-haired duty nurse continued to chat on her phone. If her patient's identity had been revealed, the news hadn't filtered through to her yet. Maybe Mila had a couple of minutes. She knew she would have to run, but a wave of fatigue flooded through her and, despite herself, she slumped back onto the bed.

She needed to get up. She needed to run.

She raised herself again but once more her body rebelled, and she sank back down onto the soft pillows with a sigh. No more Adam, no more Julian. She was on her own. She needed help, and there was only one person she could reach out to now.

She opened her keypad and dialed the number she had memorized. Fifteen digits. Always fifteen digits. Phone calls are private, Adam had told her. She had to pray he'd been telling the truth.

The phone rang three times before a clicking sound told her Holly had answered.

"Hello?" she said. A gray Avatar with no face popped up.

"Holly. It's Mila," she said.

"Mila?"

"Do you remember me? You gave me a lift. And your number."

"Of course I remember you," Holly said. She sounded scared, unsure of herself. "You're on the Channels, all the Channels."

"Look, what they're saying about me, it's not true. . . ."

"They say you have a bomb in your head. Is that true?"

"No. I mean—I don't know. Someone put something in my head without me knowing. I'm not sure what. The point is, I'm not a terrorist. I don't want to hurt anyone."

"Look at this," Holly said by way of reply, and scooted a file to her. After a moment's hesitation Mila played it. She saw herself, running into the trees beside the Center. Then the camera cut to an image that must have been taken from the phone of the Special Agent who attacked her by the barn. She saw her own face, pale and full of fury as she launched herself toward the camera. Then there was a graphic, showing the device in her head. A voiceover warned Citizens against approaching her.

Mila's mouth ran dry. "So now everyone . . ."

". . . Will be aware of who you are, yes."

Including the nurses, Mila thought. At least, those monitoring the Channels. A pop-up informed her she now had another Watcher. She opened the box and saw Holly alongside the Techs and Rebecca.

"Where are you?" Holly asked.

"You mean you can't tell?"

"No, it looks like you're in a hospital, but . . ."

"Hang on," Mila said, her addled brain struggling to make sense of this. "I've only just woken up. My phone was reset while I was asleep. Whoever started Watching me after that must have no idea where I was while I was sleeping."

"Err, yes, I suppose so."

"I'm so tired, Holly. So weak. I don't know if I can run."

"Maybe you should give yourself up," Holly said.

"They'll kill me," Mila replied.

"I don't think they will," Holly said, gently. "The Agency—"

"I saw what the Agency is capable of," Mila said, a little sharply. "They killed their own guards back at the Center. They bombed a truck stop and killed Citizens. I don't expect you to believe me—but I'm not giving myself up. I can't think straight. I can hardly walk. But I'll never stop running from them."

"Well," Holly said, after a slight pause. "There is a little trick you can do with your phone, to wake yourself up."

"Really?"

"Yeah, we students use it quite a lot when we're up all night writing essays. It's some kind of device test the Techs use before implanting a new phone. It produces a small electrical surge. You're not supposed to do it when the phone's in your head, but everybody does."

"Tell me," Mila said.

"Go to the settings, click on power output and enter the code 76GhB-8."

Mila did as Holly instructed, then clicked enter.

The effect was as if someone had jabbed an electrical cable into the back of her head. A massive surge of energy filled her senses, and she sat up, taking a huge breath, her eyes wide.

"Good, huh?" Holly said.

"Thanks," Mila said, when she'd recovered slightly.

"You can only do it once every few days," Holly said. "The phone needs to recharge properly first."

"Recharge?" Mila gasped.

"It runs off your body's electricity," Holly explained. "It draws tiny amounts of energy from your nervous system and stores it. You've just released ninety-five per cent of the charge into your head. It'll take a while to recover. The phone, I mean, not your head."

Mila stood and tested her legs. She felt fine. Wonderful, in fact.

"Are you still there?" Holly asked.

"Yeah, I'm still here. I've just realized Rebecca's probably lying to me. She doesn't have Agents waiting outside. She's only just figured out I'm in a hospital."

"There can't be that many hospitals in the area though," Holly pointed out. "You don't have long."

"I need your help," Mila said. "I need you to try and get in contact with someone who works for the Agency. He'll tell you that you can trust me. His name is Adam . . . something. I don't know his surname. He works in Applicant Control. Give him my number, we lost contact—"

"I don't know . . ." Holly said, breaking in.

"You've met me," Mila pointed out. "Did I try to hurt you? Did I seem like a terrorist?"

"Well, no . . ."

"I'm an illegal immigrant, it's true. I have no right to be here, but I'm not a terrorist. Holly, you have to believe me."

"They keep showing videos of you killing Agents," Holly said, guardedly.

"Special Agents. They sent Special Agents after me, to kill me. I had no choice." Mila sensed she was losing Holly. "Look, I'm sorry if I put you at risk. But you remember what I told you about the Center? That it was the Agency who bombed it. It's the truth. Check out the pictures. There was no fire; that building was hit by a dirty great bomb."

"I just don't want to get mixed up—"

"Please. I don't want to hurt anyone," Mila said, pleading. "I just need to find out the truth."

"And what are you going to do?"

Mila could hear the nurse outside, still chatting. She knew as long as that cheerful conversation continued, her exact location hadn't been discovered.

"I need to find out what this thing is in my head," Mila said. "It has something to do with Beverley Minster. The man who put it in my head told me to phone Beverley Minster if I was ever in real trouble."

"You know who put it in your head?" Holly asked, sounding curious despite everything. "Who was it?"

"He's dead. He was a friend."

"He put something in your head without you knowing it? Are you sure he was a friend?"

Mila had the feeling Holly was coming around.

"That's what I need to find out. I need to know who he was. I've got to get to the Minster."

Rebecca was still pinging. Mila had given up rejecting the calls. She let the chime sound, ignoring it, trying instead to concentrate on what Holly was saying.

"Do you want me to come down there?" Holly asked. "It's really close."

"What? No! It's too dangerous. I just want you to try and find the phone number at Beverley Minster."

It sounded like a lot to ask. Of course, she knew what Holly was going to say. . . .

"Okay, I'll do it."

Mila's mouth dropped open. "Oh, Holly, that's amazing, thanks so much."

"Buildings don't usually have phone numbers," Holly said. "But maybe there's an official contact person or something. I'll do some digging."

"Thanks!"

"I can call you back on this number?" Holly asked.

"Yes, I think so," she said. "I'll set you up as a Contact. I don't have many."

"Okay," Holly said, laughing nervously. Suddenly a little picture of a smiling Holly appeared in place of the gray Avatar and a pop-up text read, CONTACT SAVED!

"Look, Holly, gotta run," Mila said. "Literally."

"Okay, I'll call later."

"Yep. And thanks again."

"Good luck, Mila," Holly said.

As the Avatar disappeared, Mila heard the nurse outside stop talking, mid-sentence. A few moments later she heard her say, "Oh my god!"

Someone who'd been watching the Channels had recognized the new patient. If there weren't already Agents on their way, there would be soon.

Rebecca called again, an urgent and insistent chime, and Mila finally answered.

"Hello?" she said, brightly. "Mila speaking."

"If I were you," Rebecca said, pent-up fury dripping from her words, "I'd get back into bed and leave your hands where they can be seen. An armed unit has just entered the building. They are authorized to shoot to kill in the event of any resistance."

"Did they stitch me?" Mila asked.

"What?"

"This wound on my side. Did they stitch it?"

Rebecca was momentarily disconcerted. "They would have used skin fusion. Much stronger than stitches."

Mila crossed the room to the wardrobe and found her clothes, cleaned and repaired.

"I like this hotel," she said, pulling on her leggings.

"Are you back in bed?" Rebecca asked, seven seconds behind.

"Yes, Mum," Mila lied.

Her backpack lay at the bottom of the cupboard. She opened it. No knife. Just the waterproofs, the bottle, the trail food and the folded-up paper with Holly's number on it.

She pulled the backpack on and closed the cupboard. A thin nurse was watching her from the door of the room, a look of fear on his face. He stepped back and the door shut automatically.

"Time to go," she said to herself.

She strode toward the door, selecting the passepartout icon. The door opened and she walked through. Three nurses and an orderly turned and fled as she appeared. She looked up and down the corridor and decided to turn left. She moved gingerly at first, testing out her injuries. Her knee felt painful but she seemed to be able to run. She heard the clattering of booted feet coming up the stairs behind her as she reached the window.

"You fool," Rebecca said. "They will kill you."

"They can try," Mila replied.

The window was open, looking out over a small side street, lined with ornate, old-school lampposts. Mila turned and took a few steps. The Agents burst through the door, pulling out their weapons, ready to fire. She spun around and sprinted hard. She heard the double sound of the weapons firing behind her as she dived away from them, through the open window. The sill splintered and cracked as the bullets hit. Mila's palms slapped against the cross-piece of the lamppost below and her momentum swung her up and around. She arrested her motion with a foot against the post and slid down, landing neatly on the pavement. A pedestrian stared in astonishment, which turned quickly to fear as his phone recognized hers and told him who she was. Or at least who the Agency said she was.

Mila turned and ran, back out into the shopping street, ducking between shoppers on foot or on bikes, toward the Minster. Pop-ups flicked in and out of view, informing her about the shops, inviting her to browse. Passing a bus stop, the destination and times of departure flicked up in an instant.

"Hey, that's the girl!" someone shouted. "Stop her."

But no one took the risk. In fact the crowd parted to let her through.

She opened her Map App and recognized the large square she needed to head for. If she could just keep ahead of her pursuers long enough to get to the Minster and find the number. Then what? Would she dial it? What if there was a bomb in her head? What if Julian had betrayed her?

She ran on, ducking down side streets and across parks. She leapt a high fence and found herself running through someone's garden. On she went, between two houses, over a gate, and back onto an empty street. She was struggling now. The surge she'd got from the phone had sharpened her wits, but her body had not had time to recover from its injuries. Her lungs were tattered, her legs full of water, rolling and heavy.

Following the map, she soon came out onto a busier street. People recoiled as they recognized her. A gunshot rang out behind; they'd found her again. She risked a quick look; they were some distance away. A group of five or six Agents, running hard.

She turned and sprinted again, her lungs protesting. How long could she evade her pursuers, now that everyone in the country was an Agent?

Rebecca was having troubles of her own. She could Watch Mila's Feed again, as could the Agents, but the damn delay was making pursuit difficult. She had the Feed of the lead Agent open on the left side of her IDS, and Mila's Feed open on the right.

Mila had turned into a side street. The ID plate popped up and a tiny map in the corner of Rebecca's IDS tracked her progress.

"Left into Eastgate," Rebecca called unnecessarily. The Agents could see Mila's Feed themselves.

"Got it," the senior Agent replied. There were six of them. Each carried a handgun, except for one, the marksman, who ran at the back with a sniper rifle, waiting for a clear shot.

But as they turned onto Eastgate, suddenly Mila disappeared from the lead Agent's Feed. On Mila's own Feed, she was still running down the street. But that had been seven seconds ago.

"She should be there. Can you see her?" Rebecca asked, knowing the answer already. If she couldn't see Mila, neither could the Agent.

The officers ran down the street, pedestrians cowering from them in shop doorways. Citizens were not used to such open displays of military force.

Then, looking at Mila's Feed, Rebecca saw her duck into a tiny shop and slide behind a rack of clothes.

"She's in a shop," Rebecca said, urgently. "Stop! Turn around!"

Sure enough, as Rebecca Watched via the delayed Feed, the Agents sprinted past the shop without a glance. As soon as they were gone, Mila was out the door and running back the way she'd come.

On the real-time Agent's Feed, Rebecca saw they had turned and were running back down the road. But a sprinter can go a long way in seven seconds.

"She went that way!" a Citizen called.

"Now you tell us," Rebecca commented, bitterly. "Maddie, find open, undelayed Citizen Feeds in Beverley. Flick between them."

"What am I looking for?" Maddie asked.

"Mila," Rebecca said. "What the hell did you think?"

Mila was flagging. She was aware of the drugs in her system, blocking the pain, but her body had been battered around a lot lately. A good night's sleep and a vitamin drip had gone little way to restore it. She needed rest and proper food.

But that would be impossible now. Everywhere she went, she'd be recognized. It wasn't just Adam and a couple of Techs Watching her Feed, it was every Citizen. She'd noticed the streets had grown suddenly quieter. Had there been a warning? Had they been told to clear the town Center?

She found a quiet alley and risked stopping for a second or two, to catch her breath. A pop-up informed her she had another Watcher. She opened the box and saw she had 137 Watchers in total. She wondered if Adam had posted a message in the chat box, giving his number, urging her to make contact. But there were hundreds of messages to scroll through, uncomplimentary messages, many in caps, wishing her dead, telling her to throw herself under a bus, to go back where she came from. She closed the box and ran on, taking a zigzag course to try to confuse anyone following her progress on a map. Wherever she ran, the Minster loomed, its gray stone clock tower gazing down, stern and disapproving.

"Got her! She's on Flemingate, heading toward the Minster."

Maddie scooted Rebecca the recording she'd taken from the Feed of a Citizen looking out a window onto the street. Mila ran past, looking tired.

"Get a team there."

"On their way already," Maddie replied. "We have Blue Assault Team on Eastgate."

"This Feed we're Watching, is it delayed?"

"Yeah. Oh, wait, I've got another one. No delay."

This time the shot was from a different angle. It showed a distant Mila, seen by a Citizen standing inside a shop directly in front of the Minster. Maddie told the Citizen to remain calm and continue looking out through the window.

Mila came closer, all the time looking up at the Minster. She was loping rather than running, favoring her left side slightly. Rebecca smiled. This was real time now.

"Where's the team?" she asked.

"Should be in line of sight any time . . . now!"

A burst of gunfire sounded through the Citizen's Feed, and in his surprise he hit the deck, obscuring the view.

"Dammit! Get me another Agent's Feed."

Via the Agent's Feed Rebecca saw a hail of tracer fire from four or five weapons on the other side of the square in front of the Minster. She couldn't see Mila. The noise was horrendous and automatic filters clicked in to reduce the sound to a manageable level. Someone was firing torrents of lead across the square, apparently indiscriminately, clear from a massive weapon. Stone chips flew from the church wall. The shop fronts were dotted with black holes. Glass scattered itself across the plaza.

The Agent ran forward, firing as he went, aiming at a low stone wall that bordered the churchyard. Mila must be behind there, Rebecca realized. The Agents were trying to flank her, to get a clear shot. The heavy and unseen gun kept up its random battery, splintering an oak tree in the churchyard, knocking over an ancient gravestone.

And suddenly a movement caught Rebecca's eye. There was Mila, flipping over the wall, a dozen meters from where the fire was being concentrated. The Agents corrected their aim, but too late. She had ducked behind a heavy gravestone. The Agents kept up a grounding fire, trapping her where she crouched.

"We have another team approaching from Highgate," Maddie said.

This was the team Mila had dummied earlier. Rebecca saw them appear at the far end of the Square, skirting the wall, not wanting to get hit by errant fire from Blue Team. The marksman leaned hard against the wall of a shop and took a bead toward Mila's gravestone.

Reading Rebecca's mind, Maddie scooted her the marksman's Feed. Mila was in his crosshairs.

"Take the shot!" Rebecca cried.

But the sudden clatter and whine of the Blue Team's bullets caused the marksman to duck.

"Hold your fire!" someone shouted and the roar of the guns stopped.

Mila was away and running, seizing this unexpected opportunity.

The crosshairs lurched alarmingly as the marksman moved into the clear. Rebecca felt briefly sick. But there Mila was again, running hard for the door of the Minster. The marksman tracked her, waiting for a good shot. And fired. Once.

The theft increases as the food supply at home decreases. Mila's uncle is drinking more and more. Her aunt takes out her fury on the children, particularly Mila, who gives as good as she gets. Whenever the school is closed, which is increasingly often, Mila will escape the atmosphere in the apartment, the stench of stale alcohol and simmering recriminations, meet up with Vaclav, and they'll go stealing. The war rages down on the plains and scrap metal is in demand for making new planes and bombs and guns. The crumbling buildings are stripped quickly, thousands of rusting old cars disappearing overnight. Fences, disused railway tracks, pylons, everything not in immediate use, is taken for the war effort. Soldiers appear on the streets to protect the steel structures, which are still needed. Looters are shot on sight. Two of Mila's classmates have been killed in this way.

But in the ruined suburbs, where there are no businesses, no shops, no residents, metal can still be found. Mila and Vaclav wheel an old trolley through the dusty streets pulling sheets of aluminium, iron poles, and occasionally, an overlooked piece of copper pipe. They wheel their treasure to the army base where a foul-smelling sergeant wakes himself up, inspects the booty with a grunt and gives them a few coins for it, always less than they'd expected, always less than they need. Always less than the day before.

They split the money and Mila gives half of it to her aunt, who never seems quite as grateful as Mila would like. "And where's the money from the sale of the farm?" she feels like saying, but manages to hold her tongue. The rest of the money she spends on food, which she shares out among her younger cousins. They at least are grateful, and they understand the importance of keeping their mouths shut. Otherwise the food Mila brings might end up in the bellies of their parents.

One day Mila and Vaclav are heading back to the army base with a disappointing haul. The sky is as dusty as the ground. If there is a sun up there still, Mila hasn't seen evidence of it for a week at least.

"I'm turning sixteen next month," Vaclav says.

"So?" Mila says. She is tired and her wrist stings from where she has slashed it on a sharp piece of broken concrete. They spent an hour trying to free a tangled mess of iron palings from a lump of concrete only to give up eventually. A waste of time and energy.

"You can join the army at sixteen now," he says.

"You?! In the army?"

Vaclav looks hurt. "Sure, why not me?"

Mila doesn't reply. She is shocked, and scared. She can't lose Vaclav. He is all she has—apart from the occasional stolen hour at school when she is able to explore the dog-eared old books in the library.

"You sure they'd want you?" she says eventually. "Don't you have to be quite tall to be in the army?" She knows she is being hurtful. Vaclav is sensitive about his height, but she can't think of any other way to discourage him.

He looks straight ahead and leans against the squeaking trolley to push it up the slope.

Suddenly there are others surrounding them. Five boys and a filthy girl with an eye patch. Mila recognizes a few of them. Feral kids from the east side of Köls, the even rougher side. She knows the name of the leader, Malachi Kovic. He is the oldest, maybe seventeen or eighteen, though not much bigger than her, his growth slowed by malnutrition.

Vaclav hasn't noticed him yet.

Kovic holds out a hand and stops the trolley's progress.

"Thanks," he says, grinning nastily. "We'll take it from here."

"That's ours," Vaclav says. He is scared, but unwilling to let go.

"Not any more," Kovic says. He steps forward and punches Vaclav in the face.

Vaclav falls back. One of Kovic's gang takes his place and continues pushing the trolley up the slope. The girl with the eye patch watches Mila sullenly, perhaps wondering if she can steal an eye as well.

"Give it back," Mila says quietly.

The boy pushing the trolley doesn't stop. But Kovic senses a chance for some sport and turns around. He raises an eyebrow.

"Or what?"

"Or I'll hurt you," Mila says.

Kovic pauses for a moment, surprised, then laughs. The boy with the trolley stops. They are all watching her now.

"Not them," Mila says. "Just you and me." She raises her fists.

"Leave it, Mila," Vaclav says. "We'll get more."

"And have them steal it again?" she snaps. "No, we stand up for ourselves."

Kovic tuts and moves toward her eagerly. He swings a fist, expecting to finish with her quickly. But to Mila it seems as if he is moving through treacle. She moves her head slightly and his fist misses, throwing him off balance. There is all the time in the world for her retaliation. His guard is open and she punches him on the nose, bloodying it. He steps back in surprise and touches his face, inspecting his crimson fingers. Then he snarls and comes at her again.

But this time he grabs a length of iron piping. He swings it violently and Mila has to leap back. The burred tip slashes her shoulder and she feels a sharp pain. She continues backward, trips over a pothole and goes over onto her behind. She sits up only to feel the solid thump of a boot as he launches a kick into her face.

Mila is on her back, her vision blurred. She looks up at Malachi

Kovic, his mad face framed by teetering buildings, backlit by the dull glow of the afternoon sky. He raises the iron bar. He is going to kill her, of that she has no doubt.

But then something thumps into him and sends him sprawling. A dark shape. Vaclav.

Kovic doesn't lose his footing entirely, but Vaclav does. He falls to his knees and the furious Kovic raises the iron bar again, sweeping it around his head. Mila watches, horrified as he smashes the bar into Vaclav's temple, cracking his head and releasing a thin spray of blood, spurting in time with his heartbeat. Vaclav sways for a moment, then sinks slowly sideways onto the road, the dust around him black with blood.

Mila's breath stops. Time stops and things happen that she doesn't know about. When it is over, and the darkness retreats, the gang has fled, Malachi Kovic lies mangled and dying on the road next to Vaclav and the iron bar in her hand has more than one boy's blood on it.

Then Julian is there, approaching her cautiously, his eyes full of concern and something else. It is admiration. He takes away the bodies. He takes her home.

The black-painted doors to the Minster were half open, and Mila clattered through, just as a large-caliber round took a huge chunk of stone out of the archway above. Bullets skipped and whined outside, one finding its way through the door and destroying a small wooden bench.

It took her eyes a moment to adjust to the lack of light.

Slowly the vision formed of a vaulted heaven, lit with spheres and adorned with the bodies of angels. There was nothing like this in Köls, and if there were cathedrals still standing in the U, she had never been near them. So much space; so much beauty. The roof seemed to be held up by God and by hope. Forcing herself to move, she scuttled along the nave toward the rear of the church, hoping to put some thick pillars between herself and the inevitable bullets that would be coming her way soon.

She rested against a column and waited. Seconds passed, then a minute. What were they doing out there? Planning the assault? Maybe they didn't want to damage the Minster; too much bad publicity if they blew the place to pieces? Was this sanctuary?

Mila started as her phone pinged. Rebecca.

She answered.

"Hello?"

"Come out with your hands up. We are prepared to storm the Minster if necessary."

"Let me think about it," Mila said, before hanging up. That would give her a few minutes perhaps. Rebecca phoned back, but she ignored it. She was getting good at ignoring things.

A figure appeared before her and she organized herself into a fighting stance before realizing it was the vicar. She relaxed slightly. He seemed taken aback, but after a pause took a firm step toward her, apparently unafraid. Mila was sure that at any moment the door would swing open and he'd be cut down by a hail of bullets meant for her. He was visible from the main doors.

"Can I help you?" he asked.

"Do you know who I am?"

He nodded briefly.

"But you want to help me anyway?"

"That's why I'm here."

"I just have one question," Mila said, fighting the urge to turn and watch the door.

"Ask away," the vicar said. Mila noticed his hand trembled slightly.

"Does the Minster have a phone number?"

He blinked. "I'm sorry?"

"A number. Is it possible to call the Minster itself?"

He shook his head. "No. How can a building have a number? Do you mean like an old-fashioned landline?"

"I suppose," Mila said.

"We don't have those anymore." He said it gently, as though talking to an imbecile.

Everything was quiet outside, which suggested to Mila they were organizing themselves to rush the church. It seemed a good idea to move the vicar away from the door, behind some heavy stone pillars. If they came in, she'd run and he would be safe from the crossfire.

"Can we walk and talk?" Mila asked, leading the way into the depths of the church. After a moment's hesitation, the vicar followed.

"Is there some other number associated with the church?" she asked. "It's just I've been told I need to phone Beverley Minster and I don't understand what that means."

The vicar looked thoughtful. "Not that I can think of. I'm happy to give you my number if you like?"

"Thanks," Mila said, "But I don't think that's the answer."

"Maybe you should give yourself up," the vicar said. "You won't be hurt, I'm sure."

"I don't trust them," Mila said. "They've already tried to kill me a number of times."

"They are trying to protect the public," the vicar said gently.

Mila sighed. It was useless trying to convince the residents of the Isles that their government was capable of such terror. She turned to check behind her again, and her attention was caught by a moving figure close to the door. Her heart surged with panic, expecting an Agent, but saw instead an elderly woman, walking slowly along the pews, distributing prayer books. Mila watched her nervously.

"I don't want to hurt anyone," she said. "I just need to get away."

"From them?"

"From them, from here, from the Isles. I'm not welcome here, and I'm putting you in danger."

The vicar shook his head and opened his mouth to speak. But his words were lost in the sound of the main doors slamming open and the crunching chatter of a heavy machine gun.

Two Agents stood in the doorway, framed by sunlight, and fired rivers of depleted uranium into the church. The wooden pews disintegrated, blasted into clouds of splintered wood, soaked in blood where the torso of the elderly lady had landed.

Mila dived behind a pillar, pulling the vicar with her just as the light-dazzled gunners finally located them and unleashed their fire. Heavy shells sprayed across the pillar. She could feel the vibrations of the bullets thudding into the ancient stone. Then they stopped and Mila heard the sound of two grenade launchers, followed by the thin clank and tell-tale hiss of gas canisters.

Rebecca was calling again.

This time Mila answered.

"Your Agents just killed an old lady," she said.

"Her death is on your conscience."

"You're insane," Mila said. "The world will see what you're doing here today."

"The world will see what we want it to see," Rebecca replied. "The entire building is Cloaked. Your Watchers will see nothing."

"Cloaked?" Mila asked.

"A dampening field over the area," Rebecca replied. "No connection to the Web. Phone calls only."

Interesting, Mila thought. If she wasn't being Watched, maybe that was the advantage she needed.

She hung up. She could hear the footsteps of the Agents approaching and detected the first tang of the gas. She grabbed the vicar, still crouching in shock and confusion, and pulled him to his feet.

"Do you have a back door?" she hissed urgently.

The vicar struggled to focus at first. His world view had been comprehensively shattered in the space of a few seconds. But somehow he held himself together.

"Follow me," he said.

Together they ran deeper into the church, the pillars still affording them protection from the gunners at the door. One of the Agents must have moved farther in, however, as another hail of fire opened up, obliterating pews to their right. They ducked and carried on, Mila coughing as the acrid gas hit the back of her throat.

The vicar brought them to a tiny door at the back of the church. He fumbled with a set of keys as bullets ricocheted off the wall above and to their right. The gunners were having difficulty with their sight-lines. Mila risked a look and saw one of them approaching along the right side of the church, firing when he had a clear shot. She couldn't see the others but guessed they'd be appearing soon, and on the other side.

Finally the door opened and the vicar ushered her out. She turned to help him through the narrow portal but he shook his head.

"Follow the passage," he said. "It will bring you to an external door." He thrust an ancient iron key into her hand. "Use this."

"You're not coming?"

"I'm not leaving my church," he said.

"They may kill you," she said. "They don't care who gets in the way."

"My Feed is open," the vicar said. "God and the world will see what they are doing."

"They've Cloaked the building," she said.

"Well, just God then," the vicar replied with a wry smile.

"I'm sorry I brought this on you," Mila said.

"Whatever you've done," he said, "Whoever you are, you don't deserve this. You are not responsible for this." His eyes were a mix of sadness, anger and something else. Determination.

"God speed," he said, and closed the door firmly. She heard the key turn in the lock.

Halfway down the passageway Mila heard the guns open up again. Her shoulders dropped. She swallowed hard and carried on.

Coming to the external door, she had trouble finding the keyhole. When eventually she found it, she inserted the key. It didn't turn. She jiggled it furiously without effect, and let out a strangled sob of despair. She thought she heard the door at the other end of the passage being rattled. More haste, less speed, she heard Julian say, and she forced herself to take a deep breath. She inserted the key again and moved it cautiously until it caught on something. She twisted and, with surprising ease, the lock gave a soft clunk and the door swung open. Light hurt her eyes and she waited a couple of seconds before cautiously sticking her head out. A crunching noise from down the corridor told her the Agents hadn't found the other key and were trying to batter the door down.

Mila stepped out into the sunlight. Could they be so stupid as to not cover the rear of the Minster? A fresh breeze tickled the hairs on her arms and she smelled cordite from the earlier firefight. Before her was a grassy graveyard. Then a low stone wall and, beyond that, the plaza. It was a lot of open ground to cover. And what would she do then?

Her phone rang and she glanced at the display, expecting it to be Rebecca again. But it wasn't. It was Holly.

"Mila? Where are you?"

"I'm at the Minster," Mila said quietly. A huge crunch told her the gunners were through the inner door.

"I know that," Holly replied. "I mean which end? I'm here in my car."

"You came? I told you it was dangerous."

"You sounded like you needed help. I've been Watching your Feed, but it dropped out a few minutes ago."

"Did you see what happened to the old lady?"

"Old lady? What happened in there?"

"I'll tell you later," Mila said. "But I need to know that you believe me now."

"I believed you before."

Mila heard heavy footsteps in the corridor behind her. She had no choice.

"I'm at the south end of the building."

"Wait there for me. I'm on my way."

"I can't wait," Mila said. "I have to run."

Mila is unsure exactly what Julian does for the Corporation. He is vague when she asks, and she gets the feeling he doesn't want to talk about it. The Corporation building has a gym, rarely used. On weekends Julian opens it up for her and teaches her the range of martial arts he knows, which is idiosyncratic but extensive. He tends to favor the offensive moves and uses them against her often and without warning. Mila quickly learns how to counter him, how to defend herself, which is of course his intention.

She asks him why he is teaching her. Why he helps her. Time has passed; she is a young woman now. She knows what drives boys and men. She has begun to understand her power. She knows she is beautiful.

He stands there, in the loose, black outfit he wears for these sessions, his low forehead shining in the bright overhead lights. He smiles a sideways smile.

"You've got no one else," he says. "I want to make sure you can look after yourself. You can't rely on other people. They'll always let you down."

"Will you let me down?" she asks.

He pauses before he answers, then shakes his head.

"No," he says, "You can trust me to the ends of the earth, Mila."

Mila doesn't bother going back to school. It is too painful now Vaclav is dead. Instead, Julian offers her a job in the Corporation mailroom. It is a terrible job but she is happy. The money is poor, and her aunt and uncle take most of it, but she has a small amount left over and is able to eat a little better now. She works alone, unless you count a SEMINT mail-sorter that continually malfunctions. It is Mila's job to remove jammed letters and parcels and to relabel those pieces of mail that the machine can't read. Her English is already reasonable but quickly improves. Julian makes her work hard on her accent. They watch the Channels together and she practices the vowel sounds. She's a natural mimic, Julian tells her. The other employees are mistrustful of her. Only Julian comes to see her regularly, bringing doughnuts and sandwiches from the kitchenette upstairs, which she tries not to wolf down too fast, at least when he's watching.

It is clear Julian detests his employers. "The things they make us do, Mila," he says, shaking his head. "We're supposed to be here helping you. Trying to develop the Third. But it's basically just legalized theft, what we're doing."

Mila doesn't understand at first, so he brings down great reams of paper, armfuls of printouts showing her what he is talking about. How the country produces enormous amounts of food but it all gets shipped off to the First.

"You grow the food; they eat it," he says. "How is that developing anything?"

"But they pay for the food," Mila says, remembering her lessons. "We need the money."

"How do they pay?" Julian says, stabbing a fat finger down on the printouts and biting off a huge chunk of doughnut. "Not with currency. They don't use currency. They pay in 'services.' They pay by building roads and aqueducts and . . . dams."

"But we need those things to grow," Mila points out.

"They're not being built for your benefit," Julian says, laughing at her naivety. "They build dams and aqueducts so you can water the crops. They build roads so they can take the crops back to the First."

"We get nothing?" Mila asks, puzzled. "But why do we allow this?"

"Because the guys who run your country are in the pocket of the First's corporations. They get looked after. They get schmoozed; they get phones and hard currency; they get promises of Citizenship on the Isles, or in the States."

Mila thinks this over, chewing her doughnut. "This is terrible," she says. "Why are you telling me this?"

"I hate them," Julian says, jumping up onto a counter and dangling his legs. "They hate me. I don't really fit in here."

"Where are you from?" Mila asks. She realized some time ago that Julian is not originally from the First, as she'd first assumed because of his clean clothes. None of the Corporation employees are from the First, she is surprised to find, though they all hope to be allowed to retire there.

"Here and there," Julian says.

She has also realized Julian does not like to talk about himself. She is curious about him and about his interest in her. He has not tried to be inappropriate with her, but he could just be biding his time.

One day Julian asks her if she wants to go for a drive. He is being sent off on some tedious errand and is given a four-wheel drive. He drives fast through the dusty streets and Mila chatters away excitedly and throws half-doughnuts out of the window to the children running alongside, like a bona fide Corporation employee.

Julian's errand turns out to be an inspection of the recently completed dam wall. As they get closer, and Mila realizes where they are heading, she grows quiet. Julian stops the car on a spur beside the top of the dam wall. He sits for a while, looking straight ahead while the engine ticks and cools down. Mila feels sick and is relieved when he gets out of the car and walks over to the wall. After a couple of minutes she gets out and follows him. It is hot and dry. A stiff breeze scours her face with tiny grains of sand. It hasn't rained for months.

Together they stare out over the valley. The river looks tiny down below but its water is pooling well enough.

"How long will it take to fill?" Mila asks, peering down to see her little farm.

"A few months," Julian says. "They can only trap a little at a time, or else farms downstream will complain."

"I used to live down there," she says.

"I know," he replies. "I'm sorry."

"It's not your fault," she says, trying to hold back the tears. If she lets them come, they will fill the valley in minutes, not months. Julian says nothing. They stand for a while, the wind whipping their hair. The hills opposite are dark green and Mila can see the little road that she cycled up with her father a couple of years ago.

"I had a farm once," Julian says eventually.

"Here?" Mila asks, glancing at him. He squints against the wind and she sees his eyes are watering.

"On the Isles," he says. She is surprised. Julian rarely talks about his past. "In an area called Yorkshire. It was on a hill a few miles from town, and when the weather was clear I could see the twin towers of the big church there. It was so beautiful. I was happy there."

"What happened?"

He shrugs. "I was offered a job. Didn't have much choice. I owed someone a favor."

"Who?"

"A man I did some work for. Some . . . difficult work. He gave me the farm as payment. I thought it was all square between us but he wanted more."

"Can you go back now?"

He shrugs again. "Maybe. Not sure I want to. I'll never be left in peace there."

"That's what you want? Peace?"

He nods. "Doesn't everyone?"

She nods too.

Mila ran through the graveyard, its headstones green with lichen, their inscriptions unreadable, hurdled the wall and set off across the plaza. Just to the left, turning out of a side street, she saw Holly's little car and darted toward it, arms pumping, legs like pistons.

She very nearly made it.

Three-quarters of the way across the plaza, as Holly got out of the car and stood, holding out a hand toward her, Mila went down. They'd covered the back after all—with a sniper. She had exposed herself. They weren't as dumb as she'd thought.

"Well done, Rebecca," she murmured. "Congratulations."

She lay there a long time. Out of the corner of her fading vision she saw Agents sweep away a screaming Holly. They did not approach Mila. Unable to move, she lay face down, shivering with pain, blood draining out of her and teeth chattering as a deathly cold crept through her. She could see the row of boutiques overlooking the plaza and a little café with tables outside in the sun. It was beautiful here. A good place to die. A better place to live. What a shame, she thought.

Something dark and heavy cloaked her and she saw nothing.

11

"Approach with care," Rebecca said as the two teams of Agents moved closer to the small figure, drenched in crimson. "Remember, she has a bomb in her head. It could be primed to go off once she's dead."

In the periphery of the Feed Rebecca was Watching, she saw a heavy vehicle nosing its way into the square from Eastgate.

"Who's that?" she asked.

"Bomb Squad," Jason replied.

"Good, let them deal with her," she said. "Can you get me their commanding officer?"

There was a pause as the Tech pinged the truck. Rebecca watched the vehicle drive up to the church wall and stop by the iron gate. Two figures got out, fully armored, black helmets obscuring their faces. One carried a roll of black material.

"Phones are off," Jason said. "They're not responding."

"Well, get the Bomb Squad headquarters then," Rebecca said. "I want to know where they'll take the body."

"Move back," she heard one of the Bomb Squad call to the surrounding Agents. "Keep the area clear!"

The officer holding the material unfurled it over Mila's body. Rebecca had expected them to perform some checks, scan the corpse's skull or something, but they simply rolled the body up and, between them, carried it back to the truck.

"Got Bomb Squad HQ, ma'am," Jason said. "Captain Baines."

"Captain?" Rebecca said as the officer's Avatar popped open on her IDS.

"Ma'am?"

"These officers attending this fatality, are they yours?"

"Yes, ma'am."

"Why are their phones not on?"

The captain hesitated. "It may be that they are concerned there is a risk of triggering the bomb with phone signals."

Rebecca nodded. That made sense. "Where will they take the body?"

"A secure facility in London," the Captain said. "A heavy bunker where the bomb will be removed and made safe."

"I wish to attend the procedure." She scooted him the Minister's authorization.

"Yes, ma'am," he said.

A moment later the details appeared in Rebecca's address book. She ended the call and watched the truck crawl slowly out of the square. Two of the Agents gave each other a high-five. Rebecca allowed herself a small smile.

Job done.

Mila woke in heaven. She was floating in a warm cloud and felt amazing. A flood of well-being spread through her body. She hadn't felt so good . . . well, ever. She could hear nothing but a gentle, soothing hum.

She hung, drifting for a while, enjoying the sensation of weight-lessness, vaguely wondering what might happen next, in no hurry to do anything which might disrupt her current serenity.

"She's awake." A woman's voice, muffled.

Something swam into view and materialized into a blurry face. She leaned forward, moving slowly though the thick substrate.

"Hello, Mila."

"Adam?" she tried to say, but found something obstructing her speech. Suddenly she didn't feel quite so pleased with herself.

"Don't try to talk," he said. "You have a breathing apparatus in your throat."

She looked down and saw a black tube snaking up.

"There's a keyboard inside the tank," Adam continued. "You can type on that."

She looked around. A small black keyboard was fixed to the inner glass. She moved forward, suddenly conscious that she was entirely naked. She typed:

Where am I?

"You're in a rehab tank," Adam said. "Your body is being re-paired. You nearly died."

I thought I had died.

She was slightly disappointed to find she wasn't in heaven.

Who's the girl?

"That's Clara. She's an . . . old friend. You can trust her."

How did . . . how did I get here?

"Clara and I collected you," he replied. "She's Bomb Squad . . . ex-Bomb Squad. She lent me some armor. We drove in, collected you, and drove out again."

You're going to be in such trouble.

He laughed, his voice sounding warm and comforting in her ear. It was good to hear it again.

"Maybe," he said. "We'll see."

How did you know I was going to be there? Bleeding to death like that?

"We didn't. Once I'd lost contact with you, the plan was just to head to Beverley and collect you from the hospital. We expected the staff would be happy to release you into our care if we dis-guised ourselves as Bomb Squad. It also meant we wouldn't be recognized. But when we got there you'd woken up and all hell had broken loose. We followed the sound of gunshots, and there you were."

Sorry about all that. I'm not a morning person.

"I'm pleased to see you still have your sense of humor," he replied.

Why did you do it? Why risk yourself for me?

There was a pause before Adam replied.

"I just didn't want you to die, that's all."

I'm glad you came for me.

Rebecca sat in a vacant office at the Ministry, her elbows resting on the table, fingertips pressed together, pressed against her lips as though she were praying. The florid face of Captain Baines' Avatar peered anxiously back at her.

"So, Captain, let me get this straight," she said, slowly. "You're telling me you have no idea who the identities were of the two Bomb Squad officers who arrived at the scene in a Bomb Squad vehicle from your unit, with Bomb Squad armor from your unit. Is that what you're telling me?"

"It must have been someone with high-level security clearance," Baines said, his jowly neck wobbling. "They took the vehicle and the equipment but didn't leave any records."

"How is that even possible?"

"Our record-keeping is highly secure," he blustered. "We can't let just anyone have access to the names of our officers, or where they are. Missions are kept secret. We don't just write things on paper."

"It seems you didn't record this mission anywhere!"

"But we did. Oh, we did! The problem is, the record has been deleted. We don't know which of our officers took the vehicle."

"Who could delete such a record?"

"Only someone with extremely high-level clearance, like I said. Well above my level."

So, Rebecca thought, the girl has some powerful friends. Alternatively there were people in positions of power who were prepared to take huge risks to get hold of her corpse.

"Are there no recordings of the vehicle leaving the headquarters?" Rebecca asked.

"Oh, yes, but the windows are blacked out. We couldn't see the driver."

"And was the vehicle tracked on its way to the scene?"

"No, ma'am. No Tech available."

Rebecca sighed. How could she be expected to operate effectively with her hands tied like this? The sooner the Minister's proposed reforms were implemented the better. She felt anger welling up inside her, filling her chest, and she took a deep breath, told herself to be patient. Inquiries were still proceeding. Someone must have seen the "officers" escaping the car park with the body of the girl. Something would come up.

Adam set a steaming cup of coffee down in front of Mila and sat down at the table beside her. Mila had her bare feet up on the chair, hugging her knees, and was staring at the Smartwall. The wall showed a Feed from a London rooftop, a breathtaking panoramic cityscape. The quality was astonishing, and Mila kept having to remind herself this wasn't a high-rise apartment, but a basement.

She'd been out of the tank a couple of days and was just starting to feel like her old self. Adam had explained that the house, or at least the basement area, was Cloaked. There was no phone signal down here, though he could link locally to a server, which gave him access to the Web if he chose to.

"Can you show other views?" she asked.

"Of course," Adam said. He concentrated on his IDS for a second and a view of the Great Wall of China sprang up onto the wall. Then Edinburgh Castle, then Times Square in New York, all of which Mila recognized from photographs.

"I mean London," she said. "Can I see other views of London?"

"Where do you want?" he asked, sipping his coffee.

"The Thames," she said. "I want to see the buildings along the Thames."

Adam switched the view. "You can control the direction and the resolution yourself," he said, sending her an App.

Mila spent a while zooming up and down the river. The Smart-wall was huge and offered sound as well as real-time images. It felt as though she were flying. The App had an ID function, so she could see what each building was called, who worked in there and other information.

"Here's your office," she said, focusing on a hulking Regency building overlooking the river not far from Waterloo Bridge. "So how come you were at the Center to interview me if you work here?"

"Rebecca and I were called down from London," Adam said. "You were a person of interest."

"I'd like to think I still am."

"You are," Adam said glancing over at her. "But for different reasons now."

He looked back at the Smartwall. "I doubt I'll be going back there in a hurry."

"I'm sorry," Mila said.

"Don't be," Adam replied, laughing. "I was a terrible Agent."

"Someone has to be the good cop," Mila said.

"Good cops aren't supposed to be so good they let people escape."

"What's going to happen to you?" she asked.

"Don't worry about me," Adam said. "I have friends who will look after me. You need to think about yourself. I think you need to get away from the Isles. You'll be safer on the Continent."

"Back in the U?" she said, a feeling of dread welling up.

"Some parts aren't so bad, I hear," Adam said, unconvincingly. "France? Northern Spain?"

Mila nodded weakly. She'd been through most of the countries in the U. Returning there wasn't an appealing prospect. But he was right. What choice did she have? Part of her had wondered . . . hoped he might be more eager to have her remain. A crazy hope. She'd caused him enough trouble.

"Can I see Beverley?" she asked.

Adam nodded, concentrated for a moment, and there it was,

the Minster, filling the screen. He handed the controls over to Mila, and she swooped and zoomed around it.

"Why are you so fascinated by the Minster?" Adam asked after a while. "I would have thought you'd want to forget all about it."

Mila was about to tell him what Julian had said, but held her tongue just in time. It wasn't that she didn't trust him, but she wasn't sure she trusted the mysterious Clara. No one but Holly knew about Julian's last instruction on the bridge. She wanted to keep that to herself for now.

"It's pretty," she said. "I wanted to have a good look around when I visited recently but I ran out of time." Feeling his eyes on her she zoomed away and swept out over countryside.

"Where is the camera?" she asked.

"This one's not real time," Adam explained. "It's a computer reconstruction. These shots would have been taken over months, or years, from dozens of different cameras. The computer has put them all together and filled in the gaps."

"It's amazing," Mila said. She passed over a tiny farm, with smoke trailing upward from the chimney. Tiny sheep dotted the fields, carved out between swathes of ancient woods. A crooked river wound its way through the countryside, reminding her of the river near her home.

"That's enough," she said, looking away.

Adam switched the view back to rooftops.

"Whose house is this?" Mila asked, changing the subject.

"Clara's husband's," he said. "He's someone she—we—trust."

Mila detected something in his tone.

"You and Clara? What's the deal there?"

He hesitated, looking away from her and over to the rooftops on the Smartwall. A small flyer buzzed close to the camera. A passenger looked their way, a smiling girl, about Mila's age. Then she was gone.

"We were together," Adam explained. "But we're not now."

"Married?"

"No. I was too young to get married."

"But she wasn't? How old is she?"

Adam grinned. "It's rude to ask a woman's age. She's a few years older than me."

"An older woman, eh?"

Adam shrugged. "Age difference isn't so important on the Isles."

"How old is her husband?" Mila asked, regretting it immediately.

Adam's grin faded. "I dunno. A few years older than her, I suppose."

A twinge of something. What was it? Jealousy? How disappointed Julian would be! How old was Adam? she wondered. Early twenties? Five, maybe six years older than Mila. In some ways he seemed older. In others, he seemed just a boy.

"And now she's with the guy who owns this house?" Mila said.

"Yes."

"Do you have a house this big?"

He laughed. "No."

"Do you have a magic tank in your basement?"

"No, I don't. Only very important people have magic tanks. But that's not the reason she left me."

She left him.

"It might have played some part."

"Perhaps," he said, smiling.

"She must still feel something for you though?" Shut up, Mila, she told herself. Just stop talking.

Adam tilted his head, quizzically.

She was unable to stop herself. "To take this risk. . . ."

Adam shrugged. "She knows me. She knew this was important to me. That you were important to me."

A flower began to unfurl deep within Mila.

"But she'll get in trouble for this, won't she?"

"Her husband is an important man," Adam said. "He's an MP in the Privacy Party. And no friend of the Minister. Not everyone agrees with the current government's attitude."

"So there's the Privacy Party, who got rid of the CCTV cameras," Mila said, remembering what Julian had told her about the simplistic politics of the Isles. "But what Party is the Minister in?"

"The Security Party," Adam said. "They're in government at the moment, but with a very small majority. That's why they haven't been able to bring the cameras and Watchtowers back. Not yet."

"Clara helped a terrorist to escape," Mila pointed out. "She'll get into trouble over that, won't she?"

Adam shrugged. "Well, we have a sort of plan about that. We think she'll be safe."

"Like I said though, it's a big risk."

Adam said nothing.

"Maybe she feels guilty?" Mila suggested. Adam still didn't reply and Mila sensed she'd gone too far. Time to change the subject again. "Doesn't it scare you, sitting in a room with a terrorist?"

Adam shook his head. "I don't think you're a terrorist."

"But I have a bomb in my head. It could go off any time."

He looked at her and grinned. "I like dangerous women."

Mila blushed and the flower opened a little more.

The situation was diffused when Clara walked in. The older woman. Mila inspected her as she approached. She hadn't seen much of her since she'd come out of the tank, naked as a baby and completely healed, feeling better than she could ever remember feeling.

Clara was in her early thirties, Mila decided, tall with a muscular frame, and long dark hair. At a distance she could be in her mid-twenties. Only her eyes betrayed her true age; a deep chocolate brown, full of character, life and some regret. She was one of the most beautiful women Mila had ever seen and again felt an unwelcome twist of jealousy as Adam's head turned to watch his ex.

"How's the patient?" Clara asked her, smiling briefly.

"Fine. Brilliant, in fact," Mila replied.

"You had a broken wrist, a fractured ankle, two cracked ribs, multiple cuts, grazes, contusions and a bloody great gunshot wound in your back. You're a tough cookie."

Mila finished her coffee. "Let me wash up, by way of thanks." It was a joke but sounded sarcastic. Clara made her nervous.

"You don't need to wash up." A small hover-bot buzzed into the room and whipped the cups from Mila's and Adam's hands before disappearing again.

"I've found a surgeon," Clara said. "He's coming this afternoon."

"I thought you said I was fixed?" Mila said.

"It's for the device," Adam said. "The bomb."

"You're taking it out?" she asked, alarmed.

Clara nodded. "Don't worry, he's a good surgeon."

"Won't he ask questions?"

"Not with the amount we're paying him," Clara said.

"What if it goes off?" Mila asked.

"The basement is bombproof," Clara said. "And I've never come across a bomb that I couldn't make safe."

"Yet," Mila added, then winced at herself. Why couldn't she just say thanks?

"After that, once you've recovered, you'll have to leave," Clara said.

"Of course," Mila said. "You've done more than enough."

Clara glanced briefly at Adam before walking out of the room.

The Cloak over the house meant Mila couldn't make calls on her own phone. Later that day Mila asked Adam if there was a way she could call someone.

"You know, privately?"

"You mean securely? Don't worry, you can't be traced."

"I mean privately."

"Who are you going to call?" Adam said.

Did she detect a hint of suspicion in his face?

"Just a friend," she said carefully.

"Of course," he said, holding up a hand. "I have no right to pry. Sorry."

"It's okay," Mila said. "I can understand that you might be. . . wary."

"No, no, no," Adam said. "Not wary, just curious. I didn't realize you knew anyone on the Isles."

She said nothing, just waited.

He frowned, but then nodded. "I made a decision a while ago to trust you. I'm not going to go back on that now."

"Thank you," Mila said. "It means a lot."

"I'll arrange the connection and leave you to it. Just dial once your keypad activates. Don't worry, no one will be listening."

He left, and a couple of seconds later an App blinked into life on Mila's IDS and a keypad flashed up. An icon told her this was a secure line. Mila called up Holly's contact details and dialed.

"Mila? I thought you were dead! Oh my god. I saw them shoot you. Are you okay? Are you safe?"

"I think so," Mila said. "Look, I just wanted to call and let you know I was alive. Please don't tell anyone though."

"I'm glad you did."

"Why did you come to the Minster?" Mila asked. "I told you it was dangerous."

Holly laughed nervously. "I didn't realize just how dangerous until I got there. I wanted to help you. As soon as you ended the call I got in my car. I was worried."

"It was nice of you," Mila said, and for the second time that day she had to force back her tears.

"You're welcome," Holly said, as though she'd made Mila a cup of tea, not risked her life for her. "I've been trying to find out more about Beverley Minster. I had to do it on the Web; they've cordoned off the entire area."

"Did you see what happened in there? The vicar's Feed?"

"No, the Agency's refusing to discuss it. You know they Cloaked the entire building?"

"They can do that?" Mila asked.

"Oh, yes."

"They killed him," Mila said. "The vicar. And an old lady."

"They said you did that."

"They're lying."

"I believe you, and plenty of people are saying it was storming the church that caused the deaths. People are suspicious about the Agency being so secretive."

"Those poor people," Mila said. The truth was she did feel responsible.

"I'm afraid I couldn't find out anything useful about the number," Holly said. "There wasn't anything obvious on the building itself. I even scanned the tombstones in the graveyard."

"No, I'm not surprised," Mila replied. "I didn't think it could be so simple. What are we missing?"

"The only thing I can think of," Holly said slowly, "is that the phrase Beverley Minster might be some kind of code."

Mila paused. A code? It was possible.

"Sorry," Holly said. "I haven't been much help."

"You've been amazing," Mila reassured her. "Thanks for everything."

"I'm just so glad you're alive."

"Me too," Mila said.

"Mila," Holly began.

"Yes?"

"There are people, not just the Security Party, talking on the Channels, about bringing in new laws to help protect us from . . . people like you. Terrible laws. They'd bring back CCTV, and the Watchtowers. They want to allow tapping of people's phones."

"I'm sorry," Mila said. "I feel like I'm to blame."

"You shouldn't," Holly went on. "Like I said, some people are saying that there's a conspiracy, that you're not really a threat and that there is no need for new laws—that the Privacy Laws should be protected."

"It's good to hear not everyone thinks I'm a monster," Mila said.

"But, Mila, what if that thing in your head is a bomb? What if it goes off?"

"If that happens, then the repeal of the Privacy Laws will be the least of my problems."

Holly laughed grimly. "Yes, of course. So, what are you going to do now?"

"I don't know," Mila said. "But I think I have to leave the Isles. I've caused enough trouble already."

"I'd be sad if you go."

Mila smiled. "You don't know how much it helps, hearing something like that."

"Call again before you decide anything, yeah?"

"Promise," Mila said. "Bye, Holly. And thanks."

"Be safe."

"I'll try," Mila said.

She wiped her eyes as Holly's Avatar shrank and the call was ended. For all the wonder to be found on the Isles—the freedom, the resources, the space and the beauty—the most wonderful thing was the people themselves. Surely Julian couldn't have wanted to hurt people like Holly, or Adam, or Clara, or the vicar at Beverley Minster. She thought too of Joe and Darcie, who'd given her food and sat with her until the security forces had told her she was a terrorist. Their natural tendency had been kind and welcoming.

One day Julian comes to her aunt and uncle's house. Mila is surprised he knows where she lives. Then she remembers the day Vaclav died; the day she killed Malachi. He took her home. Her aunt gives her a knowing look as she leads the older man into the kitchen where Mila is rolling dough for dumplings. Her aunt leaves them alone, though Mila knows she will be listening from the next room. One of Mila's tiny cousins pokes her mop head around a curtain, staring at the visitor with enormous eyes.

"Boo!" Julian says, lunging at the child, who shrieks and disappears. Then he says, "I need to talk to you. There's a problem."

"We'd better go for a walk," she says.

They leave the building. Mila feels her aunt's eyes burning the back of her neck. Mila is seventeen, nearly eighteen now, and she is aware her aunt wants her married and out of the house, sorry though that she'll be losing the money Mila brings in.

They walk down to the dusty old park where the children play.

"I'm leaving," Julian says.

Mila's heart sinks. Her first thought is for her job. Without Julian's patronage, she won't be welcome there anymore. She can forget the little flat she is saving up for. Her aunt and uncle would be furious at the loss of income and would finally kick her out. Where will she live? How will she eat?

"Where are you going?" she asks, not looking at him. "You've been offered a new job?"

"Back to the Isles," he says.

"To your farm?"

"No," he sighs. "Like I said, there's a problem. I . . . I'm in a bit of trouble with the Corporation."

Mila waits for him to continue. They walk a circuit of the park, watched by hungry children with black hair and dirty T-shirts.

"I won't go into details," he says. "I have some enemies in Management, and last night . . . well, let's just say one of them woke up in the hospital this morning."

Mila stops and looks at him in alarm.

"We were drinking," he says, his hands up in defense, as though this excuses him. He is probably correct. "We were in a bar. We argued. It got out of hand. He'll be fine. But I can't go back there now."

"And neither can I, I guess?"

He shakes his head. "I'm sorry." He pauses.

"You could come with me, if you like," he says.

She stops and stares at him again.

"To the Isles? On a plane? I can't afford that!" she says. "Anyway, I don't have a passport. They wouldn't let me in."

"They won't let me in either," he says. "And I'm not going on a plane."

"You're traveling over land?" Mila asks, astonished. "Through the U?"

"I've got some money," he says. "We can buy a truck."

"Why me?" she asks.

"I feel . . . responsible for you," he says. "You've lost your father. . . ."

Mila does not question his reasons. This is what she hopes his motivation has been all along: avuncular concern. Her feet kick up little puffs of dust as she walks. Still no rain. "And what would I do on the Isles?"

"I have friends," he says. "We can get you a phone, maybe find a farm to live on. Plenty of abandoned farms on the Isles. Farming's too much like hard work for them."

They complete another circuit of the park without speaking. Mila listens to the children shrieking at each other. They've lost interest in the odd couple. She looks up at the apartment building where she lives with her aunt and uncle. Great rust stains streak the sides. Half the windows are cracked or broken. Foul graffiti covers the accessible areas. She imagines telling her aunt she has lost her job. She imagines marrying one of the black-toothed drunks her uncle works with. She has already made up her mind.

"Okay," she says. "I'll come with you."

12

To the east of the city was a large conglomeration of mega sky-scrapers. Surrounding them in a hazy ring were a couple dozen shimmering towers, reaching into the low clouds. They were hard to see clearly.

"So those are the invisible buildings?" Mila said.

She was at once impressed and slightly disappointed, the way you often are when you finally see something the fabulousness of which has been explained to you time and time again. She learned about these towers in school. Julian had also mentioned them more than once, trying, she'd thought at the time, to impress her.

In the early part of the twenty-first century there had been an intense period of construction as resource-rich corporations tried to outdo one another with ever taller buildings. Eventually the government had stopped giving planning permission for structures that restricted the views from existing skyscrapers.

The solution had been to design invisible buildings. Or, at least, nearly invisible buildings.

"Do you know how they work?" Adam asked.

"It's all mirrors, isn't it?"

"Not really," he replied. "It's a little like the Wallscreen, except there are hundreds of them covering the entire building. From inside they appear to be simply frosted glass, but from the outside, they play moving images."

"Which are the Feeds from cameras on the other side of the building?"

"Yep, but it's slightly more complicated than that. There are cameras at the corners of each of the windows. Each camera has a wide-angle lens allowing it to view pretty much everything in a 180-degree arc. The building's Brain translates these images and plays them on the screens on the opposite side of the building, using lenticular technology to project the right bit of each image in the right direction."

"Huh?"

"I mean, if a camera picks up a bird flying a little above it, and to the left, the Brain is clever enough to transmit the image through the building and out the other side in a hundred different directions. So wherever you stand on the other side, you will see the bird in the right position. In the direction it actually is, relative to you."

"Oh," Mila said. "So if I were standing directly opposite the bird with the building between us, the image would come straight through toward me, but if I were standing at forty-five degrees to the building the Brain would fire the images out at a forty-five-degree angle."

"Anyone standing in any position on your side of the building will see the bird as if the building weren't there at all. It's a brilliant feat of engineering."

"Like I said, mirrors."

Adam sighed.

"And that's all it does?" Mila went on, teasing him a little. "It just shows you what's on the other side of the building?"

"In December it shows a big Christmas tree, and different things on other celebration days. Once someone hacked it and showed a gigantic image of the Prime Minister in his underpants."

"I hear you have floating buildings too," she said, putting on a bored expression.

He laughed and shook his head.

"I'm not sure how to take you sometimes. I think you like to keep me guessing."

"There can't be that much mystery about me," she said. "You've seen me naked more than once."

He grinned mischievously. His green eyes were highlighted by the loose green sweater he wore. "I kept my gaze firmly above the neck."

"Sure you did."

"But you know that's not what I mean," he went on, his smile fading.

"What?" she asked, suddenly concerned.

He shrugged and looked back to the screen.

"Sometimes I just wish . . . things were different, that's all."

"I wish that too," Mila said, and felt as she said it that something passed between them. Something significant.

An unfamiliar feeling of happiness and excitement washed through her. But she clamped down on it quickly.

This can't happen, Julian whispered in her ear. Ignore the distractions of the heart. They will be your undoing. Mila had grown expert at clamping down on her feelings, cramming them into a dusty trunk in her subconscious and locking it tight. She couldn't let Adam, of all people, start fiddling with the keys.

She watched him as he talked animatedly about the super-light materials of the "floating buildings" and the anti-grav tech that was in its infancy. He was good-looking. She'd thought that the moment she first saw him. But it was more than that. He had a good face. A natural smile, a humorous bearing. He didn't take himself too seriously, or anything else for that matter. He was like her in that regard. He got how crazy the world was.

She sighed inwardly. She knew she should have shut him out, made it clear there could be nothing between them. Not even friendship. She didn't have that luxury.

But the flower within her was open and turning toward the light.

Rebecca watched the Minister as he stood and looked out the window at the gray London skyline. Flecks of rain pattered against the pane. She had arrived at the Ministry half an hour earlier. The Minister had made her wait.

"They found the truck?"

"Yes, Minister."

"And?"

"And it was empty. Some torn clothing; the girl's. Fragments of bandages and other evidence of first aid."

"Where?"

"A car park, in London. We tracked the vehicle with a drone. We only realized at the last moment that it wasn't going to the Bomb Squad HQ. They must have got into another car and driven out. We lost them."

"Why didn't you have a car following them?"

"The captain confirmed the officers were his. The vehicle was clearly Bomb Squad."

"And were the officers his?"

"Their IDs checked out. One of the officers had a high level of authorization. But it became apparent that Captain Baines had no proper record of their mission so we don't know who the officers actually were. No one had requested that unit's attendance."

"So you didn't follow them with one of the forty cars and three hundred Agents you had at your disposal? You sent them all home?"

"We had the drone. It wasn't considered necessary to follow with a car, sir."

"You didn't consider it necessary, you mean?"

"No, sir."

"You've been here twice already to explain your failure."

"Yes, sir."

"There will not be another occasion."

"No, sir."

Later that day, over coffee, they talked about Julian.

"Tell me what you know," Mila said.

Adam regarded her carefully.

"Julian's record is incomplete, and not having full access to the Agency database hasn't helped me. But Clara's husband has some contacts. We've pieced together a reasonable picture of who he was."

"He was an Agent?" Mila said.

"At first, yes," Adam said. "He was born in Poland. We're not sure of his date of birth but he was in his late forties when he died. He owned a civil engineering firm. But the constant wars in the U eventually ruined him. The Corporation bailed him out and effectively took over his business. That's when he came into contact with the Minister."

"He knew the Minister?" Mila asked.

"We don't know if they ever actually met. But, yes, the Minister got his hooks into Julian at that point."

"What do you mean, hooks?"

Adam sipped his coffee before continuing. "Julian was indebted to the Corporation and to the Ministry of Third Development. The Minister used his leverage to ask Julian to undertake work we suspect he couldn't ordinarily have done."

"What sort of work?" she asked, dry-mouthed.

"Clearing slums. Bulldozing shanty towns. Building pipelines across farms. Controversial projects. Things which might be expected to draw opposition. Julian's team worked with soldiers and Agents. They were armed."

Mila remembered Julian's words back in Köls; the look of regret in his eyes. The dam. That was why Julian had been sent to Köls in the first place.

Adam went on quickly, as if wishing to spare her the pain of dwelling on unwelcome truths.

"Julian was rewarded for his endeavors with Citizenship and some land on the Isles. He retired to Yorkshire."

"Beverley," Mila said.

"Yes."

"Then the records go a bit hazy," Adam said. "We know he left the Isles and was on the Corporation payroll in a city called Köls for a couple of years." Her expression must have changed because he paused.

"That's where you met him?"

She nodded. What harm could it do to tell Adam now?

"What was he doing there?" he asked.

"I don't know," she admitted. "He never really spoke to me about his work."

Adam frowned. "Well, all we can be sure of is that he suddenly went off the payroll. His phone was deactivated and eighteen months later he turns up dead in the English Channel."

"He told me he'd made enemies," Mila said. "That he'd refused to do something. Some awful job."

Adam nodded and waited for her to carry on.

"That's when we traveled across the U," Mila said. "He looked after me. Taught me how to survive. How to fight."

"He did a good job, and I know he meant a lot to you," Adam said. "But why did he bring you with him in the first place? And insert that thing in your head? That's what you need to be asking yourself—"

"You think I'm not?" Mila snapped. "I think about it all the time. It's like I can feel it in my head. A huge lump."

"We'll get it out," Adam said. "If it is a bomb, then at least you'll know."

The subtext of his statement was clear. If it turned out to be a bomb, she would know Julian had betrayed her. That he had been using her all along.

Rebecca tutted as another call came through. No ID plate but the code told her it was from someone she couldn't ignore. She answered and the Avatar of a blond, tanned man appeared. Rebecca thought he looked familiar. He bowed gently and shot her a wide smile.

"Yes?" she said.

"Special Agent Miles, ma'am."

"You don't look like Miles," she said.

"A little gene therapy," the Special Agent said. "I need to change my appearance temporarily."

"What can I do for you, Special Agent?"

"Forgive me for calling you directly, ma'am. The Minister suggested it."

"That's perfectly all right, Special Agent. I assume this is to do with the girl?"

"Mila Karenin, yes,"

"You know her surname?"

"I know a great deal about her," the Special Agent said. He pulled at the lobe of his left ear and smiled again. "I have ways of finding out all sorts of information about people."

Rebecca nodded. "I'm sure you have," she said. "So what do you need from me?"

"As I say, I have various ways of finding the information I need," he said, smoothly. "But often I find the easiest, and quickest, is simply to ask the right people the right questions."

Rebecca shrugged. "Ask away. Though I'm not sure I can be much help."

"We'll see about that. Now, your colleague, who I believe goes under the codename Adam. He is suspended?"

"What does he have to do with it?"

"Please just answer my questions, ma'am. Is Adam suspended or not?"

"He is, yes." Something about the Special Agent's manner irritated Rebecca. She didn't like to admit any failings within her department.

"And he is suspended because he was thought to have sympathies with the fugitive?"

"I thought he was becoming . . . emotionally attached to her, yes," she said. What was the point of all this? she thought.

"But his security privileges have not been revoked?"

"No. He's on gardening leave. He hasn't been formally suspended." This was technically true. No formal action had yet been taken over Adam's conduct.

The blond man looked down at his feet, shaking his head.

"And this Adam, does he have anyone close to him? A girl-friend, or an . . . ex-girlfriend, perhaps?"

Rebecca blinked, unsure where this was heading. "He recently split up with someone."

"Ah, did he? Did he?" Miles said. "And her name?"

"Clara."

"Clara. I see."

Rebecca rolled her eyes. "Where is this going, Special Agent?"

"Her surname wouldn't be Harrison, would it? Clara Harrison?"

"That was her maiden name, I believe," Rebecca said. She knew all too well it was. She'd been at enough dinner parties with them, after all.

"And what does she do for a living, this Clara Harrison?"

Rebecca thought for a moment. What did Clara do? Had Adam ever told her? Had she ever asked?

"She's in the Agency, I know that. I'm not sure what division." Suddenly Rebecca felt as though she were treading on shifting ground.

"Is there any chance you could find out for me?" Special Agent Miles asked with another small smile. "I don't have such immediate connectivity to Agency records as you do."

Rebecca had already texted the request to Jason. The answer came back almost immediately. With Level Three clearance, there weren't many morsels of information unavailable to her. Wordlessly she scooted it over to Miles.

Clara Harrison was until recently a Major in the Bomb Disposal Unit.

"Interesting," he said. "And if I'm not mistaken, Clara Harrison is now married to Gordon Urquhart, MP, CEO of WorldCorp and a big hitter in the Privacy Party."

Rebecca's mouth had dropped open and she was having difficulty closing it.

"B-but surely even a member of the Opposition wouldn't tolerate his wife stealing the body of a terrorist?" she said.

The blond man shrugged. "I do not concern myself in politics," he said. "It's simply my job to find the girl, alive or dead."

"You think she may be alive?"

"I don't particularly care," he said. "Though with the information you've given me, I will no doubt discover soon."

"I'll send some units to the Urquhart residence. . . ."

"That will not be necessary. It would be an impolite intrusion," Miles said, quickly. "Mr. Urquhart is a respected and powerful man. Please let me handle this—though I would thank you to have a back-up unit in the vicinity. No closer than hundred meters from the house."

"How will you gain access? The security arrangements are formidable," Rebecca said. The full specifications of the house were scrolling down the left side of her IDS.

"There's always a way," Special Agent Miles replied, stroking his face. "I'll be in touch."

Then he winked out.

Rebecca sat back in her chair and took a deep breath.

Mila and Adam lay on huge transparent bags filled with something gloopy, which gave off a soft light. They were half chatting, half watching some Channel show which Adam was taking direct from the home server and live-scooting to her. The little hover-bot had just finished clearing away the remains of an enormous lunch, eaten mostly by Mila.

"I've never seen someone eat an entire chicken," Adam said.

"It was tiny," Mila replied, slightly embarrassed. "Pigeon-sized."

"And a steak?"

"That was amazing," she said.

"You're full now, yeah?"

She shrugged. "Yeah. But . . ."

"What? You want something else?"

"Maybe something sweet?"

"Like what, a cake? Chocolate?"

"You don't have . . ."

"What? Go on."

"You don't have any doughnuts, do you?"

"Doughnuts? Sure. How many do you want?"

"Just one," she said.

A few minutes later the hover-bot brought a single doughnut on a plate. Soft dough, with a light, slightly caramelized sugar coating. No jam, no icing. Perfect. She took a bite and closed her eyes, in heaven.

"Good, huh?" Adam said, grinning.

"Can't we just stay here forever?" she said. "We could just eat doughnuts all day. Get fat together."

She'd already been astonished by the quality of the food on the Isles. Even back in the Center. So much taste. So much better than the limp fare her aunt used to provide in Köls. Even on her father's farm, where the food had at least been fresh, it lacked the taste, the sheer vitality of the food here.

"Is it modified?" she asked. "The food?"

"The food you have in the Eastern U is old-tech, or possibly no-tech," he explained. "We're trying to introduce modified food in certain areas, but often irrigation is the problem."

Mila pursed her lips. "So you build dams."

"Yes, dams, canals, river diversions. Though things are made difficult by all the wars you guys keep having."

Mila said nothing, stung by his insensitivity.

He must have sensed he'd upset her, as he switched off the Channel and turned to her. "Sorry," he said. "I didn't mean to—"

"Why are there so many wars in the Third?" she interrupted. "Why was there a war in the U?"

He looked surprised by the question. "The same reason there are always wars. Overpopulation, environmental pressures, scarcity of resources. When the economy of the U went into freefall after the Third Great Depression, countries started blaming each other. Waves of migrants left their homes, neighboring states resisted the incursions, atrocities ensued, and the result was civil war. Endless civil war."

"So if the Third has nothing," she said. "If we're squabbling like children over old-tech tomatoes, how is it that my country, my poverty-stricken country, exports millions of tons of food to your country every year?"

"I don't think that can be correct, Mila," Adam said, his smooth skin reflecting the soft light from the bag. "We produce all our own food. . . ."

"Don't give me that," she said, suddenly angry. "I've seen the figures. I've seen the transport orders."

"What? Where?"

"Julian showed me, in Köls."

Adam smiled. "Oh, yes, Julian, our trustworthy old friend."

"He worked for the Corporation, didn't he?"

Adam grimaced.

"Didn't he?"

"Yes."

"So he had access to the records. I saw them. And when we were traveling, we saw the polytunnels. Millions of square meters growing modified food. All for export."

"Mila, did it occur to you that Julian was showing you what he wanted you to see? He was molding you, remember? Using you for his own ends."

"That's what you think."

"Julian was thrown out of the Agency," Adam continued. "You said yourself that he'd refused to do some job and someone, possibly the Minister, had him fired. He wanted revenge."

"You don't know that," she said quietly.

"What other reason could he have had for dragging you across the U? Training you in martial arts? Sneaking onto the Isles with you?"

"I don't know, maybe he wanted to help me. Maybe he took pity on an orphan. Maybe he just wanted a quiet, peaceful life on a farm and wanted me to have the same."

"But of the billions of people in the Third, why single you out?"

"Because I was there," she answered.

Adam shook his head. "Julian chose you because you were young and impressionable. He was an angry man, and he wanted to make you angry, to make you blame the First for the problems of the Third."

"The First is to blame," she responded hotly. "You claim you want to help develop the Third, but you're busy taking all our resources."

"That's simply not true."

"You destroy people's lives. You let the wars carry on, ignore the environmental problems, as long as you get your food and your clothes and your stupid devices."

"It's not the responsibility of the First to fix the parts of the world that won't fix themselves. We're doing our best and people like Julian aren't helping. . . ."

Adam's head twitched in the telltale fashion indicating he'd received a call.

"Okay," he said out loud, then turned to look at Mila.

"What?"

"The surgeon's here."

"Have we met?" asked Adam as the blond surgeon entered. "You look familiar."

"No," the man replied shortly. "I don't believe so." He laid his case on a table and inspected the room. He smiled reassuringly, but Mila still felt nervous, remembering the nightmare she'd endured back at the Center. There was even a similar chair standing ready, one which formed itself to your body to hold you in place.

Adam stood to one side. Clara was nowhere to be seen, but Adam said she was Watching via his Feed. If the device needed defusing she would scan it remotely and enter only if necessary. Mila had told Adam he didn't need to stay. If there was a chance the bomb would go off, she didn't want him to risk his life for her again.

To her relief, he refused to leave.

"I've come this far," he said, squeezing her hand. She held his firmly, not wanting him to pull away just yet.

"This room is Cloaked?" the doctor asked.

"Yes," Adam replied. "And bombproof and soundproof."

"Is anyone Watching your Feed?"

Adam hesitated slightly before answering. "No," he said.

"Good," the surgeon said, and smiled a thin smile. "Mila, would you please sit in the Forma-seat?"

Mila swallowed and sat down in the SEMINT chair, which gripped her firmly, though without discomfort.

"Good," he said again. He opened his case, took out a gun and shot Adam in the face.

13

Mila screamed. The blond surgeon's smile widened. He returned the gun to the case and took out a small machine with a circular blade.

"I'll kill you later," he said conversationally. "First I'm going to open your head and take a look at the bomb. Not because I enjoy causing pain, you understand. I'd kill you first to spare you the agony, but I'm concerned it may be set to detonate when you're dead."

He moved behind the chair, where she couldn't see him, and the Forma-seat spun so she was on her side. Cool air against the back of her neck told her the headrest had shifted to allow him access to her skull. Apart from his shoes and bright yellow socks, Adam was obscured by the armrest. A trickle of blood nosed its way across the floor.

Mila screamed again as the saw whined into action. She clenched every muscle in her body and shut her eyes, unable to move, unable to do anything to stop the horror.

A loud bang echoed in her ears but when the pain came it was not what she had expected. The seat had released her and she'd fallen heavily to the floor. Dazed, she raised herself onto her forearms and looked up.

Clara was in the room. She had a gun but the surgeon held her wrists, forcing her against the wall. With difficulty, Mila pulled herself up. Clara had got an arm free and punched the surgeon in the jaw, to little obvious effect. Enhanced, Mila thought.

Mila sprang onto his back and wrapped her arms around his throat, dragging him backward. He grunted but clung on to Clara's wrists. To let her free her gun hand would mean instant death.

But the gun wasn't needed. With a twist and a yank, Mila snapped the blond man's neck. She felt his body relax and slide to the floor. His blue eyes stared upward at nothing, the permanent smile still there. Clara ran immediately to Adam's side. Part of Mila wanted to go too. Another part held her back. She didn't want to see. Didn't want to know.

"He's not breathing," Clara cried. "Help me!"

Mila took a deep breath and turned to look. Adam lay face down in an ever-increasing pool of blood. "What can we do?" she asked.

"We have to get him into the tank," said Clara. "Now!"

Mila's mind was a blaze of despair and self-recrimination. She could hardly bring herself to look at Adam, floating in the tank, his face hidden by a mass of bubbles as the Autodoc strived to repair the massive damage. Clara stood silently by, monitoring the readings via her phone.

"He lied," Mila said.

"What?"

"In there, the surgeon asked if anyone was Watching Adam's Feed. He said no. But you were watching."

"Of course I was," Clara said, tight-lipped, still watching her phone. "He has good instincts," she went on, her eyes flicking up toward Mila.

"Will he survive?" Mila asked, choking back her sobs and wiping her sleeve across her eyes.

"I think so," Clara said. "We got him into the tank quickly. Though it's too early to tell if there is any damage to his brain. The tank can repair physical damage, but he could lose his memories, his personality even."

"He might not be Adam?"

"He'd be able to access his recordings, of course, reconstruct his life through those, but . . ."

"But he wouldn't be the same."

"No." Clara looked at Mila, a tired look in her eyes. "But maybe that would be for the best."

"I don't understand."

"Maybe it would be best if Adam didn't remember . . ."

"Me?"

"Not just you, Mila."

Mila watched as the bright green fluid swirled: billions of nano-bots, Adam had explained, controlled by a central SEMINT brain. Maybe they could make him whole again. Make him happy. She turned to Clara, dazed, her heart leaden. "I'm sorry," she said. "I should have left as soon as I came out of the tank. I've put you and your family in danger."

"I would do the same thing again," she said. "Not just for Adam, but for you. You don't deserve to die."

"You don't think I'm a terrorist then?" Mila asked.

Clara shook her head. "No, you're just a pawn in someone else's game."

"Who? You mean Julian?"

"No. He was a pawn as well. There are powerful people in the First, Mila. People who will watch innocents die in order to advance their position."

"Politics," Mila said, bitterly.

One of Adam's hands twitched in the tank and for an instant her heart surged. But then he was still again. Just a random nervous signal fired by the subconscious.

"Not even politics. Not anymore. When you have all you could want—when food, clothes, housing, entertainment are free to all—then what is there to set one person against his or her peers? How do people show their power?"

"Social standing," Mila said.

"Yes. Who makes the greatest Contribution. Who throws the

best parties. Who is allowed to live in the grandest houses. Who gets the best seats at the opera."

"That's what drives people?"

"Some people."

"And what does it have to do with me?" Mila asked.

Clara laid her palm against the glass of the tank.

"Don't you think it odd that you were able to escape so easily?"

"It didn't seem easy."

"Oh, I don't mean to belittle your skills," Clara said. "Only someone with extraordinary resourcefulness and resilience could have managed to evade the Agency for so long."

"But you think my escape was made easier than it should have been?"

"The Agency could have killed you as soon as the device was identified in your brain. They could have had armed guards outside your cell in the Center. Once you'd escaped they could have shut down all transport networks, closed the roads. They could have reset your phone earlier. They could have flooded the countryside with Agents, filled the sky with drones. Someone made a series of decisions that gave you the opportunity to get away, more than once. Nothing overt. Nothing that could be pinned on the person responsible."

"But why? Why would they want me to escape?"

Clara turned to look earnestly at Mila. "To show up how weak and ineffective our security networks are. To demonstrate how tightly the Agency's hands are tied. This is someone who wishes to reverse the Privacy Laws and institute a regime of total security where illegals are shot on sight, where the Watch-towers go back up, where there are CCTV cameras on every corner. Where all Citizens' phones can be tapped at any time."

"But they sent Special Agents after me," Mila protested. "Why do that if they wanted me to stay alive?"

"The first two Special Agents they sent—didn't you think there was anything odd about them?"

Mila shrugged. "I don't know. I guess, they seemed pretty old."

"Special Agent Griffin, the one you killed in the woods—he was seventy-four."

"What?"

"Special Agent Fowler, who was sent to Beverley—he was seventy-one."

"Well, they looked pretty good for their age . . . and punched pretty hard."

"But they were chosen for a reason—to give you a chance. Of course, if they'd killed you, then no great harm would have been done. The Minister had what he needed as soon as you escaped from the Center and he could say it was you who blew the place up and killed the guards. But the longer you ran and the more you showed up the Security Services as weak and ineffectual, the better it was for him."

"The Minister?"

"The Minister for Homeland Security," Clara said. "Adam's boss."

Mila suddenly remembered the building overlooking the Thames, which she'd seen on the Smartwall.

"He's responsible for all this?"

Clara nodded. "Yes. He has proposed a bill in Parliament to make sweeping reforms to the Privacy Laws."

"I heard about that," Mila said.

"He wants to massively increase the budget for security, immigration control and espionage," Clara continued. "The House votes next week. This has worked out perfectly for him."

"He had those guards, those Citizens killed to win a vote?"

Clara nodded.

Mila's head reeled. "And he's got what he wants now," she said slowly.

"Yes," Clara said. "He'll do everything he needs to to kill you. That's why there is a dead Special Agent in my basement. You pose a threat to him now. If the truth got out it would be hugely damaging. There are already people willing to speak out against him. There's a call for an inquiry into what happened in the Minster."

"You know the truth," Mila said. "You and your husband. Can't you use it against him?"

"What proof do we have?" Clara said. "On the face of it, he made every effort to catch and kill you. If anything, he seems to have gone too far. He's claiming he's been let down by bungling Agents and underfunded security systems. He and his minions are on the Channels constantly, explaining why they think harsher laws will prevent these sorts of tragedies in future."

"But—"

Clara interrupted her.

"There are Agents at the door. You have to go."

"How do I get out?"

"Come with me."

Mila took one last look at Adam in the tank then rushed after her. Clara took her down the corridor and up a flight of stairs, leading to a garage. Two sleek cars sat waiting. Clara handed Mila a gun. "This was the Agent's," she said. "I don't want it in the house. You might need it."

Mila took it, nodding.

"I'm sorry, Mila, I wish I could help more, but I've done all I can."

"You've done more than enough," Mila said, hugging her. Clara was stiff at first, but then returned the hug.

"The house is Cloaked. As soon as you leave the garage, they'll be able to find you again," Clara said. "Drive to the river, downstream to Limehouse Basin perhaps. Find a fast boat, get over to the Continent. That's the best advice I can offer. You won't find any peace on the Isles."

"Are there Agents Watching the house?" Mila asked.

"I've been monitoring the situation on the house security network," Clara said. "We have drone cameras. It looks like there's just one team. You know how to drive?"

Mila nodded. Clara opened the car door and she clambered in. A SEMINT seat belt snaked around her belly, through a loop then up across her chest, securing itself to a fastening behind her right ear.

"They're not covering the rear of the house, as far as I can tell," Clara said and made to shut the door. "Good luck, Mila."

"Wait," Mila said. "Something you said before, about Julian being a pawn as well. What did you mean?"

"There's no time..."

"Tell me!"

"Julian was a Special Agent,"

"I know, then he went rogue."

"Well, maybe he did; maybe he didn't."

"What are you saying?"

"My husband thinks Julian was working directly for the Minister."

"Adam said that too, but we think they had a disagreement. Adam thinks Julian was coming to get revenge."

Clara shrugged. "It's possible they have history, those two. I wouldn't be surprised if Julian hadn't still been working under the Minister's orders. I said as much to Adam, but maybe . . . I don't know. Look, you've got to go."

The door slammed and daylight flooded the car as the garage door opened. Mila squinted in the half second before the windscreen automatically shaded over. She checked the controls; she'd seen Holly drive and it seemed straightforward enough. One pedal made you go; the other made you stop. If you kept both hands on the steering wheel you could go fast, otherwise the SEMINT brain would take over and slow you down.

"Here goes," she breathed, taking hold of the steering wheel, then pressing her foot hard on the accelerator. The car lurched forward, out of the garage and into an empty back street.

As she left the house's Cloaking field, her IDS sprang into life. Apps brightened and hopped to show her they were connected to the Web again. Adam's Avatar stayed gray. It was awful not having him there, watching her, protecting her.

She checked her speed a little; driving too fast would draw attention. At present they thought she was dead, and she wanted to keep it that way as long as possible.

She opened her Map App and considered her route. Limehouse

Basin, Clara had said. There would be fast boats there. Boats that could get her to the Continent.

She would head for the river.

Mila turned left onto a busy road. She was quickly getting used to the controls. She took her hands off the steering wheel, so she could look at the contents of the car. She should have brought food, clothes. If only there had been time. Citizens never transported anything with them. Food would always be available wherever they were going. New clothes could be picked up just about anywhere, even if they weren't the latest fashions.

Rebecca phoned. She answered the call, intrigued.

"You're alive then?" Rebecca said.

"So it would seem."

"And the Special Agent?"

"Not so special, apparently."

"What happened to him?" Rebecca asked, her voice shaking with rage.

"I'm not doing your job for you. You find out."

She hung up and checked her Watchers box. She now had 1,432 Watchers and more joining all the time. Presumably another bulletin had gone out as soon as she'd been located. It looked like every Agent on the Isles was Watching her Feed, and members of the public too. Insulting messages began appearing in the chat box, but there were a few messages of support too. She closed the box just as her phone chimed. Rebecca again. This time she ignored it. Only Adam had had a constant connection with her phone. Anyone else she could ignore.

Mila was concentrating on the road, her hands firmly on the wheel. She was relieved to be on the move again; it gave some escape from the pain. The car was nimble and responsive as she darted in and out of the slow-moving traffic. Red lights on the dashboard flashed every time she came close to another vehicle, but she added them to the list of things she was ignoring. The time for caution had passed. The one thing she couldn't ignore was the sound of sirens in the distance.

They were coming for her.

"We have two drones and a manned hover plane over the area," Maddie said.

"Get them into the line of sight and see if they can identify the car," Rebecca replied.

"Are we authorized to use airborne ordnance?"

"I may have Level Three clearance," Rebecca replied, "but I suspect dropping high-yield explosives on the Strand may be considered overstepping my brief. We'll have to take her down at ground level. Use the planes to locate her, and tell them not to strike unless there's no chance of hitting anything friendly."

"Got it."

"Don't forget the delay," Rebecca said, watching Mila slip into an impossibly small gap between two leisure vehicles. "We need to predict where she's likely to be seven seconds in the future."

"Already on it," Jason said. "How's this?" He scooted a new map to Rebecca. A red arrow showed Mila's last known position and a blue dot further up the road was her likely current position. Mila's Feed showed her turning sharply right into a side street. The red arrow changed direction. The blue dot blinked out and reappeared on another side street ahead of the arrow.

"How are you tracking her?" Rebecca asked.

"Visual clues. We're manually updating the tracking computer every few seconds."

"Follow the blue dot," Rebecca said. "Have we got a team in range?"

A moment passed as the Tech team ran through their assets. Jason spoke first.

"We have a two-car team on the bridge. If they speed up slightly they can cut her off." He patched her through to the senior officer in the lead car.

"Ma'am?" the sergeant said.

"Sergeant, pick up speed and intercept the silver BMW, ID 645RW3. Ram it if you have to; just stop the damn thing."

"Got it," he replied.

Rebecca maximized the sergeant's Feed and shrank Mila's. It was too confusing watching them at the same time, knowing that Mila's wasn't in real time.

The police car's siren screamed and its engine throbbed as it raced toward the intersection at the end of the bridge. The light ahead showed red and Rebecca watched as the policeman reached across and switched off the override that would prevent the car going through the stop light.

On the map in the upper right-hand corner of her IDS she saw the blue dot reach the intersection; the police car would be there in another second. She searched the screen, looking for the little silver car, knowing it should be there.

The police car braked suddenly, slewing across the junction and spinning round to face the way it had come. The other car also braked sharply, coming to rest half a meter away, the two cars blocking most of the intersection, bumper to bumper. The sirens had stopped traffic; there was no danger. The only car they expected to still be moving was Mila's BMW.

Only it wasn't there.

"Where the hell is she?" Rebecca screamed.

"Wait, wait, she must be—" Maddie paused.

On the predictive map, the blue dot was moving along by the river, heading east. Rebecca opened Mila's Feed up again. Seven seconds ago she was driving up a busy road, past fancy shops and hotels, toward the intersection. Suddenly she twisted the wheel to the left and drove into a tiny side street, a mews. Rebecca howled as the BMW juddered over the ancient cobblestones before turning right at the far end and disappearing up another narrow street toward Covent Garden.

"North!" Rebecca yelled, "Go north, you idiots!"

The little blue dot winked out, replaced by three paler blue dots.

"These are the potential routes she could have taken. She's on one of the streets shown," Maddie said.

"I want every unit to central London," Rebecca yelled. "Flood the streets with Agents. Shoot on sight. Stop that damn BMW!"

***

Mila found herself on the cobbles again. She'd seen blue lights flashing up ahead and had decided to ignore the tiresome, safety-first approach of the sat nav by going off-piste. She knocked over a flimsy-looking barrier, darted past a row of cafés into the plaza surrounding the old Covent Garden market building. Two Agents on foot appeared from one of the buildings and fired at the car, the bullets cracking against the side windows, which grazed, but held. Mila performed a hasty U-turn, only to see more Agents running up from the other side of the plaza. There was nowhere else to go but through the market itself.

Hand pressing the horn in warning, she shot into the mouth of the gallery leading through the market. Shoppers and stallholders scattered; wooden stalls and wheeled carts were demolished, fine china, hand-made jewelery and exotic delicacies shattered. She caught the scent of a powerful spice as the car smashed through a rack of world foods. A yellow powder coated the windshield and the wipers came on. Alarm lights, sirens, and smooth-voiced automatons told her what she was doing was dangerous, illegal and generally outrageous.

Then she was out the other side and off down another narrow street. A quick left, followed by a right. She checked the rearview mirror; no blue lights. Nothing ahead. She floored the accelerator and felt herself pressed back into her seat as the speed crept up.

Mila had picked out a twisted, roundabout route to the river, with as many turns as possible. The Map App helpfully gave directions as she went, allowing her to concentrate on driving as fast as possible. She heard her tires screech as she went around a right-hander into a shopping street, tasteful shop fronts on either side. Pedestrians stopped to watch her tear by. Did they know who she was? Had the car ID been updated to reveal who the driver was? Did it matter?

Mila knew the sat nav was taking her too far out of the way. She decided to go off-piste again. Instead of turning left as instructed, she swung right into a small side road, before realizing what the flashing display was telling her. This was a one-way street.

"That's the problem with all these damn alarms," she muttered. "They go off so often you start ignoring them, then when it's genuine, you're screwed."

Her heart sank as she saw another car turn into the other end of the road and come toward her. Its entire roof shined with a bright blue light and its siren was wailing. Dammit, she thought. She gunned the engine and raced toward it. She knew her chances were slim at best. But she had no chance at all if she didn't take a risk. She didn't much care what happened to her.

The police car slowed and stopped in the middle of the road. Two Agents got out, a man and a woman, pulled out firearms and began to shoot. Mila flinched as bullets ricocheted off the windshield, leaving deep crystal furrows but not penetrating.

There wasn't enough room to get by the vehicle on the road, so, sounding her horn, she darted up onto the pavement. A woman clutching a dog was huddling in a shop doorway. Her eyes widened with fear as Mila hurtled past and thumped back onto the road.

Immediately the officers were back in their car and reversing up the street in pursuit.

It was one thing keeping them guessing when they had only her delayed Feed to follow. But now they were in sight, things were more difficult. She had to get away from this police car.

She had to try something new.

Mila raced around a corner into a pedestrianized road. Hand on horn again she scattered the pedestrians and suddenly, swinging the car off the road, she rammed it into a fish-and-chip restaurant. The plate-glass cascaded over the bonnet, plastic chairs and tables flew in all directions. The smell of vinegar obliterated the spices. Then she was out of the car, Special Agent Miles's gun in her hand. She ran to the back of the shop, the proprietor fleeing ahead of her, and found herself in the kitchen.

She ducked behind the door.

"Come on, come on," she muttered. She had seven seconds before the Techs would tip off her pursuers. Sure enough, she soon heard the clattering of feet along the corridor and the two Agents ran in, through the kitchen and toward the doorway at the rear. She scooted back down the passage and out of the shop, glad she hadn't had to shoot.

Outside on the street bemused Citizens were inspecting the damage.

"Try the fishcakes," she called, before jumping into the front seat of the police car. More blue lights flashed as backup arrived. She ignored them and drove off.

"She was behind the door, you idiots!" Rebecca screamed. "How many times are you going to let her pull that trick?"

One half of Rebecca's screen showed Mila running out of the shop. The other half showed the confused face of an Agent, staring up and down the back alley.

"Oh, Christ!" Rebecca said as she Watched Mila get into the car and drive off. "Now she's got a damn cop car."

Mila was feeling quite pleased with herself until she remembered that Agency cars, unlike leisure vehicles, were almost certain to be fitted with tracking devices. This was confirmed when she heard the heavy roar of a hover plane overhead, closely followed by the coughing chatter of heavy cannon fire. Pieces of tarmac exploded around her. She put her foot down, turning down a narrow street lined with parked cars. The cannon stopped briefly as the plane maneuvered to get a clear shot. The pavements were deserted now, most Citizens having found cover as warnings went out.

The police car was fitted with wide-angle cameras and Mila's phone had tuned itself automatically to the Feeds. She kept half an eye on the rear camera, where the plane slid into view. She saw the white bloom of fire as the cannon opened up again. The parked car to the side of her was torn to pieces. The car ahead of it grew black holes and sprouted clouds of vaporized glass, then the next, as the cannon shells tracked her progress. She watched as the stream of fire corrected itself, just a few more seconds and—

Mila saw a gap between two cars and wrenched the wheel to the left. The police car responded beautifully, without screaming any warnings, and she shot up a ramp into a car park.

Tires squealing, she put the car into a 180-turn, recklessly scraping the side panels as she spun between two pillars. With the car now facing the exit, Mila stopped and inspected the controls. She could hear planes hovering outside. Sirens wailed nearby. She didn't have long. She could find no keyboard, but remembering her phone, she clicked on the ID App and the vehicle registration number popped. That got her into the control panel. Here she saw what she was looking for, the autodrive function. She set a random destination and, taking the gun, she got out of the car and slammed the door. The car headed off by itself. It would be seven seconds before they realized what she'd done.

Mila heard the thudding chatter of the cannon and the tortured scream of shells on steel as the police car rolled out of the car park into the firestorm. She was halfway across the car park before Rebecca caught up with her.

"Very clever," Rebecca said. "But now you have no car."

"Who needs a car?" Mila replied. She felt good. The tank had repaired her. Clara and Adam had fed her. She was strong. She could run all day if she had to.

Bright sunlight hit her as she leapt over a low wall at the far end of the car park onto Wardour Street. She ran straight across the road, into a tiny alley full of abandoned market stalls. The map on her IDS told her she was in Soho, some distance from the river and light years from the Basin. It didn't sound like she was being followed but as she neared the end of the alley a pair of police officers appeared.

Bullets whined off the walls and a shop front shattered. Mila ducked behind a cart displaying pottery.

A teapot exploded, showering her with ceramic shards. Looking down, she noticed a wedge under one of the wheels. She removed it and shoved the cart hard with her shoulder. It moved and she ran with it, pushing it hard in the direction of the Agents. At the end of the alley she sprang on the cart, her gun at the ready.

The Agents dived out of the way. Mila fired, not wanting to kill, but to keep their heads down. But she hit one of the officers, a young woman, in the shoulder and she sank to the ground. The other officer prepared to return fire. Then the cart hit the opposite curb and Mila was thrown off. She landed unsteadily but kept her feet, sprinting off down Shaftesbury Avenue as bullets skipped off the pavement behind her.

As Mila ran round a corner, momentarily losing her pursuers, a bright red bus rolled by. Her IDS revealed it to be the number seventy-three to Angel. The back was open, with a platform for jumping on and off. Mila leapt on and dropped into a seat, keeping her head down. The bus was empty, driven by a SEMINT brain. Had her pursuers seen her? If not they would catch up after seven seconds. Now that her ID App was functioning there was no way of keeping her whereabouts secret for long.

She peered through the side window until she saw another bus coming the other way. The number thirty-eight, destination Victoria. She waited til the last minute, then dropped lightly off the back of the platform. She stood in the middle of the road as the buses passed one another then hopped up onto the slow-moving thirty-eight.

"She's on a number seventy-three, heading northeast along Shaftesbury Avenue," Maddie called. "Intercept units on their way."

"Are there civilians on the bus?" Rebecca asked.

"Checking that. . . . Negative."

"Take it out."

There were a couple of passengers on the thirty-eight, teenage boys. Perhaps they hadn't got the warning about clearing the area. Or perhaps they were looking for some excitement. They'd found it now, Mila thought. They stared at her in wide-eyed astonishment and she winked back.

A few seconds later there was the roar of weaponry and the ear-splitting screech of tearing steel. Mila and the two boys turned to look at the platform, to see four armor-clad Agents firing heavy kinetic rifles at the back of the bus Mila had just got off. The windows shattered and scattered crystal across the street. Something inside exploded—the gas canisters for the air brakes, Mila guessed—punching a hole in the bodywork on the left side. The tires burst and the bus slewed to a drunken stop across the street, blocking what little traffic there was.

"This is my stop," Mila said, and she was off again.

"She's off the seventy-three!" Maddie yelled over the sound of the guns.

"What?!" Rebecca said, muting the sound for a moment.

"She got off the bus. She's on a thirty-eight heading the other way."

"Turn! Turn!" Rebecca ordered the Agents. "She's on the thirty-eight!"

But Mila was already off the thirty-eight and had darted down a narrow street, which brought her out onto Piccadilly Circus. Crossing the road, she dodged a SEMINT-driven truck. It seemed there were no human drivers in the area now, just the odd rumbling, automated vehicle, oblivious to the violent scenes surrounding it.

Mila ran at full pelt across an almost-deserted plaza. The statue of Eros seemed to watch her as she passed. An Agency car sped into the square from Regent Street, and Mila, her chest burning with the effort, sprinted downhill along a wide thoroughfare, desperate now, intent on nothing but reaching the river. The car caught up with her and she heard the crack of a pistol as some Agent fired at her from the window. She kept running. Then a plane opened fire and the wall ahead of her erupted in great gouts of smashed masonry.

"Shit, shit, shit, shit!" she squealed. She darted across the road and tore down another side road. The car overshot, unable to follow her. It reappeared soon enough though, this time ahead of her, and two officers leaned out of windows on either side, firing as the car hurtled toward her. There were more officers on foot, running from the other side of the street. She spun to see a second car behind her.

She changed direction and ran up the steps into an open building. A startled concierge stood as she came in but, ignoring him, she carried on through the building and up a marbled flight of stairs at the far end. She ran up and up until she came to a fire door which opened on to the roof. Stopping briefly to catch her breath, she saw the river a couple of hundred meters away, and a bridge. The row of buildings opposite looked as though they might offer a rooftop route down to the water's edge, but the street was far too wide to leap. The police would be halfway up the stairs by now. There was no return in that direction. She cursed herself for choosing the wrong side of the road.

Suddenly Mila's breath caught in her throat. A huge hover plane rose up before her. It turned slowly, bringing its cannon to bear. There was no cockpit; this was a drone, controlled from some remote destination. There was no escape.

Mila backed away slowly, a rising panic in her chest restricting her movement, shutting down her thought processes. Her mouth was dry as the huge black hole at the end of the stubby cannon turned toward her.

Check your exits, Julian told her. There's always a way out.

A clang and the sound of footsteps told her the police had arrived on the roof.

Where, Julian, where?

14

Mila took a deep breath and sprinted toward the raised lip of the rooftop. For a moment she was back in Köls, leaping onto the Corporation building, but there was more at stake here than doughnuts. She heard the crack and whine of bullets behind her, followed by the thudding cackle of the cannon opening fire, the tracers curving just below her arc as she flew.

She landed lightly on the nose of the plane and ran over the smooth, slick top of the fuselage, down to the flat tail, which she used as a springboard to make the leap over to the other side. She thudded down safely on the rooftop, hardly daring to believe what she had done.

The roof was slightly pitched and she scuttled up the ridge and down the other side. By the time the plane had turned and risen to find her, she was on the roof of a separate wing, projecting southward toward the river. She dropped over the edge onto a lower building, then found her way down, down, and down by drain pipes, ledges and a handily placed tree. Finally she was at ground level, in a small park by the river's edge. Scanning the area, she saw no police and trotted quickly to the water. She could hear the hover plane behind, searching through the trees. Downriver she saw two more approaching.

Rebecca phoned again.

"You've got to stop calling like this," Mila said. "It's stalking."

"What are you?" Rebecca asked.

"Seven seconds ahead of you," Mila replied. "That's what I am."

Directly below her, there was nothing but an empty jetty. The tide was out and the stony bank of the river was exposed. Fifty meters downstream Mila saw a pier with a garish yellow boat bobbing beside it. A tourist boat. She looked the other way and saw nothing but a deserted ferry pier. She frowned; needs must. She clambered over the wall and down the salty rocks to the tidal bed. Treading carefully, she ran over to the pier, scrambled up it and jumped on board the tourist boat.

The boat was around ten meters long, with two rows of double seats on either side. The engine looked big and she allowed herself to hope she might get some speed out of it. The boat had been abandoned in a hurry; the keys were in the ignition. She started the engine, then walked up to the bow to release the rope. She returned to the wheel and pulled the throttle right down to full. The boat surged over the water, the bow lifting alarmingly, too light without two dozen fat tourists. She throttled down again, pleased by the throbbing power, and turned the wheel to head downstream. She knew where she was. She'd soared up and down this river on the Wallscreen, with a grinning Adam beside her. She sped up again, controlling the throttle so the front end didn't lift too high. The boat was fast. It was built to scare tourists, and would do for her purposes.

But then she saw a stream of tracers and a blast of spray ahead of her and knew that the lead plane found her again. A second row, from another plane, opened to her left, hitting the water and sending geysers of white spume into the air. The stream corrected itself quickly, this time running right across the front of the boat. Plastic seats splintered and imploded, scattering shards of yellow plastic across the river. Mila ducked down and clenched her shoulders, waiting for the cannon shells to blow her to a thousand tiny pieces.

✳ ✳ ✳

In her office in the Ministry building, Rebecca was Watching Mila's progress on her phone. She'd given up trying to talk to her. Mila was ignoring her now. Besides, she had too many other people to communicate with. Her forces simply weren't responsive enough. It wasn't just the delay; the hover planes were too slow, suited to heavy engagements, not taking out small, nimble girls. The Agents were too few and poorly resourced; the police fat and inexperienced.

But Mila couldn't evade them forever, the girl's luck would have to run out sooner or later. When Rebecca Watched her leap into the boat and roar away from the jetty, she knew it was nearly over. Mila's first mistake: that bright yellow boat could be seen from miles away. The only vessel now moving on the river, it was a beacon for every Agent in the vicinity; the perfect target for the planes' heavy cannon, which could be used safely out on the water.

She Watched with satisfaction as the two planes opened fire, triangulating their attack to ensure the boat couldn't turn. She Watched Mila huddling in the back, holding the wheel with one hand. Side cameras on the planes gave her a view of each bank, where dozens of police vehicles, Agency cars and officers on foot were converging. Marksmen were taking up positions, ready to pick her off in case she dived into the water. At the back of the scene, on the north bank of the Thames, was the Ministry building itself.

Rebecca returned her attention to Mila's Feed, eager to watch the coup de grace. How fitting that it should occur just a stone's throw from the Ministry. She could inspect the body herself and fire a couple of bullets into it. Just to make sure.

But Mila wasn't quite finished. She slowed suddenly and the streaming fire of the two planes overshot the boat, leaving a gap in which she could turn sharply and head at a forty-five degree angle to the river bank. She opened up the throttle and the front of the boat raised itself high. Mila ran up the sloping deck and leapt, just as the boat hit the flood barrier. At the same time, the planes brought their cannon around and found their target. There was a huge explosion behind the airborne girl.

Rebecca rushed to the window. Below, on the Embankment, she saw the shattered remains of the bow wedged up against a crooked lamppost. The stern had been completely obliterated. Yellow plastic shards littered the pavement. Running officers converged on the scene, too late as ever. There was no sign of Mila.

Rebecca turned from the window and looked toward the open door to her office.

"She's in the bloody building," she said.

Everything ran in slow motion. Mila came up the stairs and through the open double doors of the Ministry building. A security guard stepped in front of her, a look of fear on his face as he pulled out his stun baton. Was she so terrifying? She supposed she probably was. She dropped and rolled, knocking the guard's legs out from under him. He hit the floor with a thud and a whoosh of air. Still holding Special Agent Miles's gun in her right hand, she snatched up the baton with her left and regained her feet.

She clicked eagerly on the building's ID plate, looking for the room she needed. There it was, first floor, end of the corridor. Could she get there in seven seconds? Make that five seconds. No time to lose.

Mila took three stairs at a time, past a startled employee who fell against the rail as she saw her approach. Round the bend and up again, then a dogleg into the corridor. She saw someone appear out of a side door and recognized Rebecca, wide-eyed. Mila punched her in the jaw. She collapsed to the floor. Mila seized the collar of her expensive suit and dragged her into the Minister's office.

Mila used her phone to close and lock the door behind her. She stood before the big desk, the stun baton in her right hand, pointing it at the Minister, the gun in her left, aimed at Rebecca. An old phone was ringing on the Minister's desk. Ancient tech, hardly recognizable. Even the old landline at her father's farm had been more modern.

The Minister watched her calmly. He said nothing. The phone continued to ring.

"Aren't you going to answer it?" Mila asked, breaking first.

The Minister shook his head. "It'll be one of my assistants warning me of your approach. Rather too late."

Footsteps approached outside and the door handle rattled. Mila felt a ping. An Agent.

"Tell them to leave us alone," Mila said.

The Minister looked at Rebecca, who had raised herself up into a sitting position, and nodded. The rattling stopped, as did the ringing of the phone.

"Now activate the Cloak," the Minister said.

"You don't have a phone," Mila observed, suddenly realizing why the Minister was asking Rebecca to do things for him.

He patted the ancient device on his desk. "This is my phone," he said. "I don't need an implant. I find them distracting."

"Your security sucks," Mila volunteered.

"I agree," the Minister said. "I could have beefed it up, of course."

"And why didn't you?" Mila asked. "You must have known there was a chance I'd come here."

The Minister laughed. "Of course, I knew. You are beautifully predictable."

The hairs on the back of Mila's neck rose slightly. Clara's words came back to her. Had this all been arranged?

"You're very cheerful for a man with a stun baton pointed at him," she said. "Do you know what these things do?"

"Oh, yes," the Minister said. "I used to own the company that makes them. I had to sell it when I decided to Contribute to the government."

"So selfless," Mila said.

"Oh, you don't know what I'm willing to sacrifice to get what I want," the Minister said, watching her steadily.

"And what is that?" Mila asked. "What do you want? To shoot illegals on sight? To cover the country in CCTV? To arm the population and make them all Agents? Spying, mistrusting, hating?"

"I want to protect the Isles, Mila," the Minister said. "I want to ensure this country is in a position to defend itself from people like you."

"Me?" she laughed. "I'm no threat to you."

The Minister pursed his lips. "And yet we have dead Agents all over the country, including three Special Agents. Dead Citizens, too."

"I had no choice," Mila cried. "I was acting in self-defense. You killed in cold blood."

"That's not how the public is seeing it, Mila," the Minister said, smiling thinly. "To them you are a dangerous terrorist, leaving death and destruction in your wake, and planning to set off an explosive device, embedded in your head."

"So it was you who arranged for this thing to be put in my brain?" Mila asked. She was suddenly scared at what he might say next. Sick at the thought that he was going to confirm Julian had betrayed her, used her.

"No, Julian did that of his own volition," the Minister said. "He was a rogue after all. Damn good idea though. If slightly dangerous."

"That's where you're wrong," Mila said. "I think Julian was playing his own game. He wouldn't have done anything to hurt me."

The Minister laughed. "Then you don't know what he's capable of."

"And what's to stop me setting off the bomb now?" Mila asked. "Destroying this whole building."

"You can't," the Minister said. "You don't know the activation code."

"Quite a big risk for you to take though, isn't it?"

"I told you I was willing to make sacrifices."

Mila stared at him, astonished. "You'd sacrifice your own life for your twisted ideals?"

The Minister regarded her coolly. "I'd be content with my legacy, should my death inspire this country to take security seriously."

Mila was dimly aware of a number of dark, hovering shapes outside the window, over the river. She was in no doubt that should she pull the trigger, the planes' cannon would pour torrents of fire into the room and this time there would be nowhere to run.

The Minister stood and pushed his chair back, his eyes shining.

"If I can put a stop to the waves of vile immigrants coming to these shores, if that's what people will remember me for, then I will have died for a reason."

Mila nodded. "I get it. It's about your legacy. About your damn reputation."

"What else is there?" the Minister spat. "All around me I see mediocrity. No one strives anymore. No one works. If they do, they make a token effort. Everyone just takes and takes. Everything's handed to them on a plate."

Mila looked down at Rebecca, curious to know how she was taking this extraordinary speech from her boss. She was only mildly surprised to see Rebecca nodding along. A bruise was starting to show on her perfect skin.

"Who will stand up?" the Minister said, almost shouting now, hectoring Mila as though she were the electorate. "Who will stand out from the crowd?"

"You know I'm recording this, don't you?" she said quietly.

The Minister gave a barking laugh. He sat down on the side of his desk, shaking with emotion.

"You're not getting out of here alive, Mila," Rebecca said. "The door is locked and secured. You can't open it now. One wrong move and the planes open fire. There are hundreds of armed personnel inside and outside the building."

Mila shifted nervously. She knew Rebecca was right.

"The room is Cloaked," the Minister said. "Nothing said here is being broadcast. We will destroy your phone and all its memories once you are dead. You have served your purpose."

Mila felt a sudden surge of despair. Had all this come to nothing? Was there nothing to be gained? She could kill the Minister, and possibly Rebecca too, before the planes took her out. But then they would have won. The Privacy Laws would be cast out. There would be no hope for any immigrant after that. No hope for the Third.

"He betrayed you," Rebecca said, twisting the knife. "Your beloved Julian, your mentor. He was working for us. But he went further than we were willing to go. He put a bomb in your pretty little head. He wanted you to kill innocent people. Ordinary Citizens. Good people. Children."

Each word added another layer to the lead encasing her soul. Mila felt her strength ebb and the hand holding the stun baton dropped slightly. What was the point?

But she took a deep breath and lifted the baton again, pointing it firmly at the Minister. The moment her aim wavered the cannon would blaze. And she had not entirely lost heart, because still there was something in the back of her mind. Something she was missing.

Call Beverley Minster, Julian had said. But only if you're in real trouble. There's something in . . .

He'd wanted her to know about the device. He'd meant to tell her once she had a phone, once he'd got her onto the Isles. Why? Was it because he was using her as an unwitting suicide bomber? Or did he have another reason for bringing her here? That had always been the question. What was Julian's real motive?

Mila turned to the Minister.

"You say you didn't know about the device?"

"No. That was his idea."

"He told me, as he died," Mila said slowly. "That there was something in my head."

The Minister's eyes narrowed.

"Why would he tell me that?"

"Because he knew he was about to die?" Rebecca suggested. "He hoped you'd set off the bomb yourself."

Trust me, Julian had said in the hospital in Frankfurt. But really she had decided to trust him long before that, when she shook his hand in the Corporation building in Köls. And she still did. She had to, because the alternative was too awful even to contemplate.

Call Beverley Minster . . .

"Drop the gun, Mila," Rebecca said. "And the baton. I won't insult your intelligence by pretending you'll escape alive if you do. But we'll make it painless. A quick injection, a dreamless sleep."

The Minister's thin hand was reaching for the phone. He pulled it toward him, the cable trailing. He lifted the receiver slowly, perhaps wondering if Mila was going to fire. She was watching his finger as he stabbed the first number. She shifted closer to the desk, peering at the buttons. She'd noticed something. Something she'd never seen before.

Each button had three or four letters printed on it, as well as the number. Number 1 had ABC beneath, 2 had DEF, and so on. Mila's mouth opened slightly.

"Give me the phone," she said.

The Minister stopping dialing and looked up at her.

"Give me the damn phone or I'll shoot you in the kneecap."

The Minister hesitated for just a moment, then pushed the handset across the desk. Mila leaned forward, scrutinizing the code, working out the number.

B-E-V-E-R-L-E-Y-M-I-N-S-T-E-R
2-3-8-3-7-5-3-9-6-4-6-7-8-3-7

Fifteen digits. She input them on her IDS. The green call button flashed, waiting for her to click.

She looked at the Minister, who looked back at her curiously. A bead of sweat rolled down his forehead. Then she glanced at Rebecca, her face impassive, waiting.

Finally she looked out of the window at the hovering planes and at the grand buildings on the opposite bank, shining proudly in the afternoon sunshine.

She shut her eyes and hit enter.

Mila felt a deep throbbing sensation at the base of her skull, like the buzz she'd got from the phone in Beverley Hospital, but magnified a hundred times. She dropped the stun baton, but clung onto the gun. She opened her eyes. The lights had gone off and through the window she saw the hover planes lurching drunkenly across the sky. She heard Rebecca let out a little cry before slumping to the ground. The throbbing in her head continued, growing in intensity.

Her IDS was grayed out.

The Minister leapt to his feet. He grabbed his phone and lifted the receiver. "There's no signal!" he said, looking at Mila. "What have you done?"

Mila shifted the gun into her right hand and lifted it unsteadily, pointing it at his face. The throbbing in her head was easing, but it felt as though something had been hammering at the inside of her skull.

"ECM blast," she gasped, as realization hit her, and relief flooded through her jangled nerves. Julian had told her about ECM. "All electronics will be disabled for a mile or so around," she added. "Your local phone networks will be out for a while."

"What happened to Rebecca?"

"I expect the proximity to the device intensified the damage to her phone. The resulting concussion knocked her out. You're unharmed because you don't have one."

"And why have you not been affected?"

"I don't know," she said, considering this. "I guess the device is designed to offer some protection to the carrier. Julian would have thought of that. My phone has no signal, but it seems to be working." The IDS had blinked back into life a few seconds after the blast. She flicked through a few drop-downs. Her record function was still working and she began recording again, even though there was no one to broadcast it to at the moment.

"Looks like you were wrong about Julian," she said.

The Minister shook his head. "He put that thing in your head so he could use you as a weapon."

"No," Mila replied. "He put it there to protect me. You people, with your suspicious minds, you made me doubt myself. You made me doubt him."

"So tell me then," the Minister said, "what was his motivation? Why did he bring you here?"

"He worked for you, didn't he?"

The Minister nodded briefly.

"You rewarded his years of loyal service with Citizenship and land in Yorkshire. Gave him what he'd always wanted."

"He was very useful to me, back then."

"But then you asked him to go back into the field. He resisted. You told him he had no choice."

"Everyone ought to Contribute," the Minister said.

"That's when he turned against you," Mila said. "The job you gave him in Köls was to build a dam. To flood a valley. Destroy farms. Ruin lives."

"Progress," the Minister said. "It was necessary."

"Necessary to provide cheap food for the First," Mila said quickly. "Well, I think Julian hated what he was doing. And when he met me, when he realized that your goons had killed my father, I think that was the final straw."

The Minister was silent now.

"He wanted to help me. He wanted me to have the chance of a quiet life in the First. The chance that had been taken away from him."

"And the device in your head?"

"I was attacked in Frankfurt. He had the device implanted for my protection, to make sure that it couldn't happen again. At least not on the Isles, where everyone has a phone that can be disabled with an ECM blast."

"So why didn't he tell you?"

Mila shrugged. "Until I was on the Isles and had a phone of my own there was no point. He probably thought that I'd be furious with him. And he was right."

"You've got it all figured out," the Minister said.

"Yes, I think I have."

"And what now?" The Minister licked his lips nervously.

Mila was ready with her answer.

"The phones you give to Special Agents," she said. "The untraceable, untappable super-phones."

"I don't know what you're talking about."

"Don't waste my time," Mila said. "There are no cannons pointing at my head now. Just my gun pointing at yours. Get me one of those phones."

The Minister hesitated.

"You've already lost," Mila said quietly. "You were wrong when you said the public were all against me. There are enough who see the truth. Resetting my phone was a mistake. Your opponents in the Privacy Party are aware of what you are doing. And now people can see how savage your Special Agents are. Public opinion is turning. You will lose your precious vote."

"You think the public are with you?" he snapped. "A few liberal commentators in their ivory towers are not the public. Most people would cheer to see your head on a spike on Tower Bridge."

"Get me the phone," Mila said.

"Or what?" he replied. "What will you do if I refuse?"

"I'll run," Mila said.

"Where?"

"To where I can find a phone signal, then I'll upload the recording of this conversation to the Web."

The Minister stared at her, blood draining from his face.

"There's your legacy. A man who kills his own Agents and murders innocents in order to advance a twisted political agenda."

"You're forgetting the Agents outside," he replied, shaking his head. "The marksmen. Do you really think they'll let you escape? You'll be dead before you can upload so much as a byte."

"Which is why you're going to order them to stand down," Mila said.

"And why would I do that?" he asked.

Mila stared closely into his watery eyes. "Because you are bluffing," she said. "Because despite your big speeches, you don't want to die. You want to live on, in your comfortable house, with your Channels and your fancy food."

She pressed the barrel of the gun to his forehead and shifted her finger slightly. She nodded toward the unconscious Rebecca.

"No one will know," she said. "It'll be our little secret."

The Minister swallowed.

"Where's your legacy now?" she asked softly.

A thin trickle of sweat rolled down the Minister's forehead. His breathing quickened and his pupils dilated.

"Okay," he said, eventually. "Okay. I'll ask them to stand down."

Mila stepped back and pushed the phone toward him.

The Minister sat slowly and dropped his head.

"And," Mila went on, "You will give me one of the Special Agent phones."

"You don't need a new phone," he said quietly.

"What's that?"

"The phones are all the same. You just need to enter the right code."

"And then?"

"Your phone will begin changing its own number. It will generate a new random number every few seconds. Each number will be valid, allowing you to access all privileges. You'll be able to travel anywhere, eat in any restaurant, be able to buy anything you like. Your credits are unlimited. And because there is a new number every few seconds, your phone will not be traceable."

"Will people be able to call me?"

"No. But you can use a voicemail service to take calls for you. That's what the Special Agents do."

"How do I know you're telling the truth?"

He looked up at her, smiling wryly. "Because I have too much to lose. The recordings in your phone are your insurance policy. But should those recordings ever be released to the public..."

"Then you'll come for me."

He nodded, shooting her a poisonous look that did more to confirm his intent than any number of words. This time he wasn't bluffing. A faint hum surrounded them, telling Mila the electricity had returned. An alarm light flashed on a monitor in the corner.

"Go on then," Mila said, nodding as the overhead lights flickered back on. "How does this work?"

"Go to your phone settings," he said, sounding tired. "Choose Set Up. Click on the base code option. You should have a pop-up window."

"Got it," Mila said.

"Type the following code: 01-Y78HK5961B3, then press enter."

Mila typed the code but paused before pressing enter. What if this were a trick? What if this code wiped out her phone? Or made it explode or something? But the Minister looked defeated. If this was a trick she couldn't read it on his face.

She hit enter.

"Nothing's changed," she said. She checked her recordings; they were all still there. She opened her Comms box. WATCHERS: 0. She smiled.

The Minister shrugged. "Your phone will operate just as before, but with extra privileges."

Mila looked at the door. Her passepartout App gave her a black padlock and she clicked on it. The door opened. In the corridor stood a number of security guards and Agents, some getting to their feet, others still out cold. Mila closed the door hurriedly. She wasn't out of the woods quite yet.

"What of your own principles?" the Minister said, sourly. "You criticize me for my heartlessness. Yet you are willing to let me wriggle off the hook to save your own skin."

Mila shifted uncomfortably.

"Once you're gone, I will continue to press for improved security," he said. "I'll push even harder for a tough approach to illegal immigrants. I can present this episode as an act of cyber-terrorism. Spin it to advance my case."

In the corner of Mila's vision she noticed Rebecca getting to her feet, holding her head and looking dazed. Mila's Contact Avatars blinked back into life. She was pleased she still had her Contacts list, stored in her phone's internal memory. Presumably, though, it didn't work both ways. Not if her number changed every few seconds. She could call other people, they couldn't call her. She clicked on Holly, and in less than a second sent her a package of recordings made in the last hour. She shook her head. "You will lose. The people of the Isles are smarter than you give them credit for. They are good people, welcoming. Even without my recordings, the facts of the case speak for themselves. A heavy-handed approach from the security services led to death and destruction and for what? To counter a threat that never materialized, not in any real way. Ten minutes without phones? That's what you tore up half the country to avoid? No. You're going to lose this battle."

"We'll see about that," the Minister said.

"I've already sent a package of recordings to a good friend of mine, to be distributed widely if I'm not in contact again in an hour. You'd better instruct your minions to let me leave the vicinity without trying to blow my head off."

"Rebecca," the Minister said, "please do as she asks."

"But, Minister," Rebecca said, "what just happened?"

"Do as I ask, please."

"Are you sure, Minister?" Rebecca said, desperation creeping into her voice. "I urge you—"

"Just do it!" the Minister screamed, slamming his hand on the desk.

Rebecca concentrated for a moment then shook her head.

"You're free to leave," she forced herself to say, unable to look at Mila.

"Thank you, Rebecca," Mila said. "Sorry I punched you so hard."

She opened the door and peered around cautiously. The Agents and guards were pointing their weapons at the floor. Slowly, holding her breath, she walked out of the room and down the corridor. The officers stood against the wall to let her pass, their faces a mix of contempt and curiosity. The girl they'd been chasing for so long was right there before them. And she was being allowed to walk free?

She was still holding her breath as she walked down the stairs. At the bottom, she stopped and forced herself to inhale deeply before continuing across the lobby, the only sound the slap of her soles against the polished marble floor. Agents and police stood silently and watched her. Mila nodded apologetically at the guard she'd knocked over on the way in. He nodded back. Then, realizing she still held the gun, she put it carefully on the reception desk before walking out of the building into sunshine.

Epilogue

She twists the apple and it comes away easily from the branch. She smells it. It is rich, full of vitality. The air has grown colder over the past few days, and the long, late summer she has enjoyed is over now. She has been bottling and storing, preparing for the cold. A quiet, peaceful winter on the farm, planning what to plant in spring, what livestock to buy. If she feels like a walk or a bike ride, Beverley is only a few miles away.

She smells a bonfire somewhere, one of her distant neighbors clearing the garden, probably. The nearest house is half a mile from hers. She's introduced herself to them as Miriam, but hasn't volunteered any more information and they haven't pressed. Not everyone here wants to show everything to the world.

And there is company if she wants it. She's met up with Holly a couple of times in Leeds and has given her the voicemail number she checks periodically. She's phoned Clara too, as securely as she can, to see how Adam is getting on. He was still in the tank when she last called, still insensible, but making good progress. Clara had asked if she had a number she could be reached on, but Mila had said no. While she has no fears for her own safety, she doesn't want to put Adam at risk. Protected by Clara and her husband, he is safe enough. It is surely best for him to rebuild his life, find a new way to Contribute, or do what she is doing, hide away. Tend his garden, pick apples, stay out of trouble. And after all, his memories may not have survived. He may not remember her at all. She tells herself she doesn't need him. Or Julian. Or even her father. She will survive just fine on her own.

But for all her mental discipline, sometimes she cries herself to sleep. There are three holes in her heart, the biggest of the three left by Adam.

She has tried to fill the gaps with hard labor. The previous tenants handed over the farm early in the summer, bored with country life, tired of the hard work it required, and there is a lot Mila needs to do to make it productive again. But most of that will have to wait until spring. For now she is concentrating on harvesting what fruits and vegetables are available. She's got a few chickens and has asked about acquiring some ducks to go with them. She has eggs, fruit and vegetables to barter with. Of course, she can buy whatever she wants with her super-phone, but wants to do it on her own as much as possible.

Mila picks up her basket and makes her way to the small barn behind the cottage. She needs to store the apples where it is cool and dry. Then she'll chop a little firewood and go inside to make her supper. As she passes the garden gate, she hears crunching on the gravel path beyond and stops to glance at the passer-by. It could be one of her neighbors, or a rambler heading back home before nightfall. A face appears over the gate, a man she doesn't recognize. Or does she? He smiles at her. It is a good face. Smooth, young, handsome.

She puts the bucket down and steps toward the visitor, looking at him more closely. It's the eyes that give it away. Give him away.

"Aren't you going to invite me in?" Adam asks.

And of course she does.

"You remember me then?" she asks, tentatively.

"I don't remember anything but you," he says.

She thinks her heart must have grown wings. How else to explain the beating, fluttering sensation in her chest?

Later, by the fire, they eat rich stew, drink red wine and talk.

"How did you find me?" Mila asks.

"The Minister gave us your address," he explains.

She is not surprised to hear the Minister knows where she is. She hasn't tried particularly hard to cover her tracks. If her insurance policy is not enough to protect her then they will find her eventually. She is surprised, though, that Adam has been in contact with the Minister.

"Let's just say we reached an impasse," Adam says. "Gordon Urquhart had me as a witness, and the recordings in my phone, which didn't portray the Minister in a good light. On the other hand, the Minister had proof that Clara harbored a suspected terrorist. They reached an agreement."

"So the Minister gets away with it?"

"I'm afraid so."

"And the Security Party won the vote?"

"I'm afraid so."

There is a darkness at the back of Mila's mind. A darkness forged by guilt that she chose to save herself and let the Minister walk free. She often tells herself that killing him would have solved nothing. But she can't quite make herself believe it. There is unfinished business.

"And part of this agreement was that the Minister would reveal my location?"

"Only to me," Adam says. "And it was more about getting me out of the way. A new face, a new life. I'm not allowed to return to London."

"Do you want to return to London?"

He shakes his head. "I want to stay here, with you," he says. "If you'll have me. I don't know much about farming, but I could chop wood? Dig up potatoes? Make chili?"

"There is a farmhand position available, as it happens," Mila says, getting up to poke the fire, her breath tight in her chest, unable to look at him. "Perhaps I could employ you on a trial basis."

"I've missed you," he says.

"I've missed you too," she replies, and when she sits back down on the sofa, it is closer to him. He puts an arm around her and she presses into his warmth.

After a while she tilts her face up toward his, and he kisses her.